DEADLY
SECRETS

SCVC Taskforce, Book 7

MISTY EVANS

ROMANTIC SUSPENSE AND MYSTERIES BY MISTY EVANS

The Super Agent Series
Operation Sheba
Operation Paris
Operation Proof of Life
The Blood Code
The Perfect Hostage, A Super Agent Novella

The SCVC Taskforce Series
Deadly Pursuit
Deadly Deception
Deadly Force
Deadly Intent
Deadly Affair, A SCVC Taskforce novella
Deadly Attraction
Deadly Secrets
Deadly Holiday, A SCVC Taskforce novella

The Justice Team Series (with Adrienne Giordano)
Stealing Justice
Cheating Justice
Holiday Justice
Exposing Justice
Undercover Justice
Protecting Justice
Missing Justice

Shadow Force International Series
Fatal Truth
Fatal Honor
Fatal Courage
Fatal Love
Fatal Vision

The Secret Ingredient Culinary Mystery Series
The Secret Ingredient, A Culinary Romantic Mystery with Bonus Recipes
The Secret Life of Cranberry Sauce, A Secret Ingredient Holiday Novella

ACKNOWLEDGMENTS

To all my readers who imagine they are the heroine in my stories. You are!

To Amy Remus whose love of Conrad Flynn inspired this story. I hope you enjoy the underlying tongue-in-cheek moments in this book.

Every book I write is a group project and I couldn't bring my stories to the world without the help of my cover artist, editors, and formatter. Thank you for making my stories shine!

As always, my writing partner in crime, Adrienne Giordano, was my sounding board and helped bring the plot of Deadly Secrets to the next level. Can't do without your evil mind, woman!

Much love and gratitude to my hubby and sons who inspire me every day to keep writing.

And to the fans who email me to let me know how much they love my stories…

This one is for *you*.

DEDICATION

To Mark, my perfect hero

The reality of the other person is not in what he reveals to you,
but in what he cannot reveal to you.
Therefore, if you were to understand him,
listen not to what he says
but rather to what he does not say.

~ Kahlil Gibran, Sand & Foam

CHAPTER ONE

Raindrops plunked loudly on the bar's metal roof as if a giant were dropping pebbles on it.

Nursing an iced tea, Brooke Heaton wished fervently she'd declined the invitation from the San Diego State University religious studies academics and headed back to her hotel room. After three days of lecturing at the university, she was ready to get back to the real world.

She discreetly checked her phone under the bar overhang for the umpteenth time, hoping for a text or call of any kind to give her an excuse to bug out. But there were no missed calls, no messages. Maybe she could pretend differently and tell her hosts that she needed to go back to her room.

But what kind of anthropological emergency would require her to beg off the company she was with?

Bars just weren't her thing—especially since at this particular one, it seemed to be prime time for Stephen Colbert-wannabes who thought their standup comedy routines were a stepping stone from San Diego to L.A. Her companions laughed at the latest joke from the young man on stage, who just happened to be a grad student from their department. Brooke smiled obligingly. For a religious studies major, the guy sure knew a variety of interesting ways to work the word "fuck" into his routine.

She'd been hungry for companionship and had erroneously thought her academic colleagues meant for their night out to include a decent meal and in-depth discussion about religious symbols of the Mayan culture. Boy, had she been wrong.

Maybe I'm just getting old. She'd much rather be in the king size bed at the hotel, eating horrible room service food and reading her latest *Journal of Forensic Anthropology,* than here listening to jokes about bathroom habits and the current administration in the White House.

Although, the two subjects did have some things in common these days.

Oh, who was she kidding? She wanted to get back to reread her favorite romance novel.

She checked her watch and blew out a sigh. Making sure no one noticed, she pulled out her cell from under the bar overhang to text a cab service.

Now all she had to do was come up with a polite excuse to bail.

There was always the universal go-to—*I have a headache.* At the rate she was going, she would indeed have one soon.

If only she didn't have yet another morning of lectures at the university the next day, she could pretend she had an early flight back to L.A.

But no, three departments had banded together to pay her speaker fee. Plus, the university had generously comped her hotel room and loaded her down with Fighting Aztec everything. No way could she carry all of it on the plane; she'd have to ship most of it home or find someone to donate it to. There was at least five pounds of shirts, scarves, coffee cups, and paperweights with the school's mascot on them to haul back.

Did anyone actually use paperweights anymore?

It was nice to be wanted, but she'd left the world of academia for a reason—she wanted to marry the past with the present. To show modern-day men and women how instrumental learning about their ancestors could be. The university bubble was comfortable and safe, and for years, it had been the perfect hideaway for her. She'd thought she could do exactly what she wanted—turn young minds on to her love of anthropology. Unfortunately, it hadn't been quite what she'd expected, and most of her students had simply taken her classes as an elective, thinking they could use religious studies and anthro class to nab an easy A.

Eventually, she'd had to break free and *do* something. Writing a book about famous fossils, and a high-profile media tour several years ago, had made her an anthropological star for about three months. A well-known Hollywood producer had taken a chapter from her book and made a web series based on the famous Lucy find of fossils from a 3.2 billion year old hominin species *Australopithecus afarensis.*

Anthropology meet pop culture.

Social media had given her another popularity boost for a few months. She'd loved seeing fossils and past cultures getting some notoriety, but it had been a strain on her personally. She'd determined she wasn't cut out for the spotlight.

An unexpected bonus had come from her brief dance with fame. She'd never dreamed she'd end up consulting for law enforcement, but with her forensic anthropology experience, research into various religions stretching back to the Sumerians, and her criminal justice degree, she'd ended up helping out Cooper Harris and his SCVC Taskforce.

There'd only been a couple of cases so far, but they'd fit into her schedule nicely and provided extra funds for her travels.

Speaking of travel... Tomorrow, after her last lecture, she'd be off to Utah and an area so remote it could only be reached by donkey. Ten miles on an ass to the dig site would be no picnic, but at the moment, it sounded like absolute heaven. Plus, it was a highly prized dig, headed by Dr. Borgman of the Smithsonian Institute. The whole situation was very exclusive and required kid gloves due to the fact the bones and artifacts were ancestors of a Native American tribe, maybe two.

From behind her, she heard loud male laughter that was out of sync with the comedian on stage. Glancing over her shoulder, she skimmed the three men making all the noise. Her gaze came back to one boldly staring at her and her stomach dropped.

Oh, no. Not him. What is he doing here?

The licorice black hair and searing blue eyes weren't to be denied. Neither was the cocky smirk on his face as he looked her up and down.

The trimmed beard was new. So was the longish hair pulled up into a man-bun. The tight T-shirt, showing off his tattoos, revealed his muscled arms and chest. He looked downright criminal.

Or the ideal model for the cover of *Muscle & Fitness.*

Roman Walsh. *Dr.* Roman Walsh. The criminal justice PhD and Homeland agent was either slumming or undercover.

Or he's stalking me.

Again.

She might have a use for that paperweight after all.

For six months, he'd been calling and emailing her, wanting to "talk shop." Last month, on a panel about domestic religious terrorism, she'd switched their seating arrangements so she was at the opposite end of the long table the panel sat at. It hadn't stopped him from openly seeking her out during the social event later that night and flirting with her. He'd told her he wanted her to consult for his taskforce.

He certainly couldn't be interested in her as a woman—a man like Roman Walsh dated models and actresses, not frumpy workaholic analysts who loved dank old libraries, dig sites, and hundred-year-old churches. But there was something beneath his invitation—both the verbal and nonverbal. She just couldn't put her finger on it.

Why do you keep turning him down? the devil on her shoulder complained. *Why don't you give him a chance?*

From across the way, his attention returned to his friends and she saw him flip one of his thumbs over his shoulder in her direction. The other men in the group looked over at her, two sets of hard eyes sizing her up.

Brooke quickly refocused on the comedian on stage, heat lacing up her neck.

I've got to get out of here.

This was why she'd refused to answer his emails or sit next to him on a panel. Working with his West Coast Domestic Terrorism Taskforce might be right up her alley; the experts on his team were top of the line. They analyzed bad guys and figured out ways to put criminals in jail and save US citizens, just like the SCVC Taskforce.

Unfortunately, there was no way in Hades she could be on his team. He made her a nervous wreck. His voice alone made her panties wet, not to mention that killer smile of his.

No man should be that mouthwateringly gorgeous. No man should be that…perfect.

Perfect men like Roman Walsh didn't flirt with women like her. She was a good girl, a professional academic who buried her head in ancient civilizations and religious rituals. Outside of her brief brush with fame over her book, she was a nobody.

Roman Walsh was a hero. High IQ, a body ancient Greeks would envy, and an arrest rate of criminals that wowed her. *If he knew how to handle a trowel, I might actually ask for his autograph.*

Behind that sexy smile and Superman complex, however, there had to be a volcano full of secrets. One that would erupt all over her and leave her heart fossilized.

And that was what scared her right down to her toes.

There weren't many men in her fields of study that actually made her drool. Most were older, balding, or at the very least, too pompous for her to tolerate. There were plenty of young, attractive co-eds who hit on her every time she visited a campus, but at thirty, she wasn't interested in stroking their egos by playing the cougar. With three failed relationships under her belt, she might just be done with men altogether.

Plus, she liked a man to be more than his looks, and while a few of the grad students who'd hit on her recently certainly had the brains, they were still a bit too young and idealistic for her taste. They believed they could save the world through studying about it.

Roman, on the other hand, was actually doing just that. He seemed determined to protect his country and her citizens with every breath he took.

A real, honest-to-God hero.

Just not my *hero.*

Because every time she even thought of saying something to him—her throat completely locked up. His intense blue eyes would lock on her and bam…it was like she'd been hit with a stun gun.

Her, a highly-educated, award-winning anthropologist and published author, who regularly spoke to auditoriums filled with students across the US, as well as to fellow anthropologists and religious leaders, struck dumb by a man?

Go figure.

It just made no sense that she couldn't handle a simple conversation with Dr. Walsh.

But there it was. She was too wise, and had been through too much in her life, not to at least be honest with herself.

Drool-worthy or not, men with secrets were a no-go. Her life had already been turned upside down by them and she wasn't about to offer her heart up to another person who would betray her.

A fresh roar of laughter went up from Roman and his pals. She told herself not to look, but the devil on her shoulder made her turn anyway.

He was eyeing her again with a fiendish look on his face. Was he drunk?

Her phone lit up, a text letting her know that a cab was on the way. *Estimated pickup time: five minutes.*

Good. She needed out of this place and fast. It had become entirely too hot in here.

She slipped off the bar stool and began making her excuses to the professors with her. They balked good-naturedly, and she feigned exhaustion and explained she needed to go over her notes before tomorrow's lecture.

Mission complete, she turned to go when a hard body smelling of whiskey stopped her.

"Hello, gorgeous." Roman invaded her personal space, pushing her up against the bar. "Damn, but you clean up nice."

He topped six foot easily and, even in her heels, she had to look up to meet his gaze. She opened her mouth to say, "What the hell are you doing?" but as per normal, her lips moved and nothing came out.

The gazes of her companions were on her and her cheeks flamed as if on fire. *Say something!* "No."

No?

Brilliant, Brooke.

"I believe the appropriate response to *hello*," Roman said, placing his hands on either side of the bar, blocking her in, "is a return greeting."

He was so close. All that masculine energy. Those sharp, intense eyes. She swallowed the lump in her throat. "Wha...?" Oh, lord. *Get it together!* "What...what are you doing?"

The words came out soft and breathy, but Roman apparently had no trouble hearing them. "My buddies over there bet me I couldn't get you to kiss me."

Holy cow! He was definitely drunk. "Ki...kiss you?"

His gaze dropped to her lips and he grinned like she was a medium-rare steak and he was one hungry man. "Yeah, kiss me, gorgeous. What do you say? Help a guy out so he doesn't lose a hundred bucks?"

He'd bet a hundred dollars that he could get her to kiss him? The nerve!

Laughter over something the comedian said erupted around them. Roman leaned in, putting his lips next to her ear, "Play along, Brooke."

Goosebumps skittered down the back of her spine. She grabbed one of his arms and pushed. It was warm and very firm. "No."

He didn't budge.

One of his hands slid behind her neck, gently grasping her by the nape as he looked deep into her eyes. The laughter and clapping in the bar receded and she saw a flicker of concern. "Things are about to get dangerous," he murmured, his lips so close to hers, she could smell his breath. It smelled like ginger and mint—not whiskey. "You need to get the hell out of here."

And then, without warning, he brought his lips crashing down on hers.

It was brutal and heavenly at the same time. Her brain raged for half a second before shutting down completely.

Her eyes closed, the devil on her shoulder hooting as her bones went molten. Roman's demanding tongue had no trouble parting her lips and slipping inside.

His muscled body pressed against hers, holding her to the bar. Against the wishes of the few brain cells still firing in her cerebellum, Brooke grasped his shoulders and pulled him closer.

And then he broke away, but his lips barely moved from hers.

"I'm serious," he said so low she almost missed it in her lust-induced haze. "Get out of here, now."

He released her as fast as he'd pinned her there, and she had to grab the edge of the bar to keep her weak knees from giving out.

As Roman returned to his friends and raised his hands in a Rocky gesture of conquest, they cheered. Still staggered from the kiss, Brooke could only watch as both men at the table slapped money into Roman's hand as he returned to his seat.

He wasn't kidding. They'd bet he couldn't get her to kiss him.

Technically, he kissed me.

The devil on her shoulder snickered.

From his chair, Roman sent her a hard look.

Get out of here, now.

Right. Something was about to go down. The kiss had meant nothing to him, just a way to warn her and not blow his cover.

Wow, some warning. Her knees shook again with something akin to disappointment.

What is wrong with me?

Brooke scanned the patrons, most watching the comedian or talking with their companions. The scandalized professors on either side of her made concerned noises and offered her another drink. She ignored them.

One guy wasn't watching the comedian or talking to his companions. The burly, bald-headed man wore a leather jacket with a local motorcycle club emblem on it. His focus was solely on Roman.

Oh crud.

Brooke turned to her companions from SDSU. "Why don't you guys share my cab? If you want, we can hit another club on the way…"

Before she could finish the sentence, the MC member stood and pulled out a nasty-looking weapon.

He fired into the crowd.

Bam, bam, bam, bullets poured out of an Uzi, peppering the place.

Roman was no stranger to the report of gunfire, the way it reverberated inside his chest as if someone were ringing a bell between his ribs. The way his mind cleared of all thoughts except *duck and cover.*

After discovering this bar was in Merton Cornell's territory, Roman had been expecting the gang leader to raise some hell. Only a couple of months ago, the bar had been neutral territory, but things had definitely changed since his last undercover op in San Diego. The thing that hadn't was the fact Cornell didn't like trespassers like the two MS-13 gang members Roman was sitting with.

Had been sitting with. At the moment, under the blaze of gunfire, he was crawling his ass as fast as possible across the floor to the bar.

Because even though he'd told her to get the hell out, Dr. Brooke Heaton was still here.

Standing at the bar, no less, with a look of sheer terror on her face. A deer caught in headlights.

Glass broke, wood splintered, people screamed. Instead of ducking, Heaton threw herself in front of one of her companions as bullets cut through the air around her.

Stupid woman.

Beautiful, brainy, accomplished woman, but obviously not one with enough common sense when it came to her own safety.

Her sexy ankles were in sight as he shimmied under the cover of a table toward her, other people's feet making haste in the opposite direction. Even under fire, the slender feet in the heels just high enough to emphasis her calves made him salivate. The conservative skirt that hit below her knees did nothing to dampen his very vivid imagination of what the rest of her legs looked like.

In his fantasies, they were just as shapely and toned as her calves. She spent long days in the field, digging up bones and other old shit, and the job kept her body in great shape.

A window broke. More screaming ensued. It was almost a shame he was going to have to grab those sexy ankles and drag her down.

Almost.

He reached for the leg closest to him, stretching to grasp it. His fingers skimmed her calf and, the next thing he knew, she kicked him, the heel of her shoe digging into his palm.

"Ow!" He jerked his hand out from under the dagger, reached another inch, and wrapped his hand around her narrow ankle. "Get the fuck down!"

She bent slightly to look at who was grabbing her, covering her ears and shutting her eyes as more shots rang out. The long, narrow skirt helped his cause as he yanked her foot out from under her. Like a tight rubber band, it kept her legs together and jerked the other out from under her as well.

"Ack!" she yelled over the commotion as she fell into his waiting arms. "Help!"

He cushioned her fall, her ass barely hitting the floor before he slid her toward him, moving them both back under the table. Her companion—the one she'd been shielding—ran for the exit at the back of the bar.

She gasped for air, kicking at him without realizing who he was, feet flailing and her hands smacking him. "Let me go!"

He was on the receiving end of several of those kicks, one coming dangerously close to his balls under the cover of the wooden table.

"Brooke." He shook her a bit as he locked eyes with her. "It's me."

Her rigid body went soft as they lay facing each other, her chest heaving as those beautiful turquoise eyes of hers grew rounder. "What are you doing?"

God, her lips were perfect, so pink and ripe for kissing. Her honey-colored skin invited the touch, a sprinkle of freckles across her nose and cheeks. "Saving your incredible backside, sweetheart. Now stay down."

Most of the people had evacuated and the gunfire had died down, but Cornell had one of the MS-13 gang members pinned against a wall. Augie already had a bullet in him, as indicated by the blood running down his right arm, and Cornell had relieved him of his weapon. Augie's compatriot was bleeding out on the floor near the kid's feet.

Cornell pointed the Uzi at Augie's chest and started in with his customary rhetoric about whose territory it was, and what were a couple of "no-good wetbacks from MS-13" doing here, etc., etc.

Roman slipped the handgun from his ankle holster and placed a finger to his lips when Brooke gasped.

Tugging her closer with his other hand, he aimed at Cornell's broad back.

Understanding what was about to go down, Brooke wrapped her arms around Roman's chest, clinging for dear life. Her breasts smashed against his ribcage, one shoeless foot wrapping around his leg. The act was so intimate, his vision went fuzzy for a second. How many times had he fantasized about the two of them being in this exact position?

Minus the gang members and the flying bullets, of course, but what was life without a little excitement?

Her lips brushed the lobe of his ear, making his cock dance. "Don't miss," she whispered. Her hair smelled like coconuts and fresh lemons. "Take him down."

Adrenaline buzzed in Roman's system, a thousand happy bees. He touched her hair, bringing his mouth close to her ear and breathing in her clean scent. Just like she had when he'd kissed her minutes ago, her body melted into his. "My pleasure, Dr. Heaton."

Roman fired.

CHAPTER TWO

Nearing midnight, Brooke sat in his Jeep as Roman covertly finished signing off with the locals, Feds, and Cooper Harris. Harris's taskforce had been working on a budding crime syndicate from Guatemala that had teamed up with MS-13 and he'd called Roman to see if he still had contacts inside the vicious Mexican gang. Not only did he still have a CI inside, he knew exactly which one wanted out of MS-13 and would flip on them.

He just hadn't realized Cornell and his biker gang had expanded their territory until he'd seen the man and his goons enter the bar.

In the end, however, Roman had saved Augie and taken down Cornell, who was still alive but not going back to his gang anytime soon. Both men would receive medical care, and Augie would get off with a light sentence if he helped Harris and his team with info on the Guatemalan gang.

"Thanks, man." Harris slapped Roman on the shoulder. They stood out of sight of the cop cars and bystanders. Since Roman couldn't publicly take credit for Cornell without blowing his undercover identity, Harris would get the credit.

Works for me. "Augie's not a bad kid, just mixed up in this crap because it's been part of his family for generations. Try not to get him killed."

Harris tilted his chin in Heaton's direction. Roman's Jeep was in the corner of the parking lot, away from prying eyes. "Sure she's okay?"

One of Harris's taskforce members, Ronni Punto, was in the Jeep talking to Brooke. They'd worked together, Dr. Heaton consulting on several SCVC Taskforce cases involving violent crimes and religious terrorists. Roman was just a little jealous. "I offered to have her checked out and she refused. Claims she's fine and just wants to go back to her hotel."

Which sounded perfect to him, even though he had a snowball's chance in hell of getting himself invited to her room.

"If she were working a case for me," Harris said, "I'd require a psych eval. The good doctor is a tough cookie, but she's not a field agent. Being shot at is not in her usual line of duty."

"That's just it, she's not on the DTT. I can't require her to do anything."

Harris frowned, crossing his arms over his chest. "She wasn't working with you tonight? And here, I thought you'd stolen her from me, which by the way, sort of pissed me off."

Roman shook his head. "Don't get your panties in a bunch, Harris. She's doing a lecture circuit at SDSU. Apparently, she came out with some of her nerd friends tonight and *bam*. Right time, wrong place."

"Didn't you try recruiting her?"

"Tried, yes. I need her on The Reverend case, but she won't take my calls."

"Huh." Harris grinned good-naturedly. "She always takes mine."

The jealousy in Roman's stomach amped up a notch. "She doesn't seem to like me, but for the life of me, I can't figure out why."

"You saved her life, tonight." Harris winked. "My guess? She'll be more than happy to take your calls now."

Roman's mood lifted as he gazed at the car. "You think?"

Harris chuckled. "I sense that you'd like Dr. Heaton to do more than consult on your taskforce."

Boy, would he. "If my Bruce Willis act tonight didn't seal the deal, nothing else will."

"Take it from me, she's more of an Indiana Jones kind of gal. You might try that instead."

Indiana Jones, huh? Roman stuck out his hand. "Thanks for the tip."

Harris shook it. "Good luck, man, but I'd be lying if I said I was happy about sharing her."

As Harris walked away, Agent Punto emerged from the car and headed toward Roman. She slowed as she neared him, but didn't stop. "She's totally lying about being okay."

"Is she hurt?"

"She's freaked." Punto stopped a few feet away, watching two Feds talking near the crime scene tape. "You need to put her to work."

"Contrary to popular opinion, she's not on my taskforce."

"Then get her on it," Punto said. "She needs a case to get her mind off what happened here tonight, and we don't have any that require her expertise at the moment. If she sits in her hotel room and stews, she'll never feel safe helping any of us again."

She shot him one searing look and went to join Harris.

Roman turned back to his vehicle and saw Brooke in the front seat, staring at him. Her hair had come loose from the bun and curly strands grazed her shoulders. She looked shell-shocked. Or was that her pissed expression?

What choice did he have? One way or another, he was going to get Dr. Brooke Heaton into bed with him.

Figuratively speaking, of course.

Roman Walsh had just saved her life.

Brooke's head swam, her ears still ringing from the gunshots inside the bar. Ronni—sweetheart that she was—thought Brooke's brain fog was the result of hitting her head, or maybe shock.

Shock was a possibility, but she had not hit her head. Dr. Walsh had made sure of that, his strong, capable hands cradling her skull after he'd jerked her off her feet.

All of her SDSU compatriots were safe. Scared, but not injured, outside of a few cuts and bruises from the mass exodus.

As Roman headed to the car, she saw the normal swagger in his step was off ever so slightly. The flashing lights from patrol cars and two ambulances silhouetted his lean but muscled frame. He glanced at her through the windshield as he approached, then his gaze darted away and he scanned the area around them.

The memory of his body against hers, his lips murmuring in her ear, sent a shiver down Brooke's spine.

Have mercy.

She'd never dreamed she would be held in those strong arms of his, much less hugging him tight and curling a leg around him, but that's exactly what had happened. She'd lost her ever-loving mind, her body betraying her as bullets rained down, and her nice, comfortable world had become one she didn't recognize.

"I don't know whether to thank you for saving my life," she said as Roman climbed into the driver's seat, "or be appalled at the way you yanked me off my feet in there."

"Too Cro-Magnon for you?" He grinned with all the nerve of a confident, egotistical shark.

"Neanderthal perhaps."

"I caught you, didn't I?" He started the car, the rumble of the Jeep dropping into a solid purr. "And I did warn you to exit the premises before the shooting began."

"Yes, I had all of three seconds to do so. Thank you so much."

His face glowed blue from the tricked out dashboard. "Are you seriously pissed at me right now?"

She held up her lone shoe. "You owe me a new pair of Steve Maddens. My other one is still in the bar."

"I'll take you shopping tomorrow. What time do the stores open? We can grab breakfast on the way." He put the car in drive. "On one condition, of course."

Oh, boy. Like she didn't know what that was. "No."

Seemed like that was one of the few words she didn't have any trouble saying to him tonight.

His gaze swung her way. "Come work for me, Dr. Heaton. I need you—your expertise."

And, oh that irritating grin was more than her heart could handle after the recent shock of the shooting.

I need you. The words sent her pulse skipping as erratically as when she'd been shot at.

A part of her wanted to smile back, maybe even grab him and kiss him to say thank you. The other part—the sane good girl, professional academic—wanted to whack him a couple times with her shoe. "I'll send you the bill for the new pair of shoes I pick out. On my own."

The grin fell. He shook his head and sighed, pulling out of his space. "Why won't you consult for the West Coast DTT?"

Because you scare the hell out of me. "I'm about to leave for a dig." The excuse came easy. "Besides, you have plenty of experts on your team."

He drove them out of the parking lot and away from the pulsating red and blue lights, quiet for several blocks. "Are you really that vain?"

Vain? "Are you really that rude? Why would you say such a thing?"

"You won't consider working for me because I have other experts on my taskforce? Your ego needs the spotlight that bad?"

Brooke squeezed the shoe in her hand so tightly her fingers cramped. "Rejecting your offer has nothing to do with my ego. I'm more than happy to work with the caliber of experts on your taskforce. *Your* ego, however, could be one of the reasons I've repeatedly declined your offer in the nicest way possible. Since that has been completely ineffective, let me state my refusal more clearly: no way in hell will I work for you."

"With me," he corrected. "You wouldn't work for me, Dr. Heaton, only *with* me."

"Your ego can't handle it."

He chuckled. "My ego can handle anything you dish out, sweetheart. I welcome the challenge."

The look he flashed her confirmed his statement, his eyes made even more intently blue in the dashboard light. The shoe clenched in her fingers didn't get a reprieve, but her solid grip was for an entirely new reason.

The devil on her shoulder liked this cat-and-mouse game. Liked how Roman was as at ease trading banter with her as he was saving her from a rain of bullets.

I need you.

How long had she waited to hear those words? From anyone?

Plus, she was actually talking to him while in the close confines of his car where she could smell the not intolerable scent of coffee and male sweat under the alcohol he must have splashed onto his shirt to convince his contacts that he was drunk. Maybe if she kept him on his toes and their dialogue laced with her honest irritation at him, she could stop feeling like a ridiculous teenage girl.

"You may enjoy a verbal sparring match, Dr. Walsh, but I find most of them to be tedious and unnecessary."

"Is that so, Dr. Heaton?"

He was just as mouthwateringly gorgeous in profile as he was full on. The right side of his mouth quirked as if he were holding back another insouciant grin. He may have been reining in the smile, but his voice was full of mocking humor.

All right. Walsh wasn't the only one who liked a good challenge. She was known for her stubbornness. "Look, Dr. Wa—"

"Call me Roman. I did, after all, save your life less than an hour ago."

He wasn't going to let her forget that she owed him. The tiniest bit of guilt sizzled in her belly.

I do *owe him.*

She dropped her head back against the headrest. She'd love to call him by his first name, but that evoked a level of friendship, an intimacy, they didn't share, regardless of his heroic act in the bar. "Even if my current work schedule wasn't already maxed, providing consulting services to the DTT would present a challenge for me. I'm already consulting with the SCVC Taskforce when needed. There could be a...conflict of interest."

"Conflict of interest?" He snorted. "Cooper Harris and I are on the same page. Our cases often overlap and we share resources, just like tonight. Thomas Mann's CI inside the MS-13 group recently went missing so I stepped in and used mine. Yes, Harris and I report to different directors, but we're all on the same side."

Arguing with him was getting her nowhere and they were nearly to her hotel. "Why me?"

The question seemed to catch him off guard, which was exactly what she'd intended. "Why *not* you?"

"No, I mean it. Why me specifically? Why are you so determined to get me on your team?"

She wasn't sure what she expected to hear, and she watched his expression intently to see if he had to comb through the reasons.

He didn't. As he pulled into the hotel lot, he put the Jeep in park and turned to her. "You're the best on the West Coast, Dr. Heaton, in all areas of your expertise. Maybe in the entire country." He gave her that irritating grin once more and took the Madden from her hand as he leaned in close. "And I only ever allow the *very* best on my team."

Before she could respond—she was once more speechless anyway—his phone rang.

The Jeep's in-dash nav system was linked to his cell by Bluetooth. The sexy nav voice told him the incoming call was from Polly. Did he want to answer?

Polly, of course. Probably his girlfriend. Brooke reached for the door latch. "Thanks for the ride."

She started to get out, but the door was locked. A hand landed on her arm as he answered the phone.

"What's up, P?"

The woman's voice sounded young, a little anxious. "You okay, boss? We heard about the gunfight with Merton."

"All limbs intact, although I'm on the hook for a pair of shoes by some guy named Steve Madden."

"O-*kay*. I can help you with that if you need it." Her confusion vanished and she went into business mode once more. "We've had another incident, looks like the work of The Rev."

"Shit." Roman shook his head, his hand on the steering wheel balling into a fist. "What happened?"

As Polly, obviously from the DTT, relayed the details of a massacre at a small church just outside the city limits, Roman put the Jeep back in gear, his face grim.

"At least thirty dead, half of them children." Polly said softly. "All were undocumented. One of the victims left a suicide video on his phone, detailing what they were doing. He referred to The Reverend as Pastor Luke."

Brooke's stomach churned. Roman punched the steering wheel. "Send the address to me. I'm on my way."

He disconnected, then turned to Brooke. In the depths of his eyes, she saw the distress at the deaths of thirty-some people, including children, underlined with determination to find their killer. "Have you heard of The Reverend?"

She'd heard of him all right. He was a serial killer targeting those in the area whom he considered 'unclean.'

Twenty years ago, she'd gotten up close and personal with the same sort of man.

"Just drive," she said. Whether she wanted to or not, she was about to help the DTT tonight. "I'm going with you."

———————

Three ambulances pulled away in quick succession as Roman drove up to the blocked off area near the church and parked. None of them had their lights on.

Bodies.

They were too late to save anyone.

Before they'd left the hotel, Roman had insisted Brooke change out of her dress and pick up shoes. He wasn't taking her to a crime scene with nothing on her feet. She hadn't said much on the drive over and he could see how deeply disturbed she was at the idea of checking out the multiple suicide-homicide with him.

Yes, the parishioners had all committed suicide, but it was the work of The Reverend who'd brainwashed them into doing it.

The Rev wasn't the first cult leader to convince his followers to do so. Jim Jones was probably the most remembered, convincing over 900 people to commit "revolutionary suicide" and drink poison. Not many years ago, just outside of San Diego, the Heaven's Gate members had killed themselves in order to enable their souls to jump on board a spaceship following the Hale-Bopp comet.

But Roman didn't believe The Reverend was a true cult leader—he didn't spend time gathering a flock and preaching to them or trying to take their money or possessions to amass his own. His targets had neither. He moved swiftly, from one group to the next, seeming to exact some kind of vengeance or justice. He was a serial killer, pure and simple, trying to rid the area of nonwhites, it seemed.

Polly, standing inside the barricades with her tablet in hand, waved him over. He flashed his badge at the police guard and guided Brooke past a group of law enforcement and crime scene techs.

Frizzy hair flying, Polly met them halfway. Roman made quick introductions, Brooke distractedly shaking Polly's hand as the DTT's crime scene expert smiled good-naturedly, not missing a beat that Roman had brought her and welcoming Brooke to the team. Brooke didn't respond other than to ask if they were sure this was the work of The Reverend.

Behind Polly, the small church, once abandoned, looked shabby and rundown in the glare of the lights.

Polly handed Roman the tablet with the details laid out in bulleted points the way he liked. She recited the details out loud for Brooke's benefit.

Death toll: 34 and rising.

Survivors: none.

Method used to kill victim(s): lethal dose of cyanide in the sacrament cups of grape juice served to each member present.

"Pastor Luke? That's what they called him?" Several other points were listed, but Roman's eyes skipped over them and he handed the tablet back to Polly. "Matthew, Mark, Luke. He's using the apostles in the New Testament. We should have seen that correlation earlier. Put out an update to the team. We need to find any and all pastors that pop up along the coast with a disciple name."

"First, middle, or last," Brooke added. She stared at the front of the church where the double doors were propped open and crime scene techs were going in and out. "He may use the apostle name as any of them. John will be next, and I'm guessing there will be a lot of Pastor Johns to vet."

Roman rubbed his knuckles across his beard. He needed a shave. "*If* he continues in biblical order." After the last few days with only five hours of sleep in sum total, he could use an energy drink to offset the exhaustion humming in his veins. "He may not."

"He will." Brooke seemed certain. "But it will be a few weeks before he starts amassing his next group of displaced immigrants and nonwhite flock. You'll have a hard time finding him because of that very type of population. They stay off the grid and, by virtue of their secrecy, so does he."

"Right," Polly said, lifting one covert brow at Roman. "Do you want to go inside?"

As her answer, Brooke marched toward the open doors. Roman fell into step beside her and Polly caught up, walking backward and typing on her tablet as she spoke. "Same scene as the previous two. There are sigils on every victim's forehead, a burnt offering was made, and of course, it's a full moon."

They were at the doors; Brooke pulled up short, gaze going skyward. "Burnt offering? Full moon?"

"That's part of The Rev's MO." Polly ushered her through the doors, pointing to a wall just inside the vestibule with a painting of the moon in its various phases. Blood cut a swath across it. "He follows the moon's cycle and apparently smears someone's blood over the painting before he leaves."

Brooke studied the painting. "That's new."

The comment was so soft, Roman wasn't sure he'd heard her correctly. "New? Both of the previous groups had the same painting. He convinces his parishioners that the Second Coming will arrive the night of a full moon and it's God's Will that they meet the angels coming to collect their souls."

Brooke studied the picture. "That's not biblical though. There are mentions of the moon in the Bible, but not exactly corresponding to sacrifices or the Rapture."

"The sigils he carves on their foreheads aren't biblical either." Polly shot him a look and Roman conceded, "At least, we don't think they are. That's why we could use you to confirm it."

"Are the bodies still here?"

Polly paled slightly. She was a CSI, and damn good at her job, but examining a mass suicide was a lot to stomach for anyone. "In the sanctuary. He delivered communion there."

Brooke started toward the sanctuary, face a grim mask. "And once they're dead, he mutilates their bodies and disappears."

An official police CSI tech with a camera hanging from her neck strap brushed past them. She'd worked with the taskforce before and she called over her shoulder, "Sending the pictures to you, Polly, as soon as Detective Clyffe gives me the all-clear."

"Thanks, Ferne!" Polly called back.

The green commercial carpeting led them to the sanctuary. Here, too, the doors were pinned open.

"Detective Clyffe?" Brooke asked Roman. "Why is San Diego PD handling the case? Where is the FBI?"

"The Reverend is our case." He stopped, seeing Clyffe at the head of the main aisle speaking on his phone to someone. Around him were empty wooden pews, the back ones displaying laid out bodies covered with white sheets. "We're stretched thin so the locals do the discovery work for us and help where they can."

Brooke hmm'd under her breath and Roman heard the criticism in her tone, although he didn't know why she cared.

Above the podium, Christ hung on the cross, staring down with sad eyes at the dead who'd died in His name.

"If you don't need me," Polly said, clutching her tablet, "I'll hang out here and notify the rest of the team about the apostle thing."

Roman nodded, then took Brooke's elbow to escort her in while waving at Clyffe. "You sure you want to actually look at a body?"

Cooper Harris's words about Brooke not being a field agent rang in his head. He'd inadvertently lured her here, but now wondered if this was a good idea. All he needed was his potential new expert to go lights out on him once she saw the body. "Polly can show you the pictures. Might be...you know." *Less graphic.*

"I'll be fine." Brooke's gaze was glued to the nearest white sheet. Her throat constricted as she swallowed hard. "I need to see what he did to them."

Her tight voice told him there was something more,

something personal here, and it hinted at the doctor already knowing more about this case than he did. Was that possible?

She started forward and he gently touched her arm to stop her. "Have you come across The Rev's work before?"

"I..." Her hesitation was accompanied by a gray pallor that washed over her face. "I'm familiar with his ritualistic killings."

Familiar, hell. She looked like she'd seen far too much of this bastard's signature work. "You've worked on a case related to him? Was it for the FBI?"

"Not exactly." Her throat constricted again. "Let's just say, I've studied him to a certain degree."

On one hand, Roman knew this was a score for him—finally, he had the expert he'd needed for the past year to complete his team and bring The Rev in.

On the other hand, there was no way he wanted to subject Brooke to the nightmares that accompanied the job he did. The things he'd seen that couldn't be unseen. Until this moment, he hadn't realized she might be in the field with him. He'd planned to keep her safe behind a desk, researching homegrown terrorists and those like The Reverend, who committed mass murder on American soil. The Reverend was no different than the Urban Warriors, a gang who blew up federal buildings, or the Outlaws motorcycle gang who killed cops up and down I-5. They all believed they were true Americans, and that those who weren't should be exterminated.

He let his hand linger on her arm. "Studying him is different than seeing his handiwork up close and personal."

She scrutinized his face for a moment, her eyes searching his. A ghost of emotion chased across her expression. "Thank you for trying to protect me. I assure you I will not lose it when I see the body under that sheet."

Tough, controlled, determined. Yep, she was going to be one hell of an asset to his team.

If he didn't scare her off.

Taking her hand seemed like a natural thing to do as he led

her to the body she wanted to examine. At first her fingers stiffened, then she stepped forward with him, her hand cool in his much warmer one. He released her, as together they bent down, he at the victim's head, and she next to the shoulder.

"Ready?" he asked, because he had to make sure. He knew what waited for them under the sheet.

She took a deep breath and seemed to hold it, giving him a nod.

With a silent prayer for the deceased, he crossed himself— his Irish catholic upbringing still in his blood. Then he peeled back the sheet slowly, revealing the woman underneath.

Dark hair and eyes, probably in her early forties. Blood had dried on the woman's forehead, outlining the sigil that had been carved there. Her eyes, still open, had a bluish tinge to them and were rolled up into her head. Her mouth showed burns from the poison she'd consumed.

Brooke's breath came out in a rush. "This poor woman." She gently touched the woman's shoulder, and Roman saw a hint of tears in her eyes as she studied the bloody sigil.

Detective Clyffe ended his call and headed their way. Abruptly, Brooke stood and whirled around, heading out of the sanctuary.

"Broo—Dr. Heaton," Roman called, replacing the sheet and straightening as Clyffe caught up to him.

Brooke kept boogying, leaving him behind. "I'll be in touch," she called.

So much for not losing it.

And how exactly, did she think she was getting back to her hotel?

Clyffe shook his hand and started reeling off the facts Polly had already shared and Roman tried to give the man his full attention. His focus, however, kept going to the open doors, waiting for Brooke to come back.

She didn't.

With a sigh, Roman keyed in on the tired, rumpled detective and got to work.

CHAPTER THREE

Even after all these years, college campuses still made Roman want a beer.

Yep, beer and hormones, all tangled up in academic pursuits.

The good old days.

As he found the lecture hall he was looking for, a pretty co-ed in flip-flops gave him a flirty smile as she passed. He smiled back, his ego enjoying the stroke.

Criminal Justice 301 and International Human Rights Law, a graduate level class, had a joint lecture today with a visiting expert. Unfortunately, he was fifty minutes late to hear Dr. Heaton's presentation on cross-border serial killers who used murder to make social, religious, and political points.

The heavy door was no quiet beast as he eased into the coolness of the lecture hall, dozens of eyes turning to see who was interrupting.

It was a standard setup with the lectern in a pit and rows of seats graduating up and out in a curve. The professor, sitting near the back, rose and came to him, speaking in subdued tones. "Can I help you?"

At the lectern in the pit, Brooke's eyes met his briefly as a kid asked her about a case she'd helped the SCVC Taskforce solve a few months ago. She was dressed in another of those conservative, form-fitting skirts and a blouse that shimmered under the overhead lights. Her hair was pulled back from her face in a tight, low bun, and decorative earrings swung from her ears every time she moved.

Roman flashed his badge at the prof, saving himself time explaining who he was. "Sorry to interrupt." He matched the man's hushed tone. "I'm here to speak with Dr. Heaton when she's finished."

The professor, barely five-five, with round spectacles and a tweed vest that was way too warm for the SoCal spring day, smiled benignly and held out a hand toward one of the seats in the back row as invitation.

Roman sat, listening to Brooke's sexy voice answer the student's question. She now ignored Roman, her slender fingers fidgeting with a paperclip. A couple times, she glanced his way, and just as quickly diverted her gaze back to the student.

He made her nervous, but he didn't understand why. Did she really think he'd let her get away so easily?

He kicked back, enjoying the fact he could throw the buttoned-up PhD off her game. She was so confident when discussing subjects she loved. It totally turned him on.

As she explained the background on the killer, she sounded more like a criminal behaviorist than a religious studies doctorate. Which in some ways, she was. Understanding various religions—some ancient or so obscure most people had never heard of them—was one thing. Understanding the killers who used those religions as a means to justify murder was another.

The next time her gaze bounced up to Roman's, he winked at her.

The paperclip slipped out of her fingers and landed on the floor. She quickly picked it up and tossed it on the nearby desk, grabbing a pen instead and nervously clicking it several times. It looked as though she was forcing herself not to look up at him.

"Are you sure it wasn't The Reverend?" the kid asked and Brooke stopped clicking the pen. "Are you sure the SCVC

Taskforce got the right guy? I heard The Rev hit another church last night. Is it true?"

A fine sheen of perspiration shone on Brooke's forehead. Understandable under the hot lights of the pit.

But her suddenly tight body language suggested she was flashing back to the previous night, seeing the body under the sheet and the bloody sigil on the victim's forehead all over again.

She'd scored a ride to her hotel from one of the local cops and hadn't answered Roman's calls or texts.

Blowing me off again.

So he showed up here to put her on the spot. He needed to know her analysis of that sigil, and he wanted to know what her relationship was to The Reverend, if any. His digging after he'd left the crime scene had revealed no official link from the doctor to the killer.

But there was one. He could smell it.

And didn't that open up a can of questions?

He didn't like unanswered questions.

"No," she finally said to the student, making work of gathering papers she'd laid out on the table. "The serial killer I helped the SCVC Taskforce apprehend in March has little in common with The Reverend. Tyson Paetro was using his own version of witchcraft and was hired by a gang leader named Lakai Cruz who wanted his enemies to die and their families cursed, including all members in their gangs. Paetro kidnapped members of rival gangs, cut out their hearts, boiled their flesh from their bones, and ground the bones into powder. Which Cruz then sprinkled over his food and consumed during ritualized ceremonies celebrating him as a king or god. He believed he was making himself more powerful when it came to exterminating his enemies."

"And how does that differ from The Rev?" a girl asked. "He's Christian, right?"

As if that were the biggest difference.

Brooke hesitated before sticking the pile of papers in her

briefcase. "The Reverend's case is an ongoing investigation, so I'm not at liberty to discuss specifics, but yes, his rituals follow a Christian-based *modus operandi*. He uses a mix of Catholic and fundamental Christian symbolism and rituals, but his victims are not gang members. I'm afraid that's all I can tell you."

The class professor stood and clapped his hands together to get everyone's attention. "I'm afraid that's all we have time for. Thank you, Dr. Heaton, for this fascinating lecture. I hope you'll come back and present for us again in the fall."

Applause was sporadic and students began talking, shoving their laptops and other stuff into backpacks and heading out.

A few gathered around the lectern, asking Brooke questions. One was the guy who'd started The Reverend conversation, and Roman saw he wasn't all that young. *Must be one of the grad students.*

The professor allowed her to answer a couple of quick questions, then shooed the students off. He shook Brooke's hand and held it a little longer than necessary, speaking in such low tones Roman had to lean forward to hear him.

"I heard about what happened last night at the bar. Dr. Reid told me. Are you all right?"

Brooke smiled, withdrawing her hand. "It was quite the evening." She chuckled, as if being shot at were an everyday occurrence. "But I'm fine. I had a"—her gaze shot to Roman, who stood and started down the aisle—"guardian angel."

Guardian angel, huh? He'd go with that, although *angel* might be a stretch.

"I would love to pick your brain over lunch," the professor said. "There's a sandwich shop on campus. My treat."

He grinned and Brooke's smile slipped off her face. "Oh, I'm so sorry, but I can't. I have…a…"

"She has a lunch date with me," Roman said, leaning on a seat in front. He looked her in the eye. "Ready, Dr. Heaton?"

She gripped her briefcase tightly and narrowed her eyes at him. "Lunch. Right."

For a second she didn't move, as if considering which was worse—lunch with Dr. Tweed or him. Finally, she offered her fake smile once more. "Thank you for having me, Dr. Olsen."

"I meant what I said about having you come back in the fall," Olsen called after them as Brooke brushed past Roman and hustled up the steps to the door.

Her only response was a wave over her shoulder. Roman jogged to get to the door first and open it for her. "I'm sorry I missed your lecture. Looks like you wrapped Dr. Tweed around your finger."

They broke out into the warm sunshine and Brooke kept walking at a pace Roman suspected was challenging in the tight skirt. He did enjoy the way it spotlighted her curvy ass though. Man, what he'd do to get his hands on that ass.

When she realized he'd fallen behind, she stopped abruptly and whirled. A second too quick, she caught him staring at her backside.

Her lips pinched and her eyes narrowed. "Why are you here?"

"You still haven't thanked me for saving your life last night."

Those pretty eyes narrowed even more. "Try again."

She really was just like a profiler, knowing he was there for a far more serious reason. He liked that she called him on his exaggerations. Most take-charge women in his line of work had to be over-the-top. Brooke's assertiveness wasn't the same. She called it like it was and didn't take crap. "You said you'd be in touch, yet you don't answer my calls or texts."

"I was being polite."

A group of students wandered past. Roman waited until they were out of earshot. "So you had no intention of discussing last night's case with me?"

"There's really nothing I can tell you about the sigil."

"Liar."

She blinked several times and drew back. Apparently she didn't like having the tables turned on her. "Excuse me?"

31

"You heard me. You're lying and I want to know why. You know damn well what that sigil is and what it means. You expect me to be straight with you? Then you be straight with me."

Her eyes closed briefly, long lashes resting against her flawless skin. "I wrote up notes for you." She blinked her eyes open and he saw a flatness covering her emotions. "I'll email them, okay?"

She turned on her heel and started marching away. He caught up to her as she entered the parking lot. "Thank you. I appreciate that."

She kept walking. He did too, right beside her.

"You cut your hair, I see."

He ran fingers through his shorter locks. "No more undercover work until I nail our guy. I didn't mind helping Cooper, but now I can't get distracted. The Rev's going down."

At the end of the sidewalk, she stopped and faced him. "Why are you following me?"

"I'm walking you to your car."

He shot her a smile, hoping that would keep her from suspecting his true intentions.

It didn't. "How gentlemanly of you, but that's not necessary."

"Come on, Brooke. Cut me some slack here."

"About what?"

"Why won't you consult for my team? Why won't you help me on this case?"

She dropped her gaze to her shoes. Nice, solid, pumps. Very college professor-ish. One toe rose, the heel digging in as she kept her focus glued to her feet. "I'm not the best person for your team."

His words from the night before boomeranged back at him. "Of course you are. You have the academic background and the real-world experience to help my team catch killers. Cooper Harris says he's never found any consultant who understands his violent ritual cases as well as you do."

In the sunlight, her turquoise eyes darkened as she met his gaze once more. "It's not the cases, Roman."

"Then what is it?"

Her lips parted to answer, but then she snapped her mouth shut and shook her head. "I'll send you my analysis. That's all I can do for now. Like I told you last night, my schedule is booked."

She left him standing on the sidewalk and he tapped a fist against his forehead. He had to be insane, or at least a glutton for punishment. Why didn't he go down his list and find the next most likely candidate to help him out?

Because I don't want anyone else.

He had to find her hot button. The thing that would lure her in. Last night, it had been the deaths of those people. Her compassion for them. Maybe that was the key.

Skirting around a pair of girls who had suddenly appeared beside him, he ignored their hellos and coy smiles, running to catch up to Brooke one more time.

She'd found her rental car and unlocked the door. As she opened it, he grabbed it and held on. "Come with me," he said. "There's an older crime scene I want you to look at."

"I told you, I'm not interested."

"The last time The Reverend hit a group, he did it at a site close to the border, out in the desert. It's a place illegals squat while waiting for relatives to get them or their fake papers to come through. He left dozens of sigils on boulders around their bodies. Come look at it with me. They're still there—the sigils. The site hasn't been disturbed; the few locals in that area believe the place carries a curse. They call it *Maldito* and won't go near it."

She sighed heavily, tossing her briefcase over to the passenger seat and looking out over the parking lot. "I'm leaving for L.A. this afternoon. I don't have time to go out to the desert."

"What's in L.A.?"

"My home. My job."

He knew that, but at least she hadn't said boyfriend. "If I make you miss your flight, I'll personally drive you to L.A."

"Why is this so important to you?"

Unanswered questions. The fear in her eyes, or whatever it had been that he'd seen last night, bugged the shit out of him. That and the fact she'd mentioned the full moon killings were "new".

"I have to stop this guy, Brooke. Now, before he kills again. I can't let him win, and I have a very strong gut instinct that you're the person who can help me get in his head and understand him in a way I haven't yet. You can help me stop him from killing other innocent men, women, and children." He watched the war going on behind her no-longer shielded eyes. "Please," he added.

She kicked off her heels and opened the back passenger door, tossing them inside and grabbing a pair of bright red kicks. Slipping those on, she pulled out a gym bag. "I'll go change and meet you at your car. What lot are you in?"

He tried to play it cool and suppress the smile that threatened to break free. "Two lots over. Same car as last night."

"Give me five," she said and walked toward the building.

He did a fist pump and said a silent, "yes" before taking off at a jog for his Jeep.

The locals were right—the place reeked of being cursed.

If only I believed in such things.

Of course, Brooke had seen some weird stuff in her career studying religion, politics, and ancient cultures. Curses and black magic were pretty much present in every civilization and culture.

Two-dozen miles southeast of San Diego, the site was a

ghost town—a sad, broken place where a mass killing had occurred. As the midday sun beat down and warmed her head, Brooke could see the desert shimmer, heat rising. In those shimmers, she saw the faces of those long dead. In the too-still, weighted air, she swore she heard the wails of their spirits.

Roman stood beside her, quiet and reverent, as if he saw and heard the same.

Although her hand automatically moved to make the sign of the cross, she stilled it. Her days of Catholicism were over. Years of studying different religions and civilizations had cemented her belief in the idea of a oneness that all living things shared, but she no longer believed there was one omnipotent God as depicted by Judaism, Christianity, and Islam. If there was, He had an amoral sense of humor.

But this place…it was so disturbing that she made the sign of the cross anyway. To protect herself as well as to honor those who'd died here.

Several hodgepodge structures stood in a semi-circle, listing to their sides, the duck cloth used as window and door coverings torn and dirty. Small pits, dug deep into the sand and rock, showed signs of old fires. Broken bowls and pots were scattered here and there, along with empty pop bottles, woven rugs, and a rusted out vehicle or two.

Turning to look north, she took a couple steps away, shaking off the goose flesh riding her skin. The dirt road they'd driven in on cut through scrub brush, funky shaped acacias, and mesquite trees created by Mother Nature's winds.

In the distance, hills and mountains formed a bowl around them, the nearest incorporated village was over six miles away.

"How did he find them?" she wondered out loud. "How did he hook up with them out here?"

"It took a while, but we traced a lead to the St. Paul Fountain of Hope Mission. He probably heard about this place from some of the folks who hang out there. A few may have come through here at one point or another. He offered to help, was brought here to perform services, and after a few months, convinced the folks to drink the Kool-Aid."

Drink the Kool-Aid. A reference to Jonestown and the cult leader who'd convinced his followers to drink poison.

Taking a deep breath and bracing herself, she walked over to the center of the camp where a large circle had been laid out with boulders. A meeting place? In her mind, she saw the people each taking a seat on one as they listened to The Reverend preach.

Now the man was long gone, having taken more lives. To what end? It seemed his goal was to cleanse Southern California of nonwhites. The groups he targeted had little access to the news and often didn't speak English. As desperate as they were, they were easy to befriend and brainwash into doing what he wanted.

The memory of her childhood friend flashed across Brooke's mind. Aleisha and her parents had been good people, so kind and happy, until the night a religious fanatic had killed all three of them.

Because of the color of their skin.

Roman's shadow appeared next to her, short under the noonday sun. "You okay?"

"You said there were sigils?"

He touched her elbow, guiding her over the rough terrain as he walked her closer to the boulders. "He laid the bodies inside this circle, heads in the center, feet facing out toward the rocks."

She saw the drawings now, the edges of some fuzzy and messed up from the rains, wind, and sun. Definitely a ritualistic killing, but why the rocks? Why hadn't The Rev drawn sigils on their foreheads in keeping with his MO?

Moving closer to one of the more detailed versions, she set her hands on the large boulder and leaned over to get a better look.

Four lines formed the sigil, but the design was wrong. A new chill swept over her skin and her stomach did a somersault.

"This isn't the same sigil he used on the people at the church. This one is similar, but different."

Roman bent down next to the boulder, the sun glinting off his shorter hair turning it from licorice to one shot through with underlying strands of graphite. He'd trimmed up his beard, too, the whole effect making him look more mature but still as sexy as ever.

His T-shirt today was an ice blue, his tattooed arms a sharp contrast. His jeans were worn in all the right places, a pair of colorful Converse shoes peeking out from the cuffs. "He leaves a different mark at each scene."

A wave of lightheadedness snuck up on her. She'd felt the same thing last night, but today's sigil hit even closer to home. "Did he carve anything onto their bodies?"

Roman shook his head. "Just the rocks."

Heat engulfed her. Her tongue stuck to the roof of her mouth. At the base of her spine, though, sat the cold prick of fear. "What about the moon photo? Was that here?"

Her voice sounded too strained, almost hopeful. She'd convinced herself last night that it couldn't be him. *Confirmation bias.* A term often used in scientific circles meaning the tendency to interpret new evidence as confirmation of one's existing beliefs. She'd convinced herself last night that the sigils were different enough, it couldn't be the same man who'd killed Aleisha.

But what if it was? This sigil was nearly the same. Not quite, but close. What if Aleisha's killer had changed his MO since that night, adding in the moon phase and ramping up his kills?

"Over there." Roman pointed to the side of one of the shacks. "On the east side."

Her legs wobbled as she walked around the circle to the leaning building. She stepped wrong on a rock and her ankle twisted, throwing her off balance.

Strong hands gripped her waist and righted her. "Whoa.

You don't look so good," Roman said. "Why don't we head back to the car and get some water?"

A part of her liked the sensation of his hands just above her hips, steadying her. Keeping her upright. Another wanted to run far away. "I need to see the..."

Her tongue was thick, her throat scratchy. All she could do was point.

Frowning, he nodded and shifted one hand to her elbow. "Lean on me."

She did, the dizziness subsiding a bit as they stepped into the shade of a tree.

Lifting her gaze, she saw the crudely painted moons, from new to full, forming an arc on the dried and rotted wood. They'd been drawn with white paint that was now faded and dull.

A rusty brown stain cut across the depiction of the full moon.

Blood.

She locked her knees, licked her dry lips, brain spinning. "*I looked when He broke the sixth seal, and there was a great earthquake; and the sun became black as sackcloth made of hair, and the whole moon became like blood.*"

Roman's gaze pinned her. "Bible verse?"

A light breeze tickled across her hand where it held onto his. "Revelation 6:12."

"Revelation? Like as in the apocalypse, Four Horseman Book of Revelation?"

"That's the one." She could breathe again.

"You said it wasn't biblical."

"I thought the moon cycle was being used as part of the ritual, but it's actually just a message. It appears he believes he's started the apocalypse."

Roman's tone was just a little sarcastic. "Great."

Brooke nearly chuckled with relief. Whoever this was, it wasn't *her* Reverend. Not the bad man her mom always warned was coming for her.

At least she didn't think it was him. The man who'd killed Aleisha and her parents had used a sigil, but there had been just the one, and no full moon reference.

This killer, whoever he was, was fixated on cleansing the world of anyone not of the white race—nothing new in the history of the world there—but his MO seemed to vary enough, she was almost positive it wasn't the man who'd altered her world forever.

Serial killers throughout history had rarely changed their signatures. They had a specific way of choosing their victims and killing them based on their motivation. Motivation differed from one killer to another, even if they had a similar goal like wiping out nonbelievers or a particular race. She'd seen it plenty of times while studying various past cultures.

"Have you seen enough?" Roman asked. "We have pictures if you want to see what the fresh crime scene looked like."

The sigil isn't the same, but so close.

That fact would keep nagging at her, she knew. She'd studied sigils for years, an all-encompassing obsession since that night when she was ten, but she'd never traced the killer's mark to anything in the ancient texts she studied. It was made up, not part of any religion or culture, at least none that had been recorded and still existed.

Could two killers make up a similar sigil? Were they working together? Had the first mentored the second and passed his notes onto his protégé?

Wouldn't be the first time, but it made her antsy to consider it.

There were too many questions. Questions the ghosts in this desert couldn't answer for her.

"I'll take that water now," Brooke said. "And I could use some lunch. I didn't eat breakfast this morning."

He helped her back toward the car. Teasing laced his tone. "Do you have time for lunch before your plane departs, Dr. Heaton?"

She removed her hand from his and put distance between them. "Won't do me much good to pass out on the plane from low blood sugar, now will it? I'll just have to reschedule my flight."

He snapped his fingers in a *darn it* move. "And here I thought I might be taking a road trip with you today."

Inside the car, he fetched a bottle of water for her from a cooler in the trunk and started the engine, wiping sweat from his forehead. He chugged his own water in several gulps and flipped the empty bottle into the backseat as his phone rang.

His face screwed up slightly. "Sorry, I need to take this."

She wiped at her own face with the sleeve of her shirt and nodded. Sipping her water slowly, the coldness tickled her throat and lingered in her stomach. She closed her eyes for a moment, the questions circling like vultures in her brain.

"Yes, Mom," Roman said.

Mom? Brooke snuck a glance at him and saw his eyes were closed as if he were searching for patience. "I will be there. I promised, didn't I?"

A pause in which he sighed quietly as a woman's muffled voice went on for a minute. He started to speak, then stopped when she wouldn't allow him to interrupt.

He opened his eyes, caught Brooke staring at him, and gave her an embarrassed grin. "I'm on a case right now, Mom. I'll call you back, okay? But seriously, I promised I'd be there and I will. Nothing will keep me from the party, I swear."

A few more reassurances were offered and he finally got off the phone.

"My parents are celebrating their 35th anniversary this weekend," he explained, sticking his phone in its car holder. "Dad has diabetes and Mom's afraid he won't be around for many more since he has a lot of complications from it. It's important to get the whole family together."

A pang of longing hit her right below her heart. "You have a big family?"

He grinned as they drove away from the site, heading back toward San Diego. "Three siblings, two with kids, and there's a bunch of aunts, uncles, and cousins."

Lucky you. "Sounds like you better not disappoint your mother."

His grin kicked up a notch. "Never. The last thing I ever want to do is let her down."

Perfect. Brooke closed her eyes and tried not to like him. *He's so damn perfect.*

And something told her she wasn't going to make a later flight back to L.A. either.

Because if there was one thing she could use a little more of in her life, it was Dr. Roman Walsh and all of his perfectness.

CHAPTER FOUR

Roman watched Brooke screw up her face as she shielded it from the sun with one hand. "Are you sure they serve lunch here?"

The wayside cafe was made to look like a Wild Wild West outpost and was the only public place in the ten-mile area. "Gas, groceries, and the best homemade bread around," Roman assured her.

Her color had returned to normal and she was steady on her feet again. Her little episode at the old crime scene left him wondering—had it been low blood sugar like she'd claimed, or something more?

Since she often worked in the blazing sun on archeological digs, he doubted it was heat stroke.

She sniffed the air and licked her lips. "Mmm. Homemade bread. I think I can smell it."

The faint aroma of warm yeast and butter drifted on the light breeze to him too, and his stomach rumbled. "They have pastries as well."

Ten minutes later, they were seated outside under a piñon tree, the dried out wood of the picnic table groaning under their combined weights. Roman popped the lid on both of their sodas, and watched as Brooke pinched off a piece of a brown sugar scone she'd said would be her dessert.

"Oh, my stars, this is delicious." Her fingers snuck another corner from the scone. "Who knew you could find bakery goods in the middle of nowhere? And they'd be really good to boot?"

The cafe's owner was a transplant from somewhere south of the border and had a keen knack for supplying locals with basic necessities, the occasional lost tourists with trinkets, and satisfying her own urge to operate a cafe. "The ice cream's not bad either."

"You come here often?" Brooke teased.

"Only when I'm trying to impress a woman."

She seemed more at ease than she had since, well, forever. "Not a bad strategy with me. I don't do fancy restaurants, but I'll kill for a decent scone."

He'd found one way to her heart. Or at least her stomach. "I'll keep that in mind."

Her pretty eyes locked on his, and for a moment, he felt that nervousness she seemed to have around him surface. "Don't do that," she said, toying with the lid of her soda.

"Do what?"

"Smolder."

He rested his elbows on the table, wishing that breeze would kick up again while they waited for their sandwiches. "Sorry?"

One of her fingers drew an air outline around his face. "You smolder, and do that thing with your voice, like every hero in every romance novel. Don't do that to me."

"I have no idea what you're talking about."

"Of course, you don't. You're a real-life hero. But you're the kind of guy they write stories about. You're just like Conrad Flynn in *Operation Sheba*. If I didn't know better, I'd bet Misty Evans, the author, based him on you."

She was so sincere, he couldn't help but grin. "A romance novel hero, huh? Hmm. I've never been compared to one of those before. Let me guess, he has staggering good looks and a heart of gold."

Thinking he mocked her, her eyes narrowed, looking almost silvery as the tree swayed in a sudden gust of breeze and a stripe of sunlight fell across her features. "Romance novels are my weakness. After years of reading academia tomes and journals, I occasionally need lighter fare. I like them. They have happy endings. And yes, Con is good-looking, although he doesn't have blue eyes, his are brown."

While he'd never admit it, he'd read one or two himself, sneaking them from his sisters when they were younger. The heroes were exactly the kind of men he'd wanted to be. The sex scenes weren't bad either. He'd learned a few tips along the way. "I wasn't judging your reading habits."

"Of course you were. Everyone does."

"Can we get back to the part where you're comparing me to this Flynn character? Is he a pirate? A cop?"

She rolled her eyes and chuckled. "He's a spy who fakes his death to save Julia, the woman he loves. She doesn't know he's still alive until he comes back to reveal there's a mole inside the CIA and he thinks it's her new boyfriend. He smolders at her all the time."

"He lied to her about his death? Ouch." He waggled his eyebrows. "But I assume this smoldering thing is one of the ways he wins her heart."

"It doesn't hurt."

"And you think I'm doing that to you."

The shield rose again. "Not for the same reasons, of course. Conrad's in love with Julia and he wants to save her from the mole. She doesn't need saving because she's a spy herself and quite competent at that, but that's neither here nor there. You want me to consult for your team, and being the hero you are, I guess smoldering comes naturally when you pour on the charm."

"I honestly didn't realize I was doing any such thing. My goal here isn't to charm you so much as prove my team needs you."

"You always get what you want, don't you?"

He snorted. "Hardly."

The owner appeared, carrying a tray with their sandwiches. Her dark hair was shot through with silvery streaks, her brown eyes crinkling at the corners as she smiled. "Two enchilada sandwiches, two chips. Anything else?"

Roman thanked her and she nodded and left. He handed Brooke her sandwich and she snagged a napkin from the stack on the tray. "So this is an enchilada sandwich." Sauce dripped from the edge of the bread. "Kinda messy, isn't it?"

"Wait until you taste it."

She bit in, sauce running down her hand that she mopped at as she moaned softly. "You're right, it's amazing."

They ate for several minutes in silence before Brooke took a drink and asked, "Did you grow up in San Diego?"

Watching her eat, her tongue flicking out to lick sauce from the corner of her mouth nearly rendered him speechless. A dab of the hot sauce ended up on her jaw and he wanted to lean over and kiss it off.

What is wrong with me?

He'd been crushing on her for nearly a year, but she'd been damn hard to access. He'd given up on his little fantasies for awhile, yet here they were, rushing back with a vengeance. She could do something completely normal, like eat in front of him, and it stirred up things down below. The image of her in the skirt from that morning surfaced, as did the memory from the previous night when she'd wound her leg around his and whispered in his ear, *don't miss.*

"Roman?"

She was watching him, waiting for him to respond, a tiny wrinkle in the center of her forehead. She'd called him by his first name and the sound was like a shot of whiskey going straight to his stomach.

"I uh… What was the question?"

A small smile lifted the corners of her mouth. "Did you grow up in San Diego?

God, he wanted that mouth on him. A fantasy of taking her there on the picnic table jabbed his frontal lobe and the stirring creature below went full-on happy.

Dropping his gaze, he focused on his sandwich, shoving a large portion in his mouth and chewing fervently as he nodded. The heat from the sauce made his eyes tear and he washed the food down with a long swig of his soda. It cooled the heat in his throat, but did nothing to alleviate it farther south. "Yep. My parents still live here. You?"

She opened her chips and picked one out of the bag. "Carlsbad until I was ten. Then we moved around a lot, mostly up north. Irvine, Ventura, Bakersfield for awhile."

"Siblings?"

"No."

He already knew the answer to these questions, having run a background check on her when he first realized how much she could add to his taskforce.

But you didn't score points with people when they realized you used your Homeland clearance to dig up every available bit of dirt on them. "You don't have much time to spend with family, do you?"

She put her sandwich down and fiddled with her napkin. "Mom has early onset Alzheimer's and doesn't know me anymore. Dad died in a car accident a few years ago." She twisted the napkin between her hands. "But you already know that, don't you?"

Busted. He started to answer, but she cut him off.

"I consult for the SCVC Taskforce. I know how things work. Cooper did a full vet of me even after Director Dupé recommended me to him. So while I give you marks for the idle chitchat, you no doubt know more about me than I do, Mr. Homeland Security."

He raised his hands in surrender. "It's not personal. It comes with the territory. And yes, I did a background check, and I knew if Harris and Dupé were using you, you must past muster. But I prefer to hear the facts directly from you. I've learned there's a lot more to a person's life than what's on paper. And it's a two-way street. Anything you want to know about me, I'm an open book. Okay?"

She looked slightly abashed and tossed the half-shredded napkin on top of her sandwich. "You're probably looking forward to seeing your family this weekend, huh?"

One landmine avoided. He went back to his sandwich. "I am. I haven't seen any of them in a couple months. I miss them."

She nodded as if she understood, but her eyes were focused on the napkins fluttering in the breeze. "Your job requires a lot of hours."

The facts on her background check didn't mention a significant other, and she didn't stay in touch with her parents. *Must be lonely.* "Yours too. You mentioned how booked your schedule is. Twice, I believe."

Her gaze rose and he smiled, taking the sting off the jibe.

A faltering smile crossed her face. She picked out a chip and crunched on it. "I'd like to see your case notes on The Reverend. If you're willing to share."

"You're joining the DTT?"

"I'll review the case and see if I can add anything of value to it. Don't get your hopes up. If the only thing I can help with are the sigils, the analysis I already wrote up will do that much. If I can help beyond that, we'll discuss my consulting terms. If not, I'll be on my way. I have a dig waiting for me in Utah."

Hot damn. Roman finished his sandwich and took a swig of soda, smiling behind the can. "Thank you, Brooke. I mean it. I have no doubt you and I are going to blow this case wide open."

She broke off a piece of scone, apparently ready for dessert. "You're doing it again."

"What?"

She waggled a finger at his face. "Smoldering."

He grinned and winked. "That's what heroes do, right?"

Her gaze dropped to her food, but she was grinning too. "Right."

"So answer me this—Indiana Jones or John McClane?"

"What?"

"Which hero do you prefer?"

"Seriously?"

"Answer the question and I'll buy you another scone for the road."

"Neither."

Hmm. "Then who?"

Her brows squeezed together. "Why do you care?"

But all of a sudden, he knew. It was written all over her face.

Conrad Flynn.

The hero from the romance novel.

Who was an accurate match for him.

"Never mind." He gathered up their wrappers and the tray. "Let's go meet my team."

———————

The Domestic Terrorism Taskforce had all the cool toys.

Brooke followed Roman through the glass doors of Laudlin Towers, a swanky high-rise on the east side of San Diego, and waited patiently as he greeted the security crew.

"Where you been, Roman, my man?" a young guard asked, sliding a sign-in form across the desk to Roman.

Roman logged them in and did some kind of fist bump-hand slap combo with the guard. "Staying out of trouble, Bijay. You taking care of things here?"

"You know it, brother. I need to see the lady's ID."

Brooke fished out her driver's license and the guard made a note on the computer in front of him before handing it back. "Any weapons?"

Weapons? "Outside of a metal nail file, no. Do you need to confiscate that?"

"We're not the airlines," he said, smiling, "but I will make note that you are armed and dangerous."

"That she is," Roman teased.

The guard actually typed something else in his computer and Brooke wondered if he was telling the truth about noting her nail file as a weapon or just making her think he was. "You all have a good day, now."

Roman tapped the desk with a fist. "Thanks, Bij. You do the same."

Roman walked her to the elevator—more glass overlooking the terrarium—and they rode it to the fifth floor.

Stepping out into a foyer, Brooke found herself once again facing a security setup, this one more like FBI headquarters in L.A. where she'd visited with Victor Dupé, head of the West Coast division.

A female guard this time, old enough to be her mother, greeted Roman with a big hug.

Everyone loves him.

As Roman walked around the security scanner without issue, he introduced her. "Sue, this is Dr. Brooke Heaton. Brooke, our number one around here is Lt. Sue Fischer. Dr. Heaton's helping with a case, so you may be seeing her off and on."

"Nice to meet ya," Sue said, her voice rough and crackly, like a woman who'd smoked too many cigarettes. A New York accent laced her vowels. "May I?"

She held out her hand for Brooke's purse. Roman interceded. "She's good, Sue."

"Rules are rules," Sue argued. "Until she has proper credentials, I can't let her through without checking her for weapons and confiscating any and all communication devices, cameras, and—"

"She's been vetted by Dupé."

Sue's eyebrows rose for a second. She swept her hand toward the doors. "Well, then. Go on in. Any friend of Victor's has the keys to the kingdom."

Director Dupé always made a good impression with those he worked with. It was a skill Brooke admired. To be considered his friend was a compliment. "Thank you, but I do understand the need for security and don't want to break any rules or get you in trouble."

Sue laughed, the sound similar to a witch's cackle, only with less evil and more good humor. "I won't get in any trouble, sugar. You go on in and kick some bad guy ass."

As Roman motioned Brooke toward the double mahogany doors a few feet away, Sue grabbed his arm and held him back, lowering her voice. "I like her. Be nice."

"Yes, ma'am," he said and Brooke had to hide her smile.

Opening the door and escorting her across the threshold, Roman gave her arm a squeeze. "Making points already, Dr. Heaton. Well done."

Brooke knew the real test wasn't Lt. Fischer. The real test would be the rest of Roman's team. They stepped into a carpeted room with soft LED lights, high-tech everything, and a giant yin/yang picture on the far wall. Under it sat a tiny water fountain on a low table with colored stones, a salt lamp, an incense burner filling the air with jasmine, and a Christian cross. Coexist was spelled out on a nearby chalkboard. Around the table were meditation cushions.

Spanish music, heavy on guitars, blasted through the room, a man singing along with a karaoke machine in one corner as two women—one of them Polly—did backup.

Another man sat with earbuds in his ears at a computer with three screens. Several soda cans and candy bar wrappers covered the desktop.

Having worked with the SCVC Taskforce, this was not at all what Brooke had expected. Cooper and his group met at a rundown building that housed a senior center and a couple low-end businesses where they could hold their meetings covertly. Since most of them worked undercover constantly, there were no desks or cubbyholes. The only equipment in the place was an old Mr. Coffee machine; they used laptops and tablets and met around a cheap conference table with awful metal chairs that had been around since the 70s.

"You call this work?" she shouted over the karaoke.

Roman put two fingers to his mouth and blew. A sharp whistle cut through the noise and four heads swiveled to look at them.

The singer jumped forward to shut off the karaoke machine, Polly and the other backup singer rushing to their desks. "Just taking a break, boss," the man said, coming forward to shake Brooke's hand. "Hi, Dr. Heaton. I'm Winslow de Soto, NSA. It's nice to meet you."

Polly stepped up, handing Roman the same tablet she'd had the previous night before she threw her arms around Brooke and hugged her. "You came! I'm so glad. I've got a desk and computer already set up for you."

Brooke gently patted the woman's back, catching the floral scent of her hair. "Thanks, but this is just a visit to look at your case files. I'm not sure I can actually help with anything."

The second woman squeezed in between Winslow and Polly and stuck out her hand. She had dark hair and eyes that looked haunted. "Nadia Fernandez, FBI. Polly told us you were at the crime scene last night."

"I briefly examined the scene and one of the bodies," Brooke told her, glad to have the case to focus on rather than her inclusion in the group. She knew the backgrounds of most of these people—at least on paper—and felt the same admiration for their work as she did for Victor Dupé. "I'd like to see the rest of your notes—any interviews, photos, etc."

"I'll be happy to go over the killer's profile with you once you're settled," Nadia offered.

Brooke smiled. "Thank you."

The man at the computer pulled the earbuds from his ears, stood and stretched. "Chatter on the dark web is all over the place," he said to Roman as he shuffled toward them. "A lot of it in favor of The Rev's tactics."

He stopped a few feet back and shoved his hands in his pocket. His hair hung down past his ears in waves, a few locks brushing his jaw as he tipped his head to nod at her. "Doctor."

"This is Shane Chandler," Roman said. "He's a freelancer, like you, only his specialty is hacking."

"*Ethical* hacking," Shane qualified. "And I was a CIA analyst."

"For all of three months," Polly added under her breath.

Brooke smiled. "Nice to meet you. All of you."

"Orion and Chelsea are in El Cajun, working undercover on one of our other cases," Polly told her. "If you stick around for awhile, you'll get to meet them too."

She didn't plan on doing that, but it was nice to feel so included. Cooper and his group had done the same.

Three large windows faced the buildings across the street, letting in tons of sunlight, but she bet they were coated with reflective film and the whole room was protected from prying ears by invisible soundproofing. "This is quite a place you have here." Near the meditation table, a cushy couch looked like a nice place to take a nap. "I'm not used to this."

"We work a lot of long hours," Roman said. "We try to accommodate everyone and keep our sanity at the same time."

"There's a full kitchen and bath, complete with a tub and shower," Polly added. "We recognize all faiths, backgrounds, and cultures. Our casa is your casa."

"No offense, but it feels more like a day spa than an office," Brooke observed.

"Shall we get started?" Roman said, holding out a hand toward a large conference room table.

Regardless of whether The Reverend was the same killer as the man from her childhood, he needed to be stopped. "Ready whenever you are. *Boss*," she added.

The corner of his mouth quirked. "Everyone, gather your things," he said to the others. Then to her, he asked, "Can I get you anything? Coffee, soda, water?"

"Water, please."

He deposited her at the conference table and went to get the requested beverage. Polly plunked down a laptop, a Diet Coke, a stack of folders, and a handful of colored pens and highlighters on the table as she took the seat next to Brooke. Slipping a blue folder from the stack, she slid it in front of her. "The basic facts of each crime, date, time, number of victims, etc. Just to get you started."

Brooke thanked her as Roman returned, the others filing in as well, each with their tablets or laptops. Roman handed her the water and took the seat at the front of the table.

"Do you want me to start with the killer's profile?" Nadia asked.

Roman shook his head, leaning back in his chair. "Dr. Heaton's going to start us off. Tell us about the sigils, Brooke. Tell us how we catch this guy."

She liked that he was ready to jump right in, but felt the weight of everyone's stares. "As I'm sure you all know, sigils are basically symbols, and the Latin term the word is derived from means seal. The general public often assumes they're only associated with the occult and various other subcultures and religions, but pretty much any symbol can be considered one. Runes, moon phases, glyphs, sacred geometry, basic alchemy signs, petroglyphs, the zodiac..."—she pointed to the picture on the far wall—"the yin/yang symbol. They're all sigils of one sort or another. Those who use them for magical purposes believe they represent a signature of a demon, or that they can be created and charged with an intention to grant the creator his desire."

Roman kicked back in the chair. "In The Reverend's case, you believe the ones he's using have religious connotations, correct?"

"Yes."

"And the moon phases?"

"The moon *is* mentioned in the Bible, so I guess it's not out of the question that he's associating the pictures as part of his ritual, but I believe he may be denoting the start of the Biblical apocalypse." Brooke wished she had her own laptop where she had an extensive database of sigils and religious symbols stored, but it was still in her car at the university. "Both modern and antiquated religions believed sigils could be used to summon demons, but also angels. He may be using them as his seal or as a way to call on a particular angel. There are thousands of universally accepted designs, but I doubt you'll find The Reverend's signature in the sigil bible."

"There's a bible?" Polly asked.

"Grimoires often list pages and pages of them. The Lesser Key of Solomon lists the sigils of 72 princes of hell. Heck, there are even apps these days where you can enter your intention and it will generate one for you. I have a database of all I've collected over the years. I can give you access to that if you'd like."

Shane typed on his laptop. "I already ran searches for all of the sigils The Rev left behind. There were no matches anywhere."

"*All* of the sigils?" Brooke frowned. "Were there more than two?"

"He leaves a different one on his victims each time," Nadia said. "Just like he changes his name."

"She's only seen two of the crime scenes." Roman motioned at Polly and her files. "Show her the first one."

Brooke's mouth went dry. The other two were close to the type left on Aleisha's forehead, but not a match. Could this other one be an exact replica?

Polly pointed at the blue folder. "Photos of all three are in there."

Brooke opened the folder and flipped through the top pages until she came to the photos, laid out side by side for comparison. She recognized the most recent from the previous night. The next one resembled the style of those on the boulders Roman had shown her earlier. Her eyes slipped to the third.

A tingling started in her fingers and the air trapped in her lungs whooshed out of her mouth.

It's not him.

Relief flooded her. The sigil from the first mass murder was not the one she'd seen carved on her friend's forehead that night. Close, like the other two, but not *the one.*

The room had gone silent, everyone waiting for her to say something. She took a swig of water and cleared her throat.

Get it together.

"Three different sigils, three different names." She glanced at Roman, who was staring at her with an expression of cautious optimism. "The sigils match the name somehow."

Roman sat forward. "Do they stand for the apostle whose name he's using? Like the seal you mentioned? Or is he using them to call on that apostle for help?"

"They're all similar, so I think the basic symbolism stands for his overall belief or goal and the slight variation may have to do with the apostle's name. He may believe he's channeling the energy of individual apostles, or..." She studied the photos again. "All of Jesus's disciples were made into saints, with the exception of Judas, so he may feel he's calling on a saint for help or protection."

"How does that help us catch the guy?" Winslow interjected. "How will figuring out the sigils give us the key to stopping him?"

The question of the hour. "To stop any killer, you have to understand his motivation, why he picks his victims, and why he kills in the manner he does," Brooke said, hoping too late that her criminology 101 speech hadn't just annoyed them. *Too many lectures lately.* "Often understanding why a killer is drawn to his victims is the key piece of the puzzle. In this case, you know his victim type—nonwhite, undocumented immigrants, but they're hard to find since they tend to stay in the shadows. I think the way to stop him is understanding everything about him in order to anticipate his next move. The sigils may actually hold more clues than you expect."

"How do we figure out the meaning of them then?" Roman asked. "Can we break them down into parts?"

"There are several methods for creating them, including various wheels of letters and numbers." Brooke glanced around the table. It was going to take them hours, maybe days, even with the insight she could give them. "Anyone here good at codes?"

CHAPTER FIVE

Five hours later, Roman had reviewed every photo, video, autopsy report, and interview with Brooke. Shane and Winslow worked on separating the parts of each sigil to find potential common links and any hidden meanings associated with them. Polly ordered takeout—it was going to be another long night— and Nadia had gone for a run to clear her head.

Roman could use one too, but Brooke was still going strong, and he was afraid if he suggested they take a break, she might realize she'd missed her flight home and bail on him.

So while the sun sank low in the west, Roman ignored the clock and his growling stomach and kept working too.

Outside of the bodies, each crime scene held few leads. Undocumented immigrants had family and friends, but finding them and getting them to open up was the trick. Some were also part of the groups The Reverend had murdered, so there were almost no leads on that end.

The lone video from the previous night had been shot outside, in the dark, and never showed Pastor Luke's face.

The interviews they had on record revolved around the St. Paul mission where The Reverend had found his second group of victims. The people who'd met him spoke of him in glowing terms, but they'd all admitted to not actually knowing him. He'd claimed to be on a quest from Jesus, going from town to town to help the poor and homeless. He'd only appeared at St. Paul's for a few days before disappearing again. Apparently, it had been enough time to make contact with a group of undocumented immigrants searching for salvation.

The descriptions of him from the volunteer staff and the homeless who frequented the daily noon food line varied considerably. Some said he was short, others tall. Some claimed he was blond, others said he had dark hair. The mission had no security cameras, nor were there any traffic cams or ATM cameras in that area.

The Reverend had chosen his research site well.

"How did he find the first and third groups?" Brooke asked, thumbing through a stack of papers. It was just her and Roman at the conference table at the moment and they'd spread out everything into segments, like a giant murder board. "Why did he need the mission to find his second group? He didn't need help finding the others."

"Maybe he did and we just haven't found the link to those yet. The only reason we discovered the mission was because one of the vics had a tract from the church in his pocket. But The Reverend's appearance there happened after the first group was killed, so it's unlikely he found them that way, and no one at the mission recognized any of the victims from the first group."

"What about last night's victims?"

"Polly canvassed the place today. No hits. The staff is all volunteer and turnover is high. Same with their clientele. We'll have to hit them up again and see if we can come up with better intel."

She gnawed on her bottom lip. "Hmm."

He saw the wheels turning in her head. "What?"

The prompt made her wiggle her lips back and forth in a gesture Roman had come to realize was her "chewing" on a theory. It was cute, reminding him of Belinda, his niece, when she was deciding on an outfit for one of her dolls. Her pursed lips would go to one side, then the other before she made her choice. Brooke seemed to do the same when deciding what to offer up in the form of working hypotheses.

She rose, kicking her chair back and pacing to the other end of the table. "Three different saints, three different sigils, one group of victims targeted through the mission, but no mission connection to the other two groups as of yet."

"Correct."

Leaning forward, she put her hands on the table, her gaze on the papers in front of her, but she didn't seem to be seeing them. She opened her mouth to speak when a sharp buzzing noise came from her purse. Her nose screwed up for a moment and she suddenly looked at her watch. "Oh, crap," she said, hustling over to her purse. She gave Roman an apologetic look. "Sorry, I have to take this."

She cut off the blaring ringtone, answering the phone and heading for the front doors, seeking privacy.

He should offer his office, but for the moment, he simply sat and enjoyed the view as she hurried away, hips swaying in her tight jeans.

During the afternoon she'd taken the pins from her hair, running her fingers through it and letting it hang loose. In her haste to get out of the office, wisps blew back from her face, the rest flowing down her back in waves created from her earlier bun.

And now he was hungry for something besides food.

"Hi, David," he heard her say. "I'm so sorry. I got completely caught up—"

She disappeared out the door mid-sentence and Roman wondered who David was and if he was going to take Brooke away from him.

Polly appeared in front of him, blocking his view. "Food will be here in 45."

"Great," he said, no longer hungry. He raised his voice so Shane and Win would hear. "Everybody take a break."

As the others did as instructed, Roman debated following Brooke into the foyer and eavesdropping. She'd been about to share an idea with him—he'd seen the light in her eyes, the one his agents got when they had an *aha* moment—and he didn't want her to lose that thought.

He didn't want to lose *her* period.

In the past few hours, she'd been like a walking encyclopedia of knowledge. She claimed not to have a photographic brain, but he wondered. She certainly retained more details and information about various religions and serial killers than he had witnessed in a single human being. And she was so determined to catch this guy.

It totally turned him on.

Sick bastard.

Not that serial killers were a turn-on. Brooke's determination, though, definitely was.

Out in the lobby, Sue was gone, the elevator locked down. Brooke loitered near the security desk, still speaking on her phone. "I promise, I'll be there as soon as I can. I have to check flights."

So she still planned on leaving him to go off on her next adventure. He could respect that, but he'd hoped she'd get caught up in the hunt for The Reverend and stay.

She must have felt his presence and turned, lifting a hand to him while speaking to whoever this David character was. "I have to go. I'll be in touch tomorrow after I reschedule my flight."

The man on the other end said something and Brooke rolled her eyes skyward. "Of course, it's important to me. I won't leave you in a lurch. It's just—"

By the way her body tensed, David must have interrupted. She listened, lips pursing.

Normally, Roman would have gone back inside and done a minute on his punching bag in order to give his guest privacy, but something inside him wanted to use David's face for the bag instead.

Brooke leaned her forehead against the far wall. Her voice lowered a notch. "David, I have never let you or the Smithsonian down before, and I certainly don't intend to now, but there are lives on the line. The people you found in Utah are long dead, and we'll get to them and make sure they are properly identified. If they're indigenous, we'll get their tribe involved. But they can wait. The people this serial killer is hunting can't."

David said something else and she cut him off. "I'll talk to you tomorrow."

She punched a button on her phone, took a deep breath, and spun to face Roman again. "Sorry, where were we?"

"We're taking a break. Smithsonian, huh? Is David a colleague?"

"I contract out with the Smithsonian on certain projects, which you already know, and yes, I answer to David Borgman when I do. Hikers found bones in a very remote site in Utah. They may date back to the Late Holocene period. It's a sensitive site because of the ancestry of the bones. They no doubt belong to indigenous Americans. Lots of hoops and red tape to get through. But if the bones and artifacts are as old as David thinks they are, it's a landmark discovery and could really help us understand the early people in that area, how they lived, the tools they used, etc. I'm excited to get there and see what we've got."

He nodded as if he understood. Past cultures and history were important, but excavating old bones in the middle of nowhere? No thanks. "Food should be here in half an hour. Feel free to use my office if you need to make any other calls."

"Thanks."

She didn't move, didn't say anything. The air snapped with electricity, and still she just stood there, staring at him. There was something behind her eyes, as if she were at war with herself.

"Brooke? You okay?"

A shake of her head and the moment was gone. "I'm fine. We should get back to work."

God, she was die-hard. Even his team of trained agents needed a break now and then. "You've been at this for hours. It's okay to clear your head for a few minutes and walk around.

Or lay down. You're free to use the couch in the main area, or the one in my office. It's quieter in there. Plus, there's a treadmill and a punching bag, if you need to work out any kinks."

"Sounds swanky." She glanced around. "This place is so..."

Her voice trailed off. "So what?"

"Expensive. Homeland must have better funding than the FBI."

"Yeah, sort of."

"Sort of?" She laughed. "Have you seen the SCVC Taskforce headquarters? It's a pit compared to this. You and your agents are lucky you're so well funded."

Yes, they were. "Guess I know my way around a budget request better than Harris. He isn't much for paperwork."

"You have to give him credit, he gets the job done."

"So do we."

"Speaking of that." She headed for the door. "I have a theory."

Bingo. "I knew you did."

She pulled up short and cocked an eyebrow. "You did?"

"Saw it on your face before you got that call."

She smiled, self-conscious. "I didn't realize I was so easy to read."

"I'm just good at my job."

The smile grew coy. "Maybe you are."

That sizzling look was back in her eyes. Was she flirting with him? *Thank you, God.* "I can't tell you how much I appreciate your help. I feel like we're making progress again on this case."

"I'm glad." She reached out and grabbed his hand. "Come on."

He was definitely making progress if she was touching him. He let her drag him back inside, enjoying the softness of her skin as well as her commanding attitude.

She released him as she walked to the white board and

grabbed a dry erase marker. He plunked one hip on the conference table and watched as she wrote Rev 1, Rev 2, and Rev 3 across the top, then drew lines to divide the columns.

"What if you have three killers?" She started filling in facts under each heading. "Reverend 1, Matthew."

Place, date, time, number of vics went in his column.

"Reverend 2, Mark." Her hand flew, the marker squeaking on the board as she filled in the next set of facts.

Polly wandered over and sat down as Brooke filled in the third column for Reverend 3, Luke. "Serial killers sometimes work in pairs, but three working together?" she asked. "That's rare."

"Three *so far*," Brooke amended. "There will be more if my theory is correct."

"We considered there could be more than one," Roman said. "How many are you thinking?"

Brooke capped the marker. "Up to twelve."

Winslow stood in the background. "Twelve?"

"Like the apostles."

"Holy crap." Polly shook her head. "You seriously think there could be twelve of these guys out there hunting people?"

"They probably don't have a Judas," Roman mused drily. "So it could be only eleven."

Brooke touched the side of her nose with one hand and pointed the marker at him with the other like they were playing a game of charades and he'd just gotten one of the words. "Agreed. At least eleven, but possibly twelve."

Nadia returned, coming through the wooden doors and joining them, her breathing still a little hard from her run. She pocketed her cordless earbuds and tossed her phone on the table. "What's going on?"

"We have a cult of killers," Polly said. "I think my brain just exploded."

63

Stars bloomed overhead as Brooke stared up through the moon roof of Roman's Jeep. Yeesh, even that was the same as Conrad Flynn in her favorite romance story. He drove a Jeep too.

Twenty-four hours after her first ride with Roman, and here she was again, letting him drive her back to the campus to pick up her rental.

"It's late. I'll just take you to your hotel," he said. His face showed the strain of several late nights—she wondered how many he'd had before last night's sting operation in the bar. "We can pick up your car tomorrow."

Since the clock showed it was already past midnight, tomorrow was actually today. "I checked out of the hotel when I left for campus this morning, not considering I'd still be around. I have to find a new place to stay tonight—what's left of it, anyway."

"Did you get your plane tickets rearranged?"

Her head felt heavy as she shook it. "Not yet. I was so caught up in the case, by the time we took a break after dinner and I called the airlines, it was too late to speak to an actual person to see what my options are."

A quick grin shot her way. "So you're literally flying by the seat of your pants right now."

"And my brain is full of serial killers and sigils. After I get some sleep, I'll deal with the airlines."

"You're welcome to crash at my place."

She wondered what that looked like. During their break after dinner, he'd taken her into his office to search some files he'd pulled together on similar religious killers stretching back to the early 1900s. As he'd mentioned earlier, there was a couch and treadmill in his office. There were also free weights, a punching bag, and some other giant bag hanging from the ceiling that fighters used. He had a small, private bathroom with a shower, filled with manly things like a razor and aftershave that had scented the entire office with a sexy, outdoorsy smell.

Not that she'd been nosy. Okay, maybe she had. She just couldn't resist asking to use his restroom so she could see what was in the medicine cabinet.

"That's kind of you," she said now, glad he couldn't see her cheeks redden at the memory of thinking about him naked in that shower stall. He'd mentioned he had to work a lot of weird hours and stay late. Sometimes he slept at the office. "But really. I just need to pick up the rental and then I'll find a hotel. In the morning, I'll figure out flights and all that junk."

He took the turn for the freeway heading to SDSU. "I have a friend who works the night shift at the Hyatt. I'll give her a call, see if they have rooms available."

A woman friend who worked at an expensive hotel? What a surprise. "Really, it's no problem. And the Hyatt's out of the budget."

"I'm picking up the tab since you helped us out. Don't worry about the expense."

They hadn't solved anything, but she'd given them more angles to look at. "Wow, you certainly throw money around for a government employee."

He shrugged off the comment. "We have a stipend for these things."

More like he was keeping secrets. She couldn't let it go. "So do other enforcement agencies, but they don't have the digs you do, or the expense accounts, apparently. You either have friends in high places, Dr. Walsh, or a pretty cool talent for stretching a dollar."

He was smiling again, but kept his attention on the road. "Could be both."

"I don't need to waste taxpayer dollars by staying at the Hyatt. I'll go back to the Days Inn. I'll be fine."

"I really appreciate all you did for my team."

"I didn't do much in all honesty. I wish I could do more."

"You gave us a new lead on there being more than one killer. Most of all, you gave the team hope. We haven't had any of that in a while."

"Determination can take you pretty far, but when you keep hitting walls, it's hard to sustain the drive. That's where hope comes in."

"Spoken like someone who's been there."

"More than my share. Few people in our present-day world see the need for archaeology or anthropology if it conflicts with progress or rewrites the history books, which it nearly always does. I believe the past can teach us many things, as can examining all the world's religions. Unfortunately, I'm afraid I'm in the minority. I've hit a lot of walls."

SDSU signs became more frequent and they left the freeway, winding around the dead campus to the designated parking area where Brooke had left her car.

Tall, overhead lamps spotlighted several others in the lot, two in handicapped slots. Roman drove past several empty rows to the rear east corner, which had been the only open spot the previous morning for her rental.

At least its still there. Not anticipating a delay in picking up the car, she hadn't paid for an overnight sticker. The last thing she needed was to get towed on top of everything else.

But in a way, she was disappointed to be here. Disappointed to see that lonely blue car waiting for her. She'd been energized and excited, helping the team understand sigils and possibly realizing there was more than one killer. Not that multiple killers was good, but they needed to know what they were up against. The more killers in the mix, the more likely one would make a mistake.

Leaving was hard, though. She had more ideas for them to investigate, all of which she'd have to write up in a document tonight while the ideas were fresh. After she slept and dealt with the airlines, she'd forget half of them.

She probably wouldn't sleep much anyway. The gruesome images in her head wouldn't go away. Aleisha's voice kept echoing in her ears. *Find him.*

Understanding religious zealots had been a driving force in

Brooke's life. It was one of the reasons she'd gotten her masters in religious studies. The depths humans would go in the name of their gods was a horrifying thing.

Roman slowed the car, the headlights shining on her rental. Brooke unbuckled her seatbelt and held out her hand. "Well, thanks, Roman. I appreciate the food and the ride. I'll send you my notes as soon as I get them all together, and I wish you and your team the best of luck stopping The Reverend and his group."

He ignored her outstretched hand and squinted at her car. "Hold on a minute."

Putting the Jeep in park, he got out. As Brooke grabbed her purse, she watched him walk to her rental and bend down.

What was he looking at? He turned on his cell phone's flashlight and something sparkled on the ground. Was that glass?

"Oh, great." She pushed out of the car, catching up to Roman who now shone the light into the interior. There was a yellow ticket on her windshield—no surprise campus security had flagged her for the lack of an overnight parking permit—but the broken passenger window was more alarming. "Someone broke into my car?"

Most of the glass had gone onto the seat, but some had fallen to the ground, likely when the perpetrator had opened the door.

Because he *had* opened it. Her suitcase was gone from the backseat.

"Dammit!" Brooke said, reaching in and popping the trunk.

"Wait." Roman grabbed her arm. "There might be prints."

He used the end of his shirt to lift the trunk, flashing a muscled midriff that made Brooke's brain hitch for a second, forgetting all about the state of her rental car.

Roman bit out a curse. "Your laptop is gone."

"Oh, crap."

Why hadn't she taken it with her? Her clothes too? Why had she been stupid enough to leave important possessions in a rental car on a major university campus?

Because I thought I'd be gone an hour or two in the middle of the day.

She snatched the ticket off the windshield. "Where was security when this was happening?"

"What time was the ticket written?" Roman asked. He punched numbers on his phone.

Brooke held the ticket up and tried to find enough light to read by. The closest parking lamp was a dozen yards away. "Ten p.m."

"So the break-in happened after that."

Someone on the other end of his call answered and he told them where he was and what had happened. A minute later, as Brooke stood, mind racing, he hung up and came to stand beside her. "Campus security has been alerted and I called one of my friends at the station. He'll be down to look for prints and find whoever did this in a few minutes."

At least she had her purse with her ID and money. "Lot of good that does me right now. Whoever did this is long gone." She put a hand to her head. "God, all my research notes for the Utah trip! My notes for you on The Reverend and the sigils! It's all gone."

"I'm sorry." Roman squeezed her arm. "Did you have backups of your research notes for the trip?"

"I made most of them on the plane here." An emptiness sat in the pit of her stomach. "There is no backup."

"Tell me your laptop is password protected."

"Of course it is, but you know kids these days. They can hack through anything."

Roman blew out a tight sigh, then went to his car, pulled out two sets of latex gloves and handed her a pair. "Let's have a look."

"What's there to look for? He even took my clothes."

"Check for your rental papers. I assume those were in the glove compartment?"

She gripped her purse strap. Yes, she'd left them inside for ease when it came time to turn the car in, but why would the criminal who'd robbed the car care about those?

Maybe Roman was just keeping her busy until his cop friend got here. She snapped on one of the latex gloves as he examined the trunk more thoroughly. Reaching inside, she made sure to avoid the ragged glass around the window and gingerly opened the plastic glove box.

The interior of the car was too dark to make out much. She reached in and found some napkins from her previous day's run through a fast food place. She tossed those out, thinking she saw a pale white square of paper.

Was that the rental papers? Couldn't be. There were several copies that she'd folded up and shoved in there.

But there was nothing else in the compartment.

She touched the white square—it felt like a notecard.

Pulling it out, she saw it was an envelope. There was nothing written on the front.

Definitely not the rental papers, so the guy must have stolen those too. Whoever this was, he had her name, home address, and insurance information—all the stuff you needed to rent a car these days—along with her laptop, which contained mountains of her research, the papers she was writing for various journals, and her contacts in the world of anthropology and religion.

Great. Just great.

Luckily, anthropology and religion weren't exactly scintillating topics to those who didn't study them. Her thief would probably see no value in her research, wipe the hard drive and sell the laptop.

Most of her stuff was backed up at home. At least she wouldn't lose everything.

"What's that?" Roman said, stepping up beside her.

"I don't know. I don't remember seeing it when I shoved the rental papers inside the glove box, but the papers are gone, by the way. Nothing else in there but this."

He took it from her hand, turning it over under the light of his phone. Handing the phone to her, he opened the unsealed envelope and drew a notecard out, slowly, as if it had cooties or something.

Opening the card, he frowned and Brooke leaned closer to see why. Fat brush strokes in black ink stared back at her and her pulse bolted.

She stumbled back, dropping Roman's phone. "The sigil. The...*one.*"

The last thing she saw as Roman reached for her was the card fluttering to the ground.

CHAPTER SIX

An hour later, Brooke sat wrapped in a blanket on Roman's couch with a brandy in her hand...the hand that shook every time she remembered the sigil on that notecard. She wasn't a drinker but after the past twenty-four hours, she might become one.

Especially with Roman sitting next to her, his eyes boring into her soul. "I will not let him hurt you, Brooke. Whoever this guy is, I will end him if he comes after you. Hell, I'm going to end him just for putting that look on your face."

Perfect Roman in his perfect little world, thinking he could stop a killer who had hunted her since she was ten. The hell of it was, she wanted to believe him. Wanted to believe she'd be safe in his perfect world where good guys always won.

Maybe I am safe here. Maybe I should tell Roman the truth.

She raised the brandy to her lips and sipped, watching the flames in the gas fireplace across the room. The alcohol burned and she welcomed it.

Roman's house, just like him, was perfect. Beautiful, and manly at the same time, with high ceilings, a stone fireplace, and deep mahogany hardwood floors, like a spread in a decorating magazine. He'd probably picked out the art on his walls personally, and regularly used the upscale appliances in his kitchen.

Perfect world or not, Roman was a hero. He stopped killers like The Reverend every day. Maybe it was time to let him into her broken, scary-ass, serial-killer-hunting-you world.

She was tired of being the good girl. 'Dependable Brooke'. 'Professional Brooke'. She needed a damned anchor right now, and there was no one but the man sitting next to her that she could grab onto.

Knocking back the rest of the brandy, she handed him the glass. "Okay, Roman. You win. Refill this glass and I'll tell you everything you want to know about me and The Rev."

He took the glass and did as she asked, taking his time pouring an inch of brandy into the snifter and then a second glass for him. Returning to the couch, he offered the expensive liquor to her, then kicked his legs up on the ottoman in front of them. "The sigil on that card is from The Reverend?"

"Yes. No." *Maybe.* She sipped the brandy, closed her eyes as she swallowed and picked through all the crazy thoughts in her head. "I'm not sure. I had a run-in with a killer when I was ten. A religious zealot who murdered my best friend and her family in their sleep. He left a sigil on their foreheads that's similar to those The Reverend has used, just not that exact one."

He tinkered with his glass, not drinking. "You were ten?"

"You didn't see it in that background check you ran on me?"

His forehead creased, his mouth turning down. "Details were scarce, and I'd rather hear the story from you."

So he did know about it. The police had kept things quiet about her in the press because of her age, and well, what had happened. A Homeland agent could dig deeper than the official reports, though.

"Short version? I was staying overnight with Aleisha, my best friend. We were like sisters. We lived next door to each other, but my mom and I were moving—the house had been foreclosed on—and it was my last sleepover at the Dunkirk's for a while—maybe forever. Around two in the morning, I couldn't sleep, not knowing what was going to happen to me and my mom, and I was worried about her, so I snuck out Aleisha's bedroom window and went home to check on Mom. She was passed out in the bathroom and had been sick on herself, so I cleaned her up, got her into bed and then I went back to Aleisha's." She tossed back the brandy and choked slightly. The burn made her eyes sting with tears. "I found my friend dead, with a sigil drawn on her forehead."

Roman reached for her, but she shrugged off his hand. A part of her wished she could climb into his arms and forget the past, but she had to get this out and she couldn't do it if she allowed any weakness. If he touched her, showed her kindness, she'd start crying and uttering unintelligent sounds and he would realize what a nutcase she really was under all her degrees and accomplishments.

She licked her lips, tasting the brandy again. "When I got back, the killer was still there, down the hall, doing the same thing to her parents. At first, I didn't realize Aleisha was dead. I saw the blood and shook her, trying to wake her." The past came barreling back, as if she were in a time machine. She saw the moonlight reflecting off Aleisha's dead eyes, felt the slack muscles in her friend's arms as she shook her. "He heard me."

Roman took his feet off the ottoman and sat forward. "What happened?"

"His footsteps were soft, but I heard them, sneaking down the hall." In her mind, she saw his shadow moving, blocking out the nightlight across from the bathroom. "I thought—hoped— it might be Aleisha's mom, coming to check on us, but then instinct kicked in, I guess. The footsteps didn't sound like hers. The shadow he threw on the wall was all wrong—too tall and bulky. I scrambled off Aleisha's bed, going for the window, but then I saw the trunk. Aleisha had a trunk her dad had used in the Navy. It was her dress-up trunk, filled with her mom's old dresses and shoes. We rarely played with any of that stuff anymore, but Aleisha still had it."

"So the killer didn't find you?"

"Almost." She set down the glass and wrapped the blanket tighter. "I was lying in that trunk, covered with dresses and scarves that smelled like Mrs. Dunkirk, trying so hard not to cry and give myself away." She blinked back tears that even now threatened to fall. "The window was still open and I heard him walk over to it, looking for me. Then he came back."

"Shit," Roman said softly. She could see by the way he gripped his glass—he had yet to take a drink—that it was all he could do not to reach for her again.

"He actually opened the trunk lid, but I guess he didn't see me."

"Thank God he didn't find you."

Thank *God*? Brooke snorted. "God had nothing to do with it. If there is a God, He wouldn't create monsters that kill innocent people in the first place."

A muscle jumped in Roman's jaw. He nodded. "Sorry."

A tightness grew in her throat. She'd shared this story with few people for this very reason—people who hadn't lived through this kind of violence couldn't understand.

But it wasn't Roman's fault that she had issues. "No, I should apologize. You've done nothing but be kind to me, and I appreciate it. God and I just aren't on good terms that's all."

Another nod. He twirled the liquid in his glass. "The killer was never caught, correct?"

"He wasn't. It was ruled a hate crime. The Dunkirks were black, living in a very white, and apparently racist, section of town. I investigated it myself later on, when I was older. The cops never even considered it might be a serial."

"I don't mean to be insensitive, and I know you were just a scared kid, but is there anything about him that stood out? You mentioned he was tall and bulky. Did you see his face? Hear his voice at any point?"

"I saw a partial outline of him through the scarf over my face. He was backlit and wearing a mask. That's all I remember—him bending over that trunk and peering into it as if he had x-ray vision. I just knew at any moment he would see me and yank me out of there. Do to me what he'd done to Aleisha." She shuddered so hard, the blanket slipped off her shoulder. "But the rest is a blank. I can't remember what happened after that moment. He must have closed the lid and left. The next thing I knew, I was in an ambulance and a cop was asking me what had happened."

"You blanked it out because of the trauma."

"The psychiatrist they sent me to afterwards said the same thing. As an adult, I've seen a bunch of therapists and I've even tried hypnosis. My brain refuses to give up any memories of what happened after the man opened the lid."

"And now, with the sigils, you're afraid he's back."

"It was my first thought, yes. There have been a few other serials through the years who marked bodies, but none like the man who killed the Dunkirks. The victim profiles and methodology don't match, however. My guy slit their throats, yours feeds his victims poison. The Dunkirks were American-born, middle-class citizens, attended church, and had decent jobs. The Reverend—and his apostles—are going after undocumented immigrants."

"Non-white victims with similar marks on their foreheads is enough for me to look into your case."

She shrugged. "I've already investigated it to the nth degree. The man who killed the Dunkirks disappeared. It's been 20 years. Serials don't wait that long between killings."

"Unless they're forced to."

"Like prison? Yeah, I thought of that, but I've combed through hundreds of men who were in that area of California when I was ten and ended up in prison shortly after. I have a database of them, in fact—the ones who seemed to fit the profile of a religious freak that hate nonwhites—and nothing matches."

"Must have taken a lot of time to create that database without access to nationwide law enforcement files."

"You have no idea."

"But tonight, someone broke into your rental car and left you his calling card. It has to be the same man from your childhood."

Her face felt stiff even though the brandy had made her body loose and soft. "Looks that way."

"Why now? Why here?"

If she knew that, she'd know how to track him down and stop him. "He found out I was investigating these new murders? He thinks I pose a threat to him, or maybe he supports The Reverend, so he's trying to scare me off his trail?"

"Or it *is* the same guy. The Dunkirks might have been his first. He's refined his technique since then."

That thought hadn't escaped her. Her hand shook again and her vision went fuzzy for a second. "I guess that's exactly what I'm afraid of."

He reached over and gently took her hand. This time, she didn't shrug him off. It felt good to share all of this with someone for once. Not hold it all in as a secret. She'd never even shared this with her best friend, Trish, who was probably already in Utah at the dig site and waiting for her to show up. It was just too much to dump on normal people.

Plus, it revealed her obsession with a killer, which people might understand up to a point because of what had happened to her, but it was still weird. Brooke didn't want the few friends she had giving her *that* look every time they saw her. Poor, crazy Brooke. The girl who'd escaped a killer, but now couldn't let it go.

Roman's hand was warm, his thumb rubbing little circles into her palm. The brandy had suffused her limbs with its warmth and the blanket was soft and comforting. She had more ideas about The Reverend, but in that moment, she didn't want to talk about serial killers and murder. She just wanted to sit there and let a man hold her hand.

Her eyelids dipped. She stifled a yawn. Those little circles Roman was rubbing into her palm sent waves of relaxation through her. All she wanted to do was lay her head in his lap and sleep.

"I have more questions," he said softly, "but they can wait.

Let's get you upstairs to bed."

If his bed was anything like the rest of the house, it would be amazing. Big, soft, *safe*. She gave him a half-hearted smile. "You coming with me?"

She hadn't meant it to sound suggestive, but the words, combined with her slightly drunk voice, definitely smacked of an invitation. The devil on her shoulder cheered.

Snatching her hand back, she shrugged off the blanket and bolted upright, nearly falling over from her drunkenness.

"Lightweight," she muttered to herself.

But the angel on her other shoulder, who seemed to disappear at inconvenient times, reminded her there was a reason she didn't drink.

Mom.

Roman stood, grabbing onto her waist and steadying her. "Easy there."

"I meant, upstairs. Are you coming upstairs?" The words tumbled from her mouth. "Not to bed. With me. I meant…"

He put a finger to her lips, shushing her, all the while a grin spreading across his face. "I know what you meant, and yes, I'll be right across the hall, within shouting distance. The security system is top-notch and armed. You have nothing to worry about."

Except falling in love with you.

Where had *that* come from?

Jeez, Brooke. The first good-looking guy who comes along and takes care of you—and whom you feel safe enough to share your childhood story with—and you fall for him.

Figured.

He was so close, looking down on her as he continued to hang onto her hips.

Brooke cleared her throat. "I'm not chasing you out of your own bed. You've already gone above and beyond what anyone should do. I can bunk down here on the couch."

"I have two guest bedrooms. I use one as an office, but I'll make up the other and sleep in there."

"I'll take the guest room. It's no problem. Really."

He was still smiling down on her. "Are you always so stubborn?"

This wasn't stubbornness, this was pure fear. "You haven't seen stubborn yet."

He chuckled. "We're going to figure this out and stop this guy. I promise."

Brooke opened her mouth to say thank you, and instead found herself going up on tiptoes to kiss him.

Few women had ever surprised Roman in his life.

Brooke Heaton was one of them.

Not only had she just confessed a secret about her past that had to be incredibly hard to share with anyone, now she was kissing him.

Her lips were soft, shy, teasing him into a response.

Truth was, he didn't need teasing. He'd been hard as a brick since she'd asked him if he was coming with her upstairs.

She was drunk and emotionally vulnerable. While every cell in his body screamed for him to kiss her back—hard and deep— he couldn't in good conscious take advantage of her.

Through years of controlling his body in and out of the boxing ring, he called up all the restraint and willpower he could. Willpower that had seen him through a lot of trying shit. It had been his savior on more than a few occasions.

Which, unfortunately wasn't enough on *this* particular occasion.

Surprise!

His lips were already responding, devouring her. His hands, locked on her hips, held her in place as he pressed his pelvis against hers.

All thoughts of backing off, of not taking advantage of her, crumbled into a thousand pieces, disappearing into the ambient light from the fireplace surrounding them. He'd wanted her from the first moment he'd laid eyes on her a year ago, telling himself he needed her only for his team.

Shit, he knew better.

Mine.

He wanted her for him and him alone.

Stroking her lips with the end of his tongue, he was rewarded when she parted them and a hushed mewing sound came from her throat. Her arms wound around his neck, fingers jetting through his hair, dragging him in closer.

He swept his tongue inside her mouth, one of his hands cupping the back of her head to hold her in place as he probed deeper. She tasted like his best brandy with a hint of raspberries—probably from her lip balm—and he wanted to drink her down, just like his favorite alcohol.

She wrapped a leg around him, running her foot up and down his calf. Her hard nipples and full breasts pressed into his chest. He was about to kiss her down to the couch when his phone rang with a familiar tone.

"I really should..."—he rained soft kisses against her mouth, her jawline—"take that."

Half-lidded eyes stared back at him as she continued to run her fingers through his hair, down the back of his neck. "Do you have to?"

The ringtone was Winslow's, and a quick check of his wall clock told him it was after two a.m. "It could be about the case. Or your laptop." Whatever it was, it was important. Winslow wouldn't call for any other reason.

"Oh." She stopped massaging his neck and stepped back, letting her hands fall to her sides. Her face was flushed. Her gaze darted away from his. "Of course."

Hating himself, he snatched his cell off the side table and adjusted his too tight crotch. "What'cha got, Win?"

"I talked to Detective Benedict. We got nothing from the campus videos outside of a guy in dark clothes. I'm running them through my friend's body recognition program, but it could be a while."

Win's *friend* was ex-NSA and worked for a covert paramilitary group based in DC with lots of high-tech toys and programs that made the FBI and CIA green with envy. The group didn't just have a facial recognition program that was top-notch, they had taken the FBI's Next Gen Identification System, which included palm prints, irises, and advanced fingerprint identification technology, and expanded it to a host of biometric measurements. They could use a person's build and gait to match perps with their respective crimes. "The guy never showed his face to the cameras, did he?"

"Doesn't matter. He wore a mask."

"A mask?" Roman turned to face Brooke.

But she had disappeared. He scanned the room, circled the couch to peer in the kitchen. No Brooke. "What kind? Like a Halloween one?"

"Ski mask."

Roman crossed the room to the steps that lead up to the second floor. He heard water running and breathed a sigh. At least she hadn't bolted on him. "Don't see those every day in Southern California."

"You do not. I had Benedict put out an APB on the guy, including his ski mask, but I doubt we'll get any hits."

Sigils, a mask, the car B&E... "Listen, this guy may be the killer that's connected to a 20-year-old case that involved Dr. Heaton when she was a kid. He's dangerous and this was no random robbery."

"You're kidding me."

"Wish I was. He left something behind for her, something very personal that few people know about and it ties in with The Rev."

"Ah, shit, I don't like this. What was it? Wait, let me guess. A sigil?"

"The exact same one a killer used on the doctor's childhood friend, a girl named Aleisha Dunkirk."

A surprised hesitation and then, "Fuck."

"My thought exactly." Roman plopped down on the couch and rubbed his eyes. It had been one long fucking day. "He has to know she's stirring things up over this Reverend killing spree, and he's coming out of the woodwork to stop her because he agrees with The Rev, or…"

"Or he *is* The Rev. That's what you're thinking, isn't it?"

"I wish I wasn't."

"Oh, man, this is bad. Where's Heaton now? You got security for her, right?"

"She's with me. Look, the guy must have followed her to the campus, or he had some kind of tracking device on the car, even though it's a rental. Maybe he's computer savvy enough to have tapped into the rental company's files and used their GPS system or he works for them. Do a background on all the employees from the company, okay?"

"I'll put Nadia on that and ask Benedict to check the car for a tracking device. He impounded it."

Roman stared at the fire. "My guess is our perp was waiting for her to return to her hotel room. When she didn't show, he got mad, found the car, and stole her stuff."

Winslow whistled softly. "He's stalking her."

"We need to pinpoint how he knew Dr. Heaton was in town and that she started consulting for us. I'm guessing the son of a bitch was hanging around the crime scene last night and saw her."

"You think he's law enforcement?"

"The media was converging on the place by the time Brooke left, and there were plenty of bystanders. See if you can get photos of the crowd and have Polly start scanning anyone outside of law enforcement through our system."

"You got it."

"And Win?"

"Yeah?"

"This guy sent a clear message to Dr. Heaton, but that doesn't mean he won't be gunning for the rest of us. If he knows who she is, he knows us as well. I want the entire team on high alert. Everyone needs to change their passcodes, up their personal security, and no one chases any leads without my okay and a partner backing them up."

"Got it. How's the doctor holding up?"

God, he was such an ass, kissing her like that when she was scared and half drunk. Once she sobered up, she would probably never speak to him again, much less work with him. Roman pinched the bridge of his nose. "She's tough, but let's find this guy and put him behind bars. We'll all sleep better."

"Amen to that."

They disconnected and Roman went through the first floor, double-checking his alarm system and making sure everything was locked up tight. Satisfied, he sucked down the untouched brandy in his glass and went to find Brooke.

She wasn't in his bedroom, wasn't in the adjoining bath. He found her in the guest bedroom lying on the bed with the lights out.

Her back was to the door and he couldn't tell if she was asleep or not. She lay on top of the comforter and he itched to cover her with a blanket, but didn't dare sneak up on her after what she'd told him.

As if she sensed his presence, she sighed heavily and spoke. "I could really use a shower. I feel…gross."

He hoped it wasn't from him groping her. "I'll get you some towels. I have a Jacuzzi tub if you want to soak for a while."

She pushed herself up so she was sitting on the edge of the bed, staring out the window. "That sounds nice, but I'm so exhausted, I'd probably fall asleep in the tub and drown."

Brooke…naked, sleepy, and wet.

His cock did a salute again.

Totally hard.

He shook his head, trying to dislodge the image of her in his tub. "I'm sorry about downstairs. I didn't mean to take advantage of you."

Her quiet laughter filtered through the shadowed room. "You didn't take advantage of me, Roman. I kissed you, remember?"

"And I returned the favor. You're vulnerable right now and I plied you with alcohol to help you relax, but I wasn't trying to seduce you."

"Of course, you weren't. I'm not your type, but that brandy is awesome stuff."

Not his type? How did she know what that was?

He walked into the room so he could see her face. Her skin was pale in the moonlight, hands gripping the edge of the bed. "I wouldn't have kissed you back if you weren't my type, Brooke, which by the way, I don't have, but if I did, a beautiful brainiac like you would definitely be it."

Her eyes widened and then she smirked. "You're doing it again."

"What?"

"Smoldering."

He covered his eyes with his hands, mockingly apologetic. "I am not!"

"It's not just your eyes. It's your voice, your mannerisms, it's everything."

He peeked at her between his fingers. "Is there hope for me?"

She pushed off the bed and straightened. "Do you suck at anything?"

"Excuse me?"

"Even Conrad has flaws. Hero-type flaws, but flaws none the less."

He played dumb. "Conrad *who?*"

"Never mind." She shook her head. "Where are the towels? I'll use the guest bath for my shower."

Roman went to the hall closet and found the plushest set he owned. He handed them to her and guided her to his room. "You're not using the guest bath."

Against her protests, he dug out one of his T-shirts and a pair of cotton shorts for her, stacking them on top of the towels in her arms. "These will be big on you, but more comfortable than your clothes, unless of course, you sleep commando."

He waggled his brows, hoping to keep things light. She rolled her eyes and headed for his en suite. "I'm calling David first thing in the morning and canceling my trip to Utah."

David, her boss. *The Smithsonian.* "You are?"

She stopped in the doorway and flipped on the light. The illumination picked up the highlights in her hair. "I'm going to catch the guy who killed my friend and her parents all those years ago and you're going to help me."

Yes. His diligence and perseverance had paid off. He held out his hands, a rush of accomplishment filling his veins. "My taskforce is your taskforce, Dr. Heaton."

"Good." She nodded. "There's just one thing."

"What's that?"

"I need a gun."

Okay, then. He held up a finger. "Hold that thought."

He went to the gun safe inside his closet, found a sweet little handgun that should fit her smaller hands and brought it out. "Glock 19, Gen 4, 9 mm pistol. Small enough to carry concealed, big enough to stop a man in his tracks. Has a dual system to reduce recoil. You know how to shoot?"

"No." She eyed the gun with a mix of interest and disdain. "But you're going to show me."

Yes, sir. The woman had balls. "You've got a deal, doc."

Her eyes locked with his. "Thank you. For everything."

"I'm glad you're here." It wasn't a lie.

Her gaze dipped, a slow scan of his body before it rose again to his face. "So am I."

She disappeared into the bathroom, shutting the door behind her.

Smiling, Roman let his imagination go wild when he heard the shower come on.

CHAPTER SEVEN

Brooke was pretty sure she was still dreaming when she woke up in Roman's king size bed on Egyptian cotton sheets and wearing his T-shirt. The aroma of freshly ground coffee met her nose as she yawned and turned over to find a cup of the freshly brewed stuff on the nightstand.

He was in here while I was sleeping? Gah! She prayed she hadn't been drooling. Or snoring.

Wiping sleep from her eyes, she felt the last, lingering snippet of a dream slide away. She'd been running from someone—a stranger—but she hadn't been scared. Not too much anyway.

Why?

Her gaze landed on a picture of Roman and another man on his dresser across the room. Roman was younger, shirtless—*my, my, my*—and wearing some god-awful silver belt around his waist. His hands were wrapped in tape and a pair of boxing gloves, tied together by their laces, hung over his shoulder.

The other man in the picture was older and beaming from ear to ear. His hair was more gray than black and she could see a familiar tilt to his eyes. The hard planes of his cheeks and jaw were similar too.

Roman's dad.

The warmth of the sheets made her want to snuggle farther down in them and stay there. Another flash of the dream skated across her memory, as translucent as smoke.

Roman. She hadn't just been running from the stranger. She'd been running *to* the man who'd given up his bed for her.

Roman had been in the dream. Probably because she was surrounded by all things Roman here in his bedroom. Even the sheets oozed his presence and smelled like his laundry soap.

Brooke sat up and reached for the coffee. What was it like to wake up next to Roman, the man himself, every morning?

Her nipples hardened at the thought, her pulse doing a happy skip.

Tell me that kiss last night was only a dream.

But no. Her lips tingled at the memory of his lips on hers. She might be able to fool her mind, but her body knew the truth. She'd kissed him, he'd kissed her back, and she wanted more.

He's put a spell on me.

A spell she would do well to ignore. He'd already gotten her to tell her secrets. Like all heroes worth their weight, he wanted to help her, save her, fix her life.

There's no fixing me.

Her past relationships, the few that even qualified in that department, had failed for one basic reason—she couldn't tell her secrets to anyone and not have them look at her funny afterwards. Even men who claimed to love her. Women who professed to be her friends. They thought she had it all together, that she was smart, accomplished, an overachiever in a world of them, who knew exactly what she wanted and was going after it full throttle.

She did know what she wanted, and yes, she enjoyed her career, putting relationships second. But underneath the satisfaction of her three degrees and her love of uncovering the past and all its history, she was downright lonely.

So far, she hadn't seen one iota of evidence suggesting Roman had a girlfriend. She suspected he had plenty of friends, the kind that came with benefits, but perhaps for all his perfection, he was lonely too.

That would explain why he kissed me back.

Had he been telling the truth when he'd claimed being attracted to brainiacs like her?

The coffee was delicious, and Brooke closed her eyes and soaked the whole thing in—the bed, T-shirt, and coffee—pretending for a moment that this was her life, not another cheap hotel room or dirty tent in the middle of nowhere. That she finally had a place to put down roots and have a committed relationship.

Ten to one, she'd get bored in the first week.

Laughing at herself for being such a nomad, she sipped the coffee, got out of bed, and tried not to care that the clock on the nightstand read 8:43.

I slept in. The thought mildly surprised her. She had an internal alarm clock that never let her sleep past seven. But she hadn't gotten to bed until after three a.m., so she considered herself entitled.

After cleaning up in the bathroom, she put her hair in a ponytail, dabbed on some mascara, and went to find her gracious host.

He was in the kitchen, dressed in sweatpants and a white T-shirt that molded against his chest as he leaned back in a chair at the breakfast bar, talking on his cell phone. His hair was mussed, looking like he'd been running his hands through it, and his jaw sported a healthy day-old beard.

When he saw her in the doorway, he lifted his chin in greeting and motioned her in.

"Hang on a minute, Win." He muted the phone, then rose from his chair, coming over to her. His blue eyes bore into hers and he smelled like a fresh shower. "Hey, doc. How'd you sleep?"

"Great." She covertly breathed in deep, enjoying his freshly showered scent and lifted her empty coffee mug. "But I'm going to need more of this excellent stuff."

He took her empty hand, leading her over to the counter.

A glass carafe like she'd seen in fancy coffee shops sat half full. "Help yourself," Roman said. "I'm just getting an update from Win about your rental car, and then I'll get dressed and we can grab some breakfast on the way to the range."

Oh, right. The gun. It was still sitting on the nightstand. She was afraid to touch it. "Yeah, about that—"

"Let me finish this call," he said, giving her a peck on the forehead that startled her before he returned to the breakfast bar and started talking to Winslow again.

She tried to listen to what Winslow said about Detective Benedict's report, but her pulse skipped and her ears rang from Roman's kiss.

It wasn't a kiss, just a friendly peck. Get over yourself.

She poured fresh coffee and opened the fridge, keeping her back to him. Even first thing in the morning, he looked like a Greek god and already had her tongue-tied. Last night was one thing—she'd been shook up and slightly tipsy from the brandy—but this morning was a whole other beast. She had to get control, quit fantasizing, stop letting him get under her skin.

There were eggs in the refrigerator, bread too. She started pulling things out, setting what she needed for omelets on the counter. Then she searched the cabinets for a skillet.

Roman appeared at her side with a half-smile on his face and led her where she needed while he talked to Win. Ignoring the tingling she felt at his nearness, she waved him off, snatched up the biggest skillet in the assortment and went to work.

While the omelets cooked and the bread toasted, she dialed David and got his voice mail. She almost breathed a sigh of relief. It was much easier to leave a message explaining why she wouldn't be flying to Utah and the dig site for several days than it was to explain it all live. She'd still have to handle his disappointment, but at least with last night's rental car ordeal, she had a good excuse to delay her departure from California.

Roman was refilling his coffee cup when she finished, finally done with his call. "No news on your perpetrator, but Win got hold of the video footage from the parking lot. He's sending it to me so we can review it." He leaned a hip on the counter. The lines around his eyes and the shadows under them told her he hadn't slept nearly as much as she had. "Thanks for making breakfast. It smells amazing."

She slid the omelets onto two plates and carried them over to the bar. "Grab the toast."

He did, also digging through the fridge to unearth some jelly and two apples. He handed one of the apples to her and sat down. His thigh bumped hers as he reached for a piece of toast. "No one but my mom has cooked for me in ages."

No girlfriend? she wanted to ask, but shoved a bite of egg into her mouth to stop the question. "Maybe you need an upgrade in your overnight company."

He chewed a big bite of toast and gave her a funny look as he swallowed. "I'm not sure I follow."

"Never mind. I'm being weird."

He bumped her leg again with his, on purpose this time. "I like your brand of weird."

She nearly choked on her eggs. Her brain searched frantically for a safer topic. "I'm afraid of that gun you gave me. I left it upstairs. I'm having second thoughts about learning to shoot."

He got up, went to an upper cabinet and pulled out two glasses. "Why?"

"I don't want to kill anyone." *Or hurt myself by accident.*

From the fridge, he withdrew a carton of orange juice and poured both glasses full before returning it. "You should know how to defend yourself."

"I'm not an agent. I'm a consultant. I sit at a desk most of the time, analyzing criminals, not going after them in person."

"I'm not talking about for protection when you're working dangerous cases." He plunked a glass in front of her. "I'm talking about for your personal safety."

The orange juice, the apple…Mr. Healthy was still taking care of her even though she'd made breakfast. "Let me guess, you're the oldest of your siblings."

His gaze darted away and she realized she'd accidentally hit a nerve. "Not quite. I had an older brother. Percy."

Had. Something had happened to Percy and Roman didn't want to talk about it. "Sorry. It's just you're always taking care of everyone and you're an overachiever. Classic first-born syndrome."

"True."

That was it. No further explanation. She sipped at the orange juice, fishing for a new topic. "This isn't fresh squeezed."

He did a double take. "What?"

"I figured you squeezed your own juice."

"You don't like it?"

Laughter bubbled up. "I'm teasing. It's just…easier to talk about orange juice than shooting someone."

He plopped back down on his seat and turned toward her. "True, but I'm not letting you off the hook. I'm taking you to the gun range after breakfast. No one on my taskforce walks around being vulnerable to a serial killer."

"But—"

"Once I show you how to handle a weapon, you won't be scared of it anymore. You'll know how—and when—to use it properly to protect yourself."

He was so confident, so sure of his talents and skills, she believed him. "You're not afraid I'll shoot you or someone on the team by accident?"

"No."

Total confidence in her this time. She relaxed slightly. "Your bed is amazing. I didn't think I'd be able to, but I slept like a baby."

He went back to his omelet, scooping up a large bite. "Maybe we can make a deal, an arrangement, doc."

She liked when he called her doc. It was cute, a nickname that she rarely appreciated, but with him it was...friendly.

His eyes cut sideways to look at her from his peripheral vision.

Okay, maybe a little more than friendly.

"What kind of arrangement?" she asked.

"You fix me a breakfast like this every morning and I'll let you stay in my bed every night."

Heat shot straight down her spine. His bed. *Every. Night.* "Um, it's just eggs with ham and cheese in them, not Breakfast at Tiffany's."

"It's my favorite type of omelet."

"Don't you cook?"

He snagged another piece of toast and slathered it with jelly. "Not if I can help it."

"Seriously?"

"What?" He shot her an incredulous look. "I burn everything."

He had to be kidding. Mr. Perfect, with his gourmet kitchen, didn't cook for himself? "The only people who install a top of the line kitchen like this either want to impress a lot of pretentious people or they really enjoy cooking. You're not the pretentious people kind of guy."

The last piece of toast received a thick layer of jelly and he handed it to her. "You sure about that?"

She accepted the toast and took a bite, sticky jelly ending up in the corner of her mouth. With her tongue, she licked it off. "Positive."

His gaze locked on her mouth. "Do we have a deal, doc?"

The tiny furnace in her lower belly kicked the heat up a notch and Brooke found herself nodding. Another night in Roman's bed...what could it hurt? "Pancakes tomorrow?"

He grinned and touched her toast with his half-eaten piece as if clinking wine glasses together. "I love pancakes."

They finished breakfast and cleaned up the dishes, talking

about normal things—the weather, their favorite meals, why Roman had such a big house.

"Did your long lost, billionaire uncle die and leave you his fortune?" Brooke asked, putting the last plate in the dishwasher.

He gave her a confused smile. "What?"

"This place must have set you back a decent penny here in San Diego. I didn't realize Homeland agents made such big bucks."

Roman tossed in a detergent pod and closed the dishwasher, chuckling. "I made some money during my boxing days, invested it wisely, and..." He shrugged, punching the on button. "I don't have anyone but myself to spend it on."

"You must have been some boxer."

One shoulder shrugged. "I did okay."

Okay? He was being modest and she got the feeling he didn't like talking about his boxing career. A new thought dawned. "The office where the DTT meets? You tricked it out on your own dime, didn't you?"

Another shrug and he started a fresh pot of coffee, using some drip mechanism and a filter over the glass carafe that seemed ultra simplistic, yet obviously yielded amazing results.

Once he'd poured them fresh cups, he placed a laptop on the breakfast bar, his face serious. "Ready to see the video of the man from last night?"

Brooke's stomach dropped. She never wanted to see the killer again, but she nodded, swallowing down her fear. Maybe this wasn't him. Maybe...

It has to be him. There was no way someone else would know that sigil. Would know how intimately it was linked to her.

"Wait," she said to Roman, placing her hand on his to stop him from hitting play. "I just... I need a moment."

"Hey." His hand took hers, pulling her closer to him. His other hand touched the side of her face. "We don't have to do this now."

She shook her head, feeling the heat of his fingers dissolving a little of her trepidation. When was the last time anyone had been worried about her?

Ignoring the brick sitting in her stomach, she used Roman's steadiness to bolster her courage. "No, it's okay. I need to do this."

He gave a slight nod and pulled her in front of him, keeping an arm around her waist as his other hand tapped a computer key.

The footage was in black and white, the camera too far away to be of much help with details, especially since the overhead lights did little to illuminate that corner of the parking lot.

But there he was, a man in dark clothes moving toward her vehicle. A shiver went down her spine.

Was this him? The man who had killed Aleisha and her family?

Roman, looking over her shoulder, played with the laptop's touch screen, zooming in on the man. The picture got grainier, and they both leaned forward.

The perpetrator kept his face turned away from the camera, but it didn't matter—he wore a mask. He checked the driver's door, and finding it locked, raised what looked like a small, black flashlight and gave the window a hard rap.

Glass exploded and he wasted no time entering the car. In the time it took Brooke to cover her mouth with her hand and blink, he popped the trunk, lifted her briefcase, and shut the trunk again. It was almost like he knew it was in there.

Roman squeezed her shoulder, his head close to hers as they watched the perpetrator return to the front seat and mess with the glove box. That must have been when he'd left the notecard. A moment later, he leaned into the backseat and grabbed Brooke's suitcase, hauling it out and looking it over.

Setting her briefcase on the top of the car, he unzipped the overnight bag, reached inside and rooted around.

Shivers went down the back of Brooke's neck. If not for Roman standing behind her, his supporting hand on her waist and shoulder, she would have taken a step back. "What is he doing?"

The man pulled out a piece of light colored clothing—one of her camisoles?—and held it up. Then he did something that made Brooke's stomach drop to her feet.

He held the piece of clothing to his face and inhaled.

Brooke's legs went weak.

———

One moment Roman was looking over Brooke's shoulder, breathing in the scent of his own soap mixed with the floral aroma of her previous day's clothes, and the next, she was sliding to the floor.

Good thing he had both hands on her—he'd been dying to touch her since the moment she'd walked into the kitchen—and now he found himself catching her as her legs gave out.

Not exactly the way he'd planned to get his hands on her. He'd been entertaining fantasies of taking her on the breakfast bar since he'd watched her building the omelets, seemingly more at home in his kitchen than he was.

"I've got you," he said in her ear, hugging her close. The bastard on the screen shoved the article of clothing he'd just sniffed into his jacket pocket. Roman hit the pause button and turned Brooke away from the screen, drawing her in for a hug.

Short, shallow breaths flared her ribcage. She shook from head to toe. "He sniffed my camisole," she said in a horrified voice.

And I'll kill him for it. "Don't let him get to you, Brooke. Don't let him get under your skin any more than he already is."

"You're right." She took a deep breath and nodded, pushing slightly away and looking up at him. "Sorry I keep acting so silly. Usually I don't lose my nerve like this. My knees keep giving out on me like I'm some soap opera heroine."

"You've been through a lot. I have the feeling all of this is bringing your ten-year-old self to the surface and she's fighting to find some safety and security again."

"I'm sure you're right, and I have enough nightmares as it is without letting this a-hole get inside my head. I have to detach from this or I'll never feel safe again."

Detachment was a vice he used often, but sometimes it backfired. In this case—at least for the moment—it was probably best if she did just that.

Roman hated to make her keep watching, but he needed her to see the entire video clip. "Do you think you can handle the rest? It's almost over."

Spinning in the circle of his arms, her hands grabbed onto his, securing his hold tighter around her waist. Her head bobbed in consent and she straightened her spine. "I'm fine. Play it."

Atta girl. Her hair tickled his cheek. "Detective Benedict caught a few seconds of the guy in another section of the parking lot as he was leaving. It's coming up."

He pressed play and on cue, the video switched to a different section of the lot and a different angle. The man didn't get in a car to leave, but walked around the corner of a building with Brooke's things and disappeared into the dark night beyond.

"Wait," she said, leaning forward again. "Go back a few seconds."

Roman released his hold on her and rewound the video. "Here?"

"Right before he hits the sidewalk."

He did as instructed, and she said, "Freeze. Right there."

The man stood immobile with one leg raised to step onto the sidewalk.

Brooke pointed at a flash of light on the man's chest. "What is that?"

It looked like one of those orb things that ghost hunters

were always capturing and claiming were spirits. Not that he ever watched those shows.

"I don't know." He played with the zoom feature, going in and out a couple times, trying to figure it out. "The outside lights on the building are reflecting on it. Must be metal of some kind."

Her body tensed. She rubbed her head. "A necklace? A pin of some sort?"

"Shane can do amazing things to clear up blurry photos and videos. I'll ask him to run this through his software and see if he can get a better image for us." He closed the laptop and turned her to face him once more. "You okay?"

"Of course," she said, and then, she sighed deeply and shook her head. "Who am I kidding? That guy—he has to be the man who killed Aleisha. *Has* to be. Which freaks the hell out of me. And he knew that was my rental car. He targeted me! And…and, oh God, he sniffed my cami."

She visibly shuddered. Her skin had a gray cast.

Roman made her sit on the barstool. "You're sure it's him, the guy you saw that night?"

Her teeth bit her bottom lip. "I can't ID him from a physical standpoint, no. I didn't get a good look at him that night, nor can we get a physical description from that video, but… Who else knows about that particular sigil and my relationship to it?" Those haunted eyes of hers came up to meet his. "He was wearing a mask, just like my childhood attacker. The sigil… It has to be him, Roman."

She was tough, but realizing that the killer from her youth was stalking her now was a blow. The vulnerability in her eyes, the fear making her tremble under his hands drove him crazy.

He couldn't help himself. He wrapped his arms around her and drew her head to his chest. "I won't let him hurt you, Brooke. Ever. I will find him and stop him. I promise."

Her arms went around his waist, her hands touching his back tentatively. "Thank you. You can't know how much this means to me. Just to have someone I can talk to about…"

Her voice was soft and… *Ah, shit.* Was she crying?

He stroked her hair. "You're staying with me. We'll pick up some clothes and toiletries in town after we hit the gun range. Otherwise, I can ask Polly to get some stuff for you if you don't want to shop."

She raised her head and he saw the tears on her cheeks. "What if this *is* The Reverend? If I'd gotten a better look at him all those years ago, maybe I could have stopped him before now. He wouldn't have killed all those innocent people."

She was blaming herself for The Reverend's sick actions. "Brooke, you were ten and he was wearing a mask."

"I know." Her eyes closed for a moment. "But I still feel guilty. I should have done something. Pulled his mask off. Hit him over the head. Anything! I wish I could remember more about that night."

What if she had seen the killer and he knew it? But if this bastard knew she could finger him, why wait twenty years to go after her?

The answers would come, Roman was sure of it. For now, he needed to stop Brooke's guilt train and get her back on solid footing. "Stop beating yourself up. We don't know for sure that the guy who broke into your car last night is, in fact, The Reverend. You said it yesterday, the sigils on the deceased don't match, the victims are different, and there may be more than one killer this time around."

"That little stunt last night? He's the same guy. I can feel it. He knows I'm working with you, and he's scared. He knows we're going to nail his ass." A tiny expression of hope spread across her face. "And if he's scared, he's going to make a mistake."

Control. He could see that mixed with the hope on her face. The two ingredients Roman knew everyone needed in order to feel safe.

He was going to give her another. The quickest way to gain

self-confidence was to do exactly what you were afraid to. "I'll have Shane get to work on cleaning up that video. Grab the gun I gave you. It's time for a shooting lesson."

An hour later, he had her at the range, gun in hand and ear protection ready.

Since Brooke's hands were smaller than his, he'd picked the Glock 19 on purpose. It was the most compact of his collection. A properly fitting handgun had less recoil in general and was more enjoyable to shoot. A shooter's overall enjoyment increased proficiency.

Even when practicing wasn't necessarily for fun.

"I don't have a license," she said.

"Nadia is working on a concealed carry license for you as we speak."

"You think of everything, don't you?"

He motioned at the Glock. "If you want one of these for home defense, you probably want a larger framed handgun, as long as it still fits your hand, but for concealed carry, this one is accurate and reliable."

"Good to know."

"If you don't like this one, I'll find you some others to try."

"I'm sure this will be fine."

"You're trusting your life to it. You want to be sure you have one that you like."

"You, I trust with my life. This gun? No way. But I get the gist. Show me what I need to know to shoot it."

They ran through the basics of stripping the gun and rebuilding it, then the basics of stance and holding the weapon to fire.

"Don't lock your elbows." He stood behind her, his arms around hers as she aimed at the target. It felt good to be so close. Too good. His cock was going crazy. In his book, there was nothing better than a sexy woman with a gun, trusting him to show her how things worked.

"If you lock your elbows, the recoil will go straight to your shoulders and take you longer to recover. Your elbows are your shock absorbers."

She leaned back into him, her hair tickling his chin like it had earlier in the kitchen. Using his chest to shift her weight slightly forward once more, he reminded her about her stance. "Keep your weight forward. You control the gun, Brooke. Don't let it control you."

"Right. If I lean back, I lose stability."

God, he wanted to nuzzle her ear. She was too much of a distraction.

He silently inhaled, letting her scent invade his lungs. Settling his hands softly on her hips, he wondered how he was going to keep his attraction to her under control. Mixing business with pleasure had never been an issue for him before. As leader of the DTT, there were clear-cut lines that he never crossed. Had never wanted to.

Now he did.

Not a surprise. He'd wanted her all along. He just hadn't thought it through, nor had he suspected she'd end up being the target of the serial killer he was after.

"Knees soft," he said in her ear. "Take a deep breath and clear your lungs. When you're ready, take another and let it out halfway. Squeeze the trigger slowly and steadily. Don't jerk it."

She nodded and he stepped back. "Ear protection on, and then give it a try."

They both donned their earplugs. Resuming the stance he'd shown her, she controlled her breathing and…

Bam, bam, bam. She fired, sure and steady.

And missed the target completely.

He didn't need to push the button to bring the paper outline in for inspection. He flipped off his ear protection and grinned at her.

"I missed," she said, sounding miffed. "I'm definitely not trusting this gun with my life."

"It's your first time. You need practice."

By the fifth round, she was hitting the target center mass.

"You're a quick study," he told her, enjoying the pride in her beaming smile.

"You're a good teacher."

If he had his way, he was going to be much, much more than her gun range instructor.

CHAPTER EIGHT

There were times in a woman's life when she just had to stand back and admire a man.

Roman's feet were planted, arms up and muscles rippling as he fired at the paper target a dozen yards away. His large hands clasped the stock of the much bigger gun he used, his thighs engaged as he absorbed the recoil of the blasts.

The memory of his arms around her as he'd instructed her on proper body placement sent a warm flush through her system. Power and control exuded from every inch of him.

A power and control she knew he must exhibit in the bedroom as well.

What am I thinking?

There was that pesky confirmation bias again, letting her interpret this new evidence based on her current belief in him. Maybe that was the problem—she was thinking too much. For once in her life, she wanted to turn off her constantly churning mind and just *feel*.

His kiss from that morning had made her do just that—stop thinking. Even now, when the memory of his sensuous lips taking control of hers surfaced, her brain seemed to short-circuit. Earlier, when he'd positioned her body with his, she'd completely forgotten all the instructions he'd given her. Instead of focusing on the target, all she could think about was turning in his arms and kissing him. Running her hands over his solidness and feeling anchored again.

He muddled her thoughts but made her body come alive. It had been nearly two years since her last relationship, and that one had been almost asexual. Gordon was passionate about many things, but sex hadn't been one of them. At least not with her. He'd left her for a younger version. A younger, ditzy version who didn't know the difference between a trowel and a toothbrush.

Roman fired off another round of bullets, and even from her distance behind him, she could see the clean hole in the center of the paper man's chest that Roman expanded with every squeeze of the trigger.

Deadly.

Commanding.

Totally in control.

Another shiver went down her spine.

For half a second, her wild imagination took over. In the last chapter she'd read of *Operation Sheba*, Conrad and Julia had made up, their hot passion nearly sizzling the pages of the book, and making Brooke wish she could trade places with a fictional character for just one intimate night with a hero. A hero who would risk his life to save hers, and do it with a cocky smile and wink.

As Brooke watched Roman shooting his weapon, she imagined she was bold enough to write her own romance. To take control over her own world. She'd take that weapon from Roman and guide his hands to her own trigger.

"Brooke?"

She jumped. Roman had stopped shooting and removed his ear protection. He was staring at her.

"Um, yes?"

"Everything okay? You were a million miles away."

She hadn't gotten to finish *Operation Sheba* yet. Of course, she'd already read it at least a dozen times, so she knew what happened at the end, but still. It was her favorite book.

It had been in her suitcase, which was now in the hands of the masked man. Where she'd stopped, Julia was just about to get caught stealing top-secret information.

I need another copy of that book. "Just picking up tips from your extremely perfect form."

He flipped the switch to pull in the paper target, a small, very male grin on his face. "Like what you see, Dr. Heaton?"

Flirting with me. Again. It was still too good to be true, but what the hell? She had nothing to lose. Julia certainly didn't thumb her nose at Conrad's flirting once she'd forgiven him for faking his own death. "I think I'm in good hands."

His blue eyes caught hers for a moment, heat and desire pulsing between them. "I guarantee it."

And *ho-boy*, it took all of her nerve to hold that bold gaze of his. She hoped she'd never have to use the gun he'd loaned her on a real, live human being, but she sure didn't mind his tutelage in learning to handle one.

Over the next few minutes, conversation ceased, but the easy silence felt normal, natural. They stripped and cleaned their respective weapons, multiple law enforcement officers, both current and retired, speaking to Roman in passing.

He knows everyone. And they all seemed to like him. The handshakes, comments, and pats on the back kept interrupting their quiet time, but Brooke didn't mind.

An older man with a buzz cut stopped at the table where they sat. "Roman Walsh, is that you?"

Roman did a double take and stood, the chair legs scraping the floor. "Ludacris? When did you get back?"

The two men clasped fists and did a manly hug with exaggerated back slaps. Ludacris glanced Brooke's way, back to Roman. "Two weeks ago. I didn't think I'd ever make it out, but they finally got sick of me."

They both chuckled. Roman shook his head. "Never thought I'd see you retire."

"Never thought I would." He put his hands on his hips,

reminding Brooke of a boot camp instructor. "Hey, I was sorry to hear about Percy."

Roman's casual stance stiffened. His attention focused on his gun again. "Yeah, thanks."

"He was a good man. I never had any trouble with him. But all those tours,"—Ludacris shook his head—"it messes with guys, you know? Then to get hurt on top of that and need those damn pain killers. What a waste."

Roman stepped back and fiddled with the stock of his gun. "Tell me about it," he muttered.

His fingers twitched and the utter sadness enveloping him had Brooke jumping to her feet. She stuck out a hand, moving in close to Roman. "Brooke Heaton. Nice to meet you."

Ludacris gave her a half-smile and they shook. "Ludacris Van Pelt. You a friend of Roman's?"

He winked at her, emphasis on the word friend.

"We're working together. He's teaching me to shoot."

"Working together, huh? You still with the Domestic Terrorism Taskforce?" he asked Roman.

"Absolutely." Roman touched Brooke's back. A subtle thank you, she thought. "Dr. Heaton is consulting for us."

"Doctor, huh?" Ludacris gave her another look. "Well, you're working with an awesome team. Take care of my boy, here."

She smiled sweetly. "You'll excuse us. We need to get back to the office."

Ludacris shook Roman's hand, saying they should get together for lunch some day and catch up. Roman agreed, but Brooke knew he was lying.

"Thanks," he murmured to her, as they resumed their seats. He started snapping his gun back together.

She gave him an innocent look. "For what?"

He glanced up. "You know what."

"We all have things we don't want to talk about. I don't like to talk about my mom, you don't want to talk about your brother. I got your back."

Guns cleaned and in working order again, Roman took her hand and led her out of the range. A day ago, Brooke realized, it would have been awkward and she would have pulled away. Instead, she entwined her fingers with his, her steps buoyant and light as they made their way across the parking lot to his car.

"Is there a bookstore around here?" she asked as Roman helped her into the passenger seat.

He eyed her and gave a shrug. "I suppose I can find one, why?"

"There's a reference book I need that might help the case. As long as we're picking up some clothes and shampoo for me, I thought I'd check the bookstore."

His eyes narrowed as if trying to see through the lie. "A reference book."

Yep, he definitely wasn't buying it, but she didn't care. She gave him a stern look. "The key to successfully solving a case is in the research, Roman."

And boy, did she need some Julia-type research to handle the hero staring back at her.

The *smoldering* hero staring back at her.

Brooke swallowed.

"You really think a book is going to help with this?"

God, I hope so. "Absolutely."

A smug smile spread across Roman's features as he shut the door and went around to his side of the vehicle. He started the car and turned to her. "I know you're top notch in the research department, but it's like learning to handle a gun. You can read how to shoot and watch a dozen YouTube videos, but until you actually get one in your hands and fire it, you'll never learn how to handle a weapon properly. So while I agree that book knowledge and research *is* important, Doc, hands-on research is vital as well."

In some ways, Roman was like a gun. "No worries there. I have every intention of getting my hands dirty with this research subject."

His brows furrowed again, seemingly in confusion this time. "Are we still talking about self-defense?"

Quite possibly.

At least where my heart is concerned.

Roman rarely enjoyed taking a woman shopping. Brooke, however, attacked it like she did everything else—with speedy efficiency.

She'd made quick work of grabbing a couple shirts, jeans, underwear, some tank tops, and a pair of flip-flops at the local big box chain store. Into the cart went shampoo, body wash, and deodorant. The store had a section of paperbacks and magazines and she wheeled her cart in that direction.

"I'll just be a minute," she said, pointing at the sporting goods area. "Why don't you see if they have any boxing stuff."

What was she up to? The place sold everything from guns to soccer balls, but their boxing equipment selection was sparse. "I'm not letting you out of my sight."

"Why?" She stopped the cart at the end of the aisle and pinned him with a look. "It's a public place in the middle of the day. I hardly think I'm in danger."

He needed to train her in evasion and hand-to-hand combat. Soon. "I don't take chances."

Her eyes narrowed slightly and she bit her bottom lip, rolling it in as she seemed to be arguing with him in her head.

Yep, she was definitely up to something, but what?

Damn, he wished he could take her back to his place rather than the office. He wanted a taste of that lip himself.

"I'm just going to grab a fashion magazine." She wheeled the cart around. "Wait here."

A fashion magazine? She didn't strike him as the type to get much out of in-depth articles on the latest runway show and hairstyles. "I thought you needed a research book."

"Don't worry about it." She waved him off. "I'll figure it out."

He checked his watch as she made her way down the aisle, then pulled out his phone. He had three texts from his team and one from Cooper Harris. That morning before Brooke had gotten up, Roman had spoken to his boss, Quinn Kuprin. Kuprin had upped Brooke's official Homeland security clearance and had also mentioned pulling in the SCVC Taskforce to lend a hand with The Reverend case.

Normally, Roman didn't like sharing. Harris's team was different. Since they'd helped each other out before, he thought it might be a good idea. Harris's resources weren't as wide and deep as Roman's, but more boots on the ground, finding leads and interviewing sources, never hurt.

The text from Harris told him Director Dupé had okayed a cross-team effort on The Reverend's case. After the latest mass suicide, the FBI and Homeland seemed to be in agreement that the killer deserved a special, temporary cross-taskforce dedicated to taking him down.

With FBI, DEA, Homeland, and NSA all working this case, Roman felt sure The Rev would be behind bars soon.

Especially if Brooke could help them.

He glanced down the aisle, making sure she was still okay and found her deep in the paperback section. She snatched a book from the shelf, tossed it in the cart and hurried back to him.

"Ready," she said, blowing by him. "You can bring up the car while I pay for my stuff."

He took the cart from her and started wheeling it toward the cashiers a mile away. "I'll take care of it."

"What?" She tried to take the cart back. "No way. It's my stuff, I'll buy it."

Gently but firmly, he pried her fingers off the handle. "Your clothes and briefcase were stolen because you were helping me with this case. I already owed you a pair of shoes. You're staying here to work with my taskforce instead of flying off to your next job helping the Smithsonian. I've got it covered, Brooke."

She huffed but turned the cart loose. "I don't feel right about it."

They walked and he kept an eye out. The Reverend didn't seem the type to do his dirty work in public, and yet he obviously knew how to use public places, like the mission, to stalk his prey. "Why not?"

"I don't let…"

She swiped a tube of mascara from an end cap.

"You don't let what?"

A long-suffering sigh. "I don't let men buy my clothes. Or my deodorant. It's…weird."

He took the makeup from her hands and tossed it in the cart. There were many things he suddenly wanted to buy her. None of which were ordinary supplies like flip-flops and shampoo. "This is business."

As they got in line at the checkout, she picked up a magazine and the paperback from the cart. "Well, these are for pleasure, so I'm buying them."

Pleasure. The things that word and Brooke stirred up when combined.

He tried to let her go first, but she insisted on paying for her stuff after him. He waited patiently, and since she seemed to want privacy, he pretended to be busy texting as she paid.

"Oh my god," the checkout girl said, holding up the paperback. "*Operation Sheba.* I love this story! The Great Conrad Flynn." She snickered like there was an inside joke. "Con and Julia make such a cool couple. I won't say anything else so I don't spoil it for you."

She winked at Brooke and the good doctor looked like she might melt through the floor. Cheeks flaming bright, she snatched the book from the cashier's hand and shoved it in her purse, ignoring the magazine she'd been covering the book with. "Keep the change."

Outside, the summer sun beat on the asphalt parking lot. Roman pressed his lips together to keep from saying anything, but Brooke caught the grin he was trying to suppress anyway.

"Not one word," she threatened.

He didn't know whether to be jealous of the fictional hero or flattered that she needed her Flynn fix after spending time with him. "Research, huh?"

"He's good with a gun. I thought I might pick up some tips to impress you."

Roman laughed and it felt good. "You've already impressed the hell out of me, Doc."

They were at the car. Brooke faced him as he hit his key fob and unlocked the doors. "I have?"

A mother with twin girls passed by. An aging couple was across from them, the man helping his wife from the car. Roman touched Brooke's face, tugging a piece of hair off her cheek. "You have."

She went up on her toes and kissed him, a light, quick kiss on his lips. "Thank you."

"For what?"

"For everything."

He pressed her back against his Jeep, sliding his hand into her hair. Her pulse throbbed at the base of her throat. "I'm the one who should be thanking you."

"I think you've already done quite enough to show me your appreciation."

He nipped her bottom lip, like he'd been dying to since they were inside. "I'm just getting started, sweetheart."

Her hands went to his back and she started to pull him in for one of those soul-sucking scorchers. It was wrong, kissing her. Exposing her in the parking lot. Crossing lines he should never cross.

But he did it anyway, shielding her from any prying eyes and letting her kiss him the way she wanted to. It started off soft, expectant, and then she parted her lips and slipped her tongue across his.

He gave her a solid kissing back, making sure she understood that this was no game to him. This was a contract. If she continued to cross that professional line with him, she was going to get everything and more.

A minute later, his phone dinged with an incoming text that brought him back to reality. He was breathing hard and so was Brooke, her lips swollen, eyes at half-mast, and her hair a mess from his fingers.

Gently, he hustled her into the passenger seat, threw the bags in the back. The elderly couple across the way were staring at him. The man gave him a thumbs up before the two teetered off toward the store.

What was wrong with him, taking chances like this?

She made him forget everything—his training, his paranoia, his professionalism. If he wasn't careful...

He got in and sat for a second, taking a deep breath to clear his head. Her fingers brushed his jawline and he looked over to find her smiling at him.

"I know I'm being completely unprofessional," she said, "and if that makes you uncomfortable, I apologize. I don't know what comes over me when I'm alone with you. It's like...nothing I've ever experienced, but if you want me to stop—"

He shut her up and answered her question by kissing her again. His hand took the back of her neck, drawing her closer and holding her as he completely worked over her mouth.

She moaned and nearly crawled over the stick shift into his lap.

He almost let her.

But then his phone rang this time with a call, not a text, blaring in the tight confines of the vehicle and making both of them jump.

Brooke sat back, once more breathing like she'd run a mile. "You should probably get that."

Probably.

He leaned forward and kissed her again, this time soft and quick. "I should."

But he didn't, instead he just stared into her eyes.

"You're an amazing kisser," she said, her gaze dropping to his lips.

She wasn't bad herself. He wondered if she'd learned to do that from a book, but no. Becoming a good kisser required practice, not research. "Just so you know, normally, I never mix business with pleasure."

"Me either." She grinned, looking like the Cheshire Cat. "But I have to admit that in this case? My personal code of ethics may need an amendment."

God, he loved this woman. He'd worshipped her from afar for so long, building all kinds of fantasies about her. In the flesh, she was even better than he'd anticipated. Smarter. Funnier. So damned sexy. "I'm just throwing my code completely out."

She laughed. "Well, okay then. I like your style."

"I like yours too."

Another bubble of laugher, this one full of deviousness. She hit the door locks, climbed over the gearshift, and started kissing him again.

CHAPTER NINE

Brooke finger-combed her hair. It was a disaster after making out in the car with Roman. Good Lord, she was turning into a wanton woman. What on earth had come over her?

She dabbed on lip balm using the mirrored panels of the elevator to check her blurry reflection. She hardly recognized the image staring back—it certainly wasn't her usual coiffed and well-heeled self.

"You look fine," Roman said, but he had a weird grin on his face, like he'd just hit the jackpot.

She was the one still tingling from their make-out session. If it hadn't been for their already delayed work day, and the fact that the front seat of his vehicle wasn't ideal for a full-on sexual encounter, he might have actually hit the pot of gold. As it was, he'd still managed to practically bring her to orgasm just from some heavy petting combined with those wicked lips of his.

She adjusted her bra. "I look like a woman who just spent half an hour getting felt-up in the front seat of a car."

"Exactly."

She smacked him and opened the package of mascara she'd bought at the store. One swipe of each eye and she dropped it into her bag just as the elevator dinged and opened on the fifth floor of the towers.

Security guard Sue was waiting. Her eagle-eyed gaze swept over Brooke, then Roman, then came back to Brooke. "You all right, sugar? You look a little flushed."

Roman snickered and it was all Brooke could do not to smack his arm again. "It was a rough night, but I'm fine, thank you."

Sue winked at her and handed her a black plastic ID badge. "This was delivered earlier."

Brooke flipped the top up and saw her picture and the official Department of Homeland Security emblem on it above her name. Sue handed her a lanyard. "Welcome to the team, Dr. Heaton."

Brooke clipped the ID to the lanyard and slipped it around her neck. "Thank you."

Sue eyed the box of pastries Roman had picked up for the team. "It's a little late for breakfast, but if those are from Sweet Annie's, I'll take one for my dessert after lunch."

Roman opened the lid and let Sue pick her favorite. She licked frosting off her fingertips as she waved them through the checkpoint. "He's a keeper," she said *sotto voce* to Brooke.

He just might be.

As they entered, a hooray went up from the team the moment Polly shouted "Annie's!" Everyone descended on them, vying for a pastry. Brooke smiled at their antics.

"I love you, boss," Polly said.

"Me too," Nadia echoed.

"Dr. Heaton." It was Cooper Harris. He leaned against the conference table, ankles crossed, a blue file folder in his hands. "Good to see you're all right after the other night."

Brooke loved Cooper. Not in a romantic kind of way—which was good, since he was engaged and expecting a baby any moment—but as a big brother. He could be gruff and demanding with his team, but he'd always been kind to her. "Agent Harris. We didn't get to speak the other night at the bar shootout. What are you doing here?"

He was over six foot, with a broad chest and tanned complexion. His coffee-colored hair showed lighter, sun-kissed streaks from hours of surfing and running on the beach.

"Crashing the party. I couldn't let Walsh have all the fun with this serial killer."

"You need coffee?" Roman asked Cooper, sliding the pastry box onto the table. He motioned at the others seated there—Thomas Mann and two people Brooke didn't know. "Sweet Annie's if any of you are interested."

"I never turn down anything from Annie's," Thomas said. Another surfer, Thomas had the matching light hair and tanned skin.

"I could use a refill," Cooper said to Roman.

Roman brought over cups for him and Brooke and a twin version of the glass carafe he had at home. Someone—probably Polly—had just made a fresh pot.

Polly, Nadia, and Winslow took their seats at the conference table, chowing down on the pastries.

"Dr. Heaton, this is Mitch Holden," Cooper said, pointing to the man across from Thomas. "He helps out the team when we need him. Next to him is his wife, Dr. Emma Collins."

Mitch stood, his longish sandy-colored hair and intense eyes giving Brooke the impression he'd seen some nasty stuff in his lifetime. He shook her hand and nodded. "We sort of met you in passing last Christmas."

She'd been on her way to Dr. Collin's ranch outside of Bakersfield to consult on a case involving famous actor, Chris Goodsman, when things had come to a head between Agent Holden and Goodsman, and Collins had landed in the hospital.

Brooke nodded at the psychologist. "It's wonderful to finally meet you, Dr. Collins. I'm glad everything worked out okay for you and Agent Holden."

"Call me Emma." She beamed like a woman in love. Her hair was pulled back in a braid and she wore dark framed glasses. "We were very lucky."

Emma declined the coffee Roman offered her. She had a cup of tea, the tiny tag indicating it was a ginger chamomile blend.

Cooper pulled out his chair and sat, dropping the folder onto the table. "Ronni and Nelson are busy and I figured you could use all the hands-on help you could get after last night."

"You told them?" Brooke asked Roman.

"We have two cases, instead of one," he said. "Your stalker and The Reverend. They could be one and the same, but with the escalation of the mass suicides and your stalker's possible involvement, we need to work the case from multiple angles. I thought it wise to pull in the SCVC Taskforce and my boss, Quinn Kuprin, and Director Dupé agreed."

Thomas swallowed a sip of coffee and nodded. "Many undocumented immigrants end up in gangs in order to survive. I have contacts inside three of the major Southern California gangs and a couple CIs who might be able to give us a lead."

"As you know, Brooke, violent crime is our thing," Cooper added. "And this asshole is leaving a trail of bodies wherever he goes. Holden and Mann can work Mann's leads, see if they can get any more on where other undocumented groups are holding religious services. Roman and I can visit all the local missions, ask more questions, and see if we can figure out who this guy is. Emma can stay here and help with profiling and figuring out our killer's next move."

Brooke had been able to forget about The Reverend for a while that morning. It had been nice to revel in the safety of Roman's world, even when she was shooting a gun.

Now hers came crashing back.

This was Roman's too, but a different side of it. She was no longer here just because of her expertise—the case was personal now.

For the next twenty minutes, the DTT brought the SCVC Taskforce up to speed. They had plenty of evidence from each crime scene, as well as speculation about the killer. They revisited the idea that it was more than one man participating in the crimes, and if that theory proved true, there could be up to 12 of them.

Roman picked out a tart with cream cheese and strawberries

and set it on a paper plate in front of Brooke while he answered questions from Thomas and Mitch. "Eat," he murmured in her ear.

Her stomach growled in response, even though they were talking about murder and mass suicides. Her breakfast was long gone and she didn't know when they'd get lunch.

She took a bite and the flavors exploded on her tongue. She gobbled down another bite and nearly moaned from the way the soft texture of the crust combined with the sweetness of the fruit and cream cheese. The group was right—this Annie gal knew her pastries.

But was it just her or did everything taste better today?

The coffee, too, was delicious, although a touch milder than the strong stuff Roman had made at breakfast.

For the next hour or so, the two groups batted around ideas about the multiple killer theory and how to pick up the trail. Brooke listened closely, trying not to stare at Roman the way Emma did Mitch.

"You've been on campus for a few days doing lectures, correct?" Thomas asked Brooke.

She nodded. "I hit the religious studies, anthropology, and criminal justice departments."

Roman fiddled with his now empty coffee cup. "Did you notice anyone out of place at your lectures? Any non-student, older males?"

Had she? She scanned over the past few days, but nothing stood out. "I don't think so. The criminal justice lecture that you popped into the other day was the largest and there wasn't anyone there over the age of twenty-five outside you, me, and the professor."

"Still, I'd like to get a list of all the people who attended the lectures, and you should talk to the professors again, see if they noticed anyone outside the norm."

Brooke went to the desk Polly had set up for her and started calling while the rest of the group continued to review the dates, locations, victims, type of poison, and the sigils. A couple phone calls later, Brooke had left messages for the three professors she'd lectured for. She returned to the group as Roman added entries to the timeline on the white board, and the group began reviewing different styles of knives that might have been used to do the carving.

Winslow put up copies of the sigils on the smart board. "Here are the three corresponding to Matthew, Mark, and Luke. There are similarities in design and the ME believes they were all drawn with a small, sharp-tipped knife."

"Like a pocket knife?" Mitch asked.

Roman added that to the board. "Or a scalpel, perhaps?"

A few more possibilities were thrown out, but Brooke was focused on the sigil designs.

Getting up from her chair, she went to the smart board where the digital photos were lined up. "Can you overlay all three of these pictures into one?" she asked Win.

"Sure."

As he typed on his laptop, Brooke pointed at the individual sigils. "You can see that they share the same root—this line here."

The main line was vertical, like a tree trunk, and each had a different line connected to it underneath some scrolling lines and dashes.

A new image appeared of the three sigils merged into one. Win had made each a different color so it was easy to see where they overlapped. Brooke used her finger to outline the center root. Then she picked up one of the markers and drew the sigil that haunted her dreams next to the projected one on screen. "This sigil was on a notecard left in my rental car last night. The same sigil carved into the forehead of my childhood friend twenty years ago."

She used a different color marker to highlight the main line. "It has the same root."

Mitch tapped his pen on the table. "Can you overlay that on the others?" he asked Win.

"I scanned the notecard before sending it off for prints," Win said. "Give me a second to project it."

More typing and then the scanned image appeared. On the smart board, it moved over the top of the merged images and dropped down.

Thomas, who'd had his long legs kicked up on a nearby chair, sat forward. "Whoa. Does anyone see what I see?"

"A swastika," Nadia said. "Not a traditional one, but sort of a 3D version."

Brooke took a step back, adjusting her view, and yep, there it was. A partial hooked cross that most people identified with Nazi Germany, only in this case, the lines were connecting on different faces of a cube. "This is actually an antahkarana."

"What's that?" Roman and Cooper both asked at the same time.

"A symbol used in Reiki—an eastern energy medicine for healing. The antahkarana is a cube, so that's why these lines appear to be 3D and the sigils look like they're connected by the center line."

She pointed to one of the hooked lines. "If this were actually 3D and you turned it, you would see the lines continue to branch off. Fill in all the lines and you have a cube. The extraneous scrolling lines and dashes are extra. They don't connect to this main sigil."

"So those are more of the individual signatures—what makes them unique," Emma theorized, "and there are more lines to come, because the other apostles have yet to add their sigils."

Brooke nodded. "The hooked cross motif is an ancient pagan symbol seen as far back as Neolithic Eurasia. Most cultures consider it sacred, denoting life, good fortune, and well being. Hitler stole it, his followers adopted it, and the rest is history as they say."

Emma made a note. "It continues to stand for the Aryan Nation and its subgroups."

"Correct." Brooke leaned against the smart board. "At the

beginning of the Twentieth Century, famous archeologist Heinrich Schliemann linked the hooked cross he found on some German pottery to a similar design at a site in ancient Troy. Many Germans saw it as a symbol of their ancestors and took up the symbol for luck. Soon it became one of Aryan identity. Those who favor a racially pure state continue to use it."

Roman sighed heavily. "Which fits with our killer's end game to take out nonwhite immigrants."

"He and his followers have bastardized the swastika once again," Brooke added.

"Any sharpening of those images from the video on campus last night?" Roman called over to Shane.

The hacker, still at his desk, jerked out his earbuds. "Yeah. I'll bring them up. Also, I tried tracking Dr. Heaton's laptop digitally, but there's no signal from it at all. The guy who stole it hasn't turned it on."

Well, that was one thing she could be grateful for.

Two new pictures appeared on the smart board, both from the campus video.

"I'm still running the guy's biometrics through the TrackREC system," Shane added. "It'll take time."

"Is that Emit Petit's system?" Cooper asked.

Roman nodded. "I can't figure out who's smarter, Emit or Bianca."

"Beatrice," Thomas said. "Remember, she changed her name?"

"Right." Roman saw Brooke staring at him with curiosity and he shrugged. "Top secret stuff you don't need to worry about. The important thing is that the best minds in the country are helping us."

Brooke eyed the masked man in the shot taken at her car. The still photo was from when he'd looked around, probably checking to make sure he was alone before he broke the window.

His eyes were the only thing clearly visible and her breath caught, her mind searching, searching, searching for any memory of those eyes.

Could it the same man as her childhood attacker?

The easy answer was yes, but serial killers were crafty, smart. They liked to play games and misdirection was one of their favorites. There would be no easy answer to her questions or this case.

The second photo was at the corner of the building. The reflection of light coming from the man's upper chest caught her eye again. She moved in closer, breath still caught in her chest, pushing a manic bubble up into her throat.

Oh no.

The barest of outlines showed in the shadow around the reflection.

A cross.

A gold cross.

Her body froze. She heard Roman say her name, but he sounded muffled, far away. Her body, her mind, was back in the trunk, back in Aleisha's room.

The man had opened the lid and stared down at her, his eyes nearly black in the shadows. He reached into the trunk, started to move the clothes.

He's going to find me!

Goosebumps ran over her skin. She wanted to yell, scream, reach out and hit him, but she was frozen. Completely and utterly unable to move or cry out at all. Moonlight caught on the chain around his neck.

Brooke saw a gold cross hanging from the chain.

"Brooke!"

Roman was there beside her, shaking her gently. She blinked at him, trying to get her knees to lock and her mind to come back to the present.

Her gaze traveled once more to the photo on the smart board. Her attacker stared back at her from behind a mask.

"It's him," she muttered. "It's definitely him."

"How can you be sure?" Roman asked Brooke.

She pointed at the reflection in the second photo. "That's a gold cross. The light is reflecting off it."

"A lot of people wear those." Win squinted at the photo. "Is there something specific about that one that matches your perp from twenty years ago?"

Brooke nodded. "I remember it."

She hadn't mentioned that before. "Just now when you saw that picture?" Roman asked.

Her face was as pale as the smart board. "The guy looked up at a sound in the hall and moonlight reflected on his cross, just like this."

A memory from the childhood attacker? Progress! "Anything else?"

She licked her lips and then shook her head. "No, but I'm sure it's the same one."

"How?" Thomas asked. "Like Win said, a lot of people wear those things."

"This one has an eye in the center." Her finger trembled slightly as she pointed to the photo. "It's inlaid with a tiny diamond. That's what caused the camera flare."

Roman moved closer. "Like an evil eye or something?"

"An all-knowing eye," Emma said. "Like on US paper bills."

Brooke snapped her fingers. "Exactly."

She continued to study the photo, but Roman could see a change come over her. A stiffness. Was she remembering more?

Roman touched her back and she flinched. "You okay?"

"Yeah, yeah." She ran a hand over her eyes. "Just a little tired."

"Everybody take a break," Roman said, keeping his attention tuned in on Brooke. "Stretch your legs, grab some lunch, whatever. We'll regroup in thirty."

Her fingers trembled slightly as he took her hand. "There will be twelve total," she muttered. "It's a cube, so six sides, with each new killer adding his mark to one side. There will be twelve sigils in all, The Reverend and eleven of his followers."

Her worried eyes met his. "There've been three mass suicides so far. There will be nine more, Roman. Nine!"

Jesus. She seemed so sure. He glanced back at Harris and Harris nodded, agreeing with her logic.

"Come on." He drew Brooke away from the board. "Let's get you some water."

"I don't have time for water. I need to figure out how to stop this bastard."

"Brooke, we're doing all we can." He guided her away from the others and down the hall. Bright sun came through the floor-to-ceiling window at the end. "We'll hit the streets this afternoon."

Inside his office, he led her to the couch, grabbed a bottle of water from his mini fridge, and tugged her down beside him. Even her lips were a pale version of their normal pink. He opened the plastic lid. "Drink."

She did, and then handed the bottle back to him. "I never recalled that cross before. Do you think Emma can help me remember more?"

"Can't hurt to try. The question is, are you ready to remember what happened that night?"

"Of course I am."

He was no shrink, but he knew she felt safe with him. Getting her to talk about the situation surrounding that night might prime her for Dr. Collins to dig deeper. "Why was your house in foreclosure?"

A perplexed look crossed her face. "What does that have to do with anything?"

He acted nonchalant. "Just curious. You mentioned your mom was passed out that night when you checked on her. Alcoholism?"

A bob of her head. "My dad left when I was nine, on my birthday, in fact. There was another woman." She looked down at her fingers in her lap, twisted them together. "Mom drank heavily after he left. Things fell apart. She was sick a lot, couldn't keep a job."

"What happened after that night? Where did you guys go?"

"Nowhere initially. Due to what happened, some people from church put together a fund and paid the bank some of the back mortgage Mom owed on the house. The police didn't want us to go far until the investigation was over. My dad showed up, talked to her about custody, and a lot of secrets came out. I probably would have been better off with him, but I couldn't leave Mom. She needed help and I was the only one she had left."

"Secrets?"

Her focus darted to the left, landing on his weights. "I heard them arguing. They thought I was asleep. Mom kept saying the bad man had finally come for me. She was drunk again. Dad told her to shut up, that she was delirious, and that the bad man story was a sham to play on their sympathies and keep them quiet about…"

Bad man? Was that some reference to the killer? Was it someone Brooke's mother had known? Or was her father correct, and the woman had been drunk and making it up?

Brooke's fingers entangled themselves again, twisting and wrenching so hard, Roman feared she'd dislocate her knuckles.

He reached out, took her hands in his and held them. "Brooke, it's okay. Breathe. Do you know who this bad man was? Why your mom was scared of him?"

Her chest hitched. She blinked several times as if holding tears at bay. "It had something to do with my…my adoption."

She was adopted? There'd been nothing in her file about that. "You never mentioned you were adopted."

She pulled her hands out of his and launched herself off the couch. A turn around the open space of the room and she stopped at his Everlast Powercore bag. "I don't know much about it myself. Didn't believe it even when I heard them talking about it that night, and yet, so many things made more sense after that. Like the fact, I don't actually favor either of them. And there are no pictures of my mother pregnant with me or of me in the hospital after I was born."

Her fingers stroked the bag that he had punched and kicked out his frustrations on many times. "Apparently it was a private adoption, very off the books, probably illegal. The woman, my birth mother, was an American living in Paris who traveled a lot. She got pregnant, didn't want me, and arranged for me to be adopted back here. I don't know who did the paperwork, but it was good enough not to show up on your background check, so that says a lot, doesn't it? For all intents and purposes, I was born to Krissy and Everett Heaton here in America."

For the most part, that was true. He had a few sources, though, that knew things even Homeland didn't. "Did your parents ever admit to it?"

"My father went back to his new family, my mother lived in a hazy world of alcohol and fear, and I was too scared to ask. I was years older when I finally confronted them. My dad told me that I misunderstood their argument that night. My mother claimed she didn't remember anything and that she'd said a lot of things that weren't true, trying to keep my dad from taking me away from her. They both lied, of course. There was too much detail, too much conviction in my mother's voice that night. I overheard her say my birth mother feared for her life and the life of her child and that's why she had to get me out of the country. Out of *Europe*. The bad man would get us both if she didn't. That's why the adoption had to be so hush-hush. No one could know about me."

"Who do you think this bad man was—is? The Reverend?"

She faced him, her arms hugging herself. "No clue. Nothing else happened to me after that night, and believe me, I kept my eyes peeled for the 'bad man.' I stopped making friends, stayed vigilant in case he tried to hurt my mom. Nothing happened. After I got older, I chose to believe my adopted parents, that Mom had made up the whole thing. The killer went after the Dunkirks that night, not me. Maybe it was just wrong place, wrong time. But I had a DNA test done several years ago. My biological parents came from Spain and Russia, with a little Romanian and Greek thrown in for good measure. The Heatons are French-Canadian and British. Everett had dusky skin and dark hair. Growing up, I thought I got my coloring from him. Once Mom's mind started going wonky with the Alzheimer's, she told bits and pieces of the same story to me, but she never knew the woman's real name and the man who'd provided the papers disappeared right after he delivered me, apparently. I never know, though, how much she's actually remembering and how much is delusion. She and Everett couldn't have children and she said once that it was like an angel had handpicked them to be my parents."

Roman sat back, wanting to go to her but understanding that she needed space. She was sorting through a lot of crap. "Do you think The Reverend could be this bad man your mom talked about?"

"If he wants me, why is he killing other people?"

That was the question of the hour.

"It doesn't make sense," Brooke added, affirming Roman's thoughts. "I feel like this could be all tied together, but I have no idea how."

"You said some people from the church put together a fund to stave off the bank after the Dunkirks were murdered. Your attacker wore a cross. Do you think he might have belonged to this church group?"

The slightest spark of hope lit her eyes. "Do you think it's possible?"

"Anything's possible." And they now had a new lead to check out. "We can get the names of the members from back then, start checking into all the men who might fit the profile Nadia came up with. See if any of them currently live in this area."

She flew back over to the couch and sat, throwing her arms around him. "I've never told anyone about my adoption or the bad man. I was always too scared. Thank you."

He hugged her back, a welcome relief at having her in his arms coursing through his system. Secrets sucked. He knew what it was like to keep them buried. "You did good today, Brooke."

Laying her head on his shoulder, she sighed audibly. "I've held that secret for so long, I had no idea what it would be like to let it out."

Roman held her close, stroking her hair, wondering if he'd ever be able to let his own horrible secret out.

A knock sounded on the door.

"Yeah," Roman called out, turning to see Cooper stick his head in.

The SCVC Taskforce leader held up his cell. "Sorry, man, but I have to bail. Celina's water just broke."

CHAPTER TEN

"I'm going with you," Brooke insisted to Roman twenty minutes after Cooper left.

The conference room was quiet, Nadia and Emma sitting at the table comparing notes on The Reverend's profile. Mitch, Winslow, and Thomas had left at the same time as Cooper to track down leads and contact sources who might provide more.

Brooke had heard back from two of the three professors at the University. Neither had noticed any strangers at her lectures and both had small classes, so they knew their students well. The third, the criminal justice professor, had yet to return her call. She sat at her loaner computer, trying to find the members from the church she'd attended in childhood.

Which was proving to be much more difficult than she anticipated. The church had dissolved fifteen years ago, and the building had been sold. The records had disappeared, probably thrown out when the membership went elsewhere. "The church membership was a good idea, but it's a dead end. I might as well go with you."

Polly was on the phone with SDSU campus security, hitting them up for more footage of the parking lot from the previous couple of days, sure The Reverend had probably scoped the area and become familiar with it since Brooke had been on campus. With the cross necklace to identify him, she planned to weed through hours of footage.

Shane worked at his computer station, searching various federal databases for perpetrators wearing religious jewelry and cross referencing everything with the hooked cross and moon signs. His source with the TrackREC system had gotten back to him with a general size and weight ratio of the person who'd broken into Brooke's rental car and over a thousand matches had coincided with the man's biometrics. Shane was busy eliminating any that didn't meet their other parameters—location, victims, method.

But they needed more in order to narrow down the list of suspects.

Roman snatched up the photos Shane had printed for him to take to the mission where the killer called Luke had visited. "Too dangerous," he said to Brooke. "Our killer or killers might be watching the place and see you."

"You and I both know that The Reverend is aware I'm working with you. I'm not hiding out here and letting him think I'm scared."

Roman took her arm, rubbed his thumb over the sensitive skin of her wrist. "I don't care what the man thinks. Your safety comes first. Besides, I want you to talk to Dr. Collins and see if she can help you access more memories from that night."

It was logical, since seeing the cross necklace had brought back a smattering of memories. They flashed in and out, never stopping nor forming a cohesive storyline she could follow. Like a dream she could only remember bits and pieces of, she couldn't make sense of them.

She hadn't told Roman because what would she say? They were such small snippets of memories, she couldn't even describe them.

But what good would it do to tell Emma about them either? They made no sense.

Not yet anyway. Maybe if she kept working on the current case, the past would continue to reveal itself.

"I will talk to Dr. Collins when we get back, I promise." She gripped Roman's hand hard. "I need to go with you. See where this Luke was, who he talked to. It might help me remember something else."

He returned her firm hand hold, his eyes revealing the war going on inside his head. "I don't like it."

"I know you don't. And I appreciate your concern." She lowered her voice, stepped closer. "You're one of the only people to ever show this much concern about my well-being, in fact, and it means a lot to me. But you wanted me on this team for a reason, and now that I'm here, I can help with more than just sigils and random biblical quotes. I won't leave your sight and the Glock is ready to go if you get us into any trouble."

A small, reluctant smile lifted the corner of his lips. "You think I need protection?"

No, she was definitely the one who needed it, especially since her heart nearly pumped out of her chest every time he looked at her this way. Lowering her voice to a whisper, she leaned in. "Mostly, I just want to kiss you again."

The smile grew. "Well, why didn't you say so?"

He still didn't like it and she was sure he would end up making her sit in the car, but at least she'd be with him. Right now, she didn't want to be anywhere else.

They gathered their things and Roman informed the others where they were going. Polly got off the phone with the campus and twirled a strand of hair around her fingers. "They want a subpoena."

"It's parking lot footage." Roman said, disgusted.

Polly shrugged. "I'll call Judge Alvarez, tell her what's up. Shouldn't be more than a couple hours."

Brooke followed Roman out, waving at Sue as they got into the elevator.

As soon as the doors closed, Roman gave her the look.

She jumped his bones.

He laughed as her body weight knocked him back against the elevator wall, her lips all over his. He grabbed her legs as she wrapped them around him and held her up. "I like...this...side of you," he said between kisses.

"I've completely lost it."

His lips nuzzled her neck and she threw her head back. He licked her skin. "I would have never guessed you were so..."

"Wanton?"

"Lusty. It's incredibly sexy."

She ran her hands over his chest, through his hair. "Really? You think I'm sexy?"

"You just attacked me in an elevator." His tongue licked her collar bone. "It's one of my fantasies."

"Maybe I should hit the stop button."

Right at that moment, the elevator dinged and the doors slid open. Brooke *eeped* and Roman let her legs slide down so her feet were back on the floor as a middle-aged man in a dark suit entered. "Am I interrupting?" he asked, shooting her a grin.

Roman shifted Brooke to the side. "Arthur, good to see you. Ground floor?"

"Unless you're hiring lawyers for that menagerie you got upstairs. I'm always available, you know." Arthur winked at Brooke and pulled a business card from his pocket. "Arthur McPherson of McPherson, Adams, and Pullman Law Offices. You need a lawyer, you call me."

Brooke accepted the card. "I'll do that."

They parted ways with Arthur downstairs, exiting the parking garage a few minutes later. Brooke's emotions were all over the place. She had never been this happy *and* miserable at the same time. "Thanks for letting me come. I know how protective you are, but it means a lot to me to do something besides sit in the office and twiddle my thumbs."

He reached across the seat and took her hand. "It goes against every cell in my body to take you to a spot where I know the killer has been."

"I'm safer with you than anywhere else."

He kept his eyes on the road, though the tenseness in his body told her he didn't agree. But he didn't argue further.

At the St. Paul mission, it was the end of lunchtime. As Roman led her to the side door, his gaze swept the homeless loitering up and down the sidewalk. Some sat with their backs against the walls, others stood. A few huddled in groups, watching them approach. At least three bugged out as if afraid of being arrested. Cigarette smoke and stale body odor hung in the air.

"You be my eyes." Roman held the door open for her. "While I ask questions and show the photo around, you watch the people. Anyone or anything that jumps out at you, make note and let me know."

"Copy that."

He gave her a look as she walked across the threshold.

"What?"

That crooked smirk lifted the right corner of his mouth. "Just doesn't sound like you, Doc."

She patted her purse where her book nestled, ready for her to dive in. "Research. I know how undercover agents talk."

The smirk turned into a full-fledged laugh. He drew out his badge as he led Brooke to a woman in a hair net behind the serving line table. "We're not undercover."

"Maybe you're not, but I am. The fearless anthropologist enters the killer's territory with her trusty sidekick Homeland agent who's as sexy as he is skilled in the ways of making people talk. She pretends she's a Homeland agent too."

His soft laugh made her smile. The woman behind the table and several others watched them approach. All eyes were on Roman, of course, his amazing body and easy stride drawing appreciative glances. His smile, and probably that seductive bedroom laugh of his, drew them in like flies to honey.

For a split second, something primal and very female hit Brooke right in the solar plexus.

Back off, ladies.

"Roman Walsh, Homeland Security." He flashed his ID

along with that smile and the woman in the hair net barely glanced down at his badge. "My agent, Nadia Fernandez, from the Domestic Terrorism Taskforce was here a few days ago about Pastor Luke. He volunteered here for a brief time?"

"Yes, I spoke to your agent. I'm afraid I couldn't tell her much."

"And you are?"

"Loretta Atkins. I run the food line around here."

Roman showed her the pictures from the parking lot footage. "Was he wearing a cross necklace?"

Again, Loretta's gaze barely registered anything but Roman. "Most people of faith in Pastor Luke's position do."

You be my eyes. Brooke forced herself to glance around at those still finishing their lunches. A few curious faces stared back, but most didn't seem to notice—or care—that she was there. One man in long sleeves and a hat abruptly got up and headed for the door. She heard metal clank on metal as he grabbed the door handle, a chunky gold ring on his finger making the noise. A second man, also dressed too warm for the spring day in long sleeves and a jacket, followed close on his heels.

Criminals? Drug addicts? Undocumented illegals? Maybe they'd simply had bad experiences with cops.

And Roman, like anyone in law enforcement, had that effect on those who stayed off the radar.

There were no security cameras, but there were bars on the windows. Behind the table was a kitchen where the volunteer staff worked at cleaning pots and pans.

"This cross has a center eye with a diamond in it. Do you recognize it?"

A young Hispanic man joined Loretta and glanced over her shoulder. "I've seen one like that."

Brooke took in his ratty jeans and two-sizes-too-big shirt. "On whom?"

Roman gave her the side-eye and she made a *sorry* face at him, even though she wasn't.

The kid took the photo from Roman and studied it more closely. "Pastor Rogers has one like that. My brother says it freaks him out. That Pastor Rogers can see all his sins."

Roman accepted the photo back. "Who is Pastor Rogers? Is he head of this church?"

"She."

The voice came from behind Brooke's left shoulder, making her jump. She turned and saw a woman in a white shirt and black pants with her hands clasped in front of her.

"And yes." The woman pulled out a gold cross from under her shirt. The center diamond flashed under the fluorescent lighting. "I run the church. What can I do to help you?"

———————

Roman didn't let his smile falter as he shook the pastor's hand and flashed her his ID. Unlike Loretta, the Pastor held out her hand to inspect the badge more clearly.

Beside him, Brooke stared intensely at the cross necklace that now dangled on the front of the woman's shirt.

Be cool, Brooke.

Rogers handed his ID back and he put it away. "This is Dr. Heaton. She's a consultant for the taskforce."

"How can I help?" Rogers asked in a voice that suggested it was the last thing she wanted to do.

Roman showed her the photo. "We're trying to locate this man, known as Pastor Luke, who came through as a volunteer a month ago."

Rogers lifted her brows. "I never met him."

"Any information you can share would be helpful."

Brooke pointed at Rogers' necklace. "Like where you got that cross."

He hadn't really expected her to stay silent and let him do the talking, but she wasn't trained in interrogation and her personal interest in the case could jeopardize his knowledge-seeking mission.

Yet, he couldn't blame her. She had the scent of the trail like he did, and her nose was part bloodhound.

Rogers rubbed the gold cross between her fingers, then slid it inside her shirt once more. "My mother gave it to me when I accepted my holy orders."

Loretta had returned to cleanup duty. The young man spoke to a bearded man in stained overalls at one of the tables, trying to get him to finish up his soup.

Roman wanted a picture of that cross. "Was Pastor Luke wearing one like it?"

"As I said, I'm afraid I never met Pastor Luke. I was upstate at the Catalyst Conference for church leaders when he volunteered here."

"So you have no last name, no idea what church he's from, and no pictures of him?"

"I'm afraid not. Like Loretta told the other agent, Pastor Luke dropped in, helped out at lunchtime, and left after two days."

"Does that happen a lot?" Roman couldn't believe how casual people were in this day and age with safety and security. "You let anyone volunteer without a background check or even getting their last name?"

He didn't need to worry about Brooke offending the pastor, he'd just done it for them.

The pastor's shoulders went back and she lifted her chin. The smile she forced to her lips, and the way she clasped her hands again, told him he was about to get schooled. "We run on a very slim budget, Mr. Walsh, and very few in the church are able to volunteer to serve the homeless and destitute. We take all the help we can get and thank God for any person who walks through that door willing to give it."

Which meant they didn't ask questions, not even basic ones.

Brooke opened her mouth and Roman touched her hand to

stop her. "Are you sure there's no one else who interacted with Pastor Luke who could give us more information about him?"

The forced smile stayed in place. "I'm afraid not, but if I hear anything, I'll be in touch."

"What about a Pastor John?" Brooke asked, hefting her purse a little higher on her shoulder. "Has he volunteered here? Pastor Matthew? Mark?"

Rogers looked confused. "What?"

Brooke wasn't done. "Where did your mother get that cross from? A store here in San Diego?"

The pastor's fingers went to the pendant, idly rubbing it again. "I took my orders in Albuquerque, and my mother lives in Bangor, Maine. I assume she bought it from a store there."

Good thought to figure out if there was a central location where The Reverend and his followers might have purchased the cross necklace. He would have Polly call around to all the local jewelry shops and get Shane on the internet shopping sites and see if they could find a central supplier.

Roman started to thank the pastor for her time when Brooke went Homeland agent on him once more. "What do you know about the moon phases?"

Rogers looked like she thought Brooke was a mental patient. "Like full moon, new moon stuff?"

"The moon, blood, the Book of Revelation. Any of that come up with your fellow ministers lately?"

"What does that have to do with my necklace and Pastor Luke?"

The young man wandered by, a now empty soup bowl in hand. "Pastor Luke had a moon glyph tattooed on the back of his neck."

Roman stopped the kid. "You saw the back of his neck?"

"Under his collar." The kid looked at Brooke as he spoke, as if more comfortable with her. "I saw it when he bent over to hand one of the guys outside a plate of food. We had lasagna that day—at least what passes for it." A quick glance Loretta's way told Roman the kid didn't want to get in trouble for criticizing the cook. "There was a family outside, illegals I think. They were afraid to come in. He took plates of food out to them, got them to sit down out back under the tree. He prayed over them, made sure the kids had plenty to eat, gave the mom some cash from his own pocket. Nice guy. We could use more like that around here."

Brooke's fingers dug into Roman's arm. Damn, this was the best lead they had yet. "Is that family here today?" Roman asked.

"Nah." The kid headed for the kitchen. "They never came back."

"Wait." Brooke started after him.

Rogers huffed. "You can't go back there."

Roman stepped in front of Rogers, cutting her off while keeping an eye on Brooke. She definitely had the scent and her instincts were good. The kid was more comfortable talking to her, so Roman would give her some leeway.

Meanwhile, he needed to keep Rogers out of her hair. "Do you know of any sites where undocumented immigrants might hold services?"

"Why? So you can arrest and deport them?"

Hostile much? "I'm trying to save their lives. Have you heard of The Reverend? He's on a killing spree and they're his target."

She wasn't stupid. He could see the wheels turning in her head, putting the puzzle pieces together. "We don't ask personal questions here."

"If you know anything that can help, it could stop another mass suicide/killing."

Her face fell. She shook her head. "I've told you everything I know. I'm sorry I can't help you."

She walked away and Brooke emerged from the kitchen, giving Roman a covert thumbs-up. "We done here?" she asked.

He took her arm. "Yep."

She called back over her shoulder to Pastor Rogers. "He has a PhD in Criminal Justice! And he's a Homeland agent! So it's *Dr.* Walsh or *Agent* Walsh, Pastor Rogers. Show the man some respect."

Roman hustled her out the door, shaking his head. He'd created a monster.

CHAPTER ELEVEN

"I gave him your card," Brooke told Roman as they parked back at the towers. "The kid, his name's Jamison LeMont, knows how to spot the undocumented. He can interact with them in ways you can't."

"What do you mean, *ways I can't?*"

She exited the car before he could help her out. He'd parked in the garage and they walked toward the secure elevators.

"Come on, Roman. You know what I mean. You saw the way some of the people at the mission took off the moment they saw us." They passed the security guard with a show of their badges. "You don't necessarily look like a cop, but you certainly don't come off as one of them."

The elevator doors opened and they stepped inside. As soon as they closed, Roman reached for her and drew her close. "Maybe I should have kept my undercover look a while longer."

She raked her fingers through his short, dark strands. "Maybe you should have."

"You did good back there."

"I like helping. I asked Jamison to let us know if he came across any information on undocumented immigrants, regardless of whether they attend worship services. They typically stay together and watch each other's backs. The grapevine is strong within their communities. All we need is one person who can point us to The Reverend and his group."

"They took a chance with this Luke character exposing himself at the mission. Why did he do that?"

"The pastor was away, Loretta is obviously good at what she does but she's overwhelmed, and the other volunteers may not pay that much attention to the people who come through there."

"He felt it was worth the risk."

Upstairs, they brought Polly, Nadia, and Emma up to speed. Polly started working on local jewelry stores, Nadia snagged the warrant they'd been waiting on for the parking lot footage from the fax machine and left, and Emma asked to speak to Brooke alone.

Brooke had been hoping they'd all forget about Roman wanting her to speak to the psychologist, and she gave Roman a look, wondering if he'd jabbed Emma on the sly, but his return glance was innocent. "Use my office," he said.

So many therapists, guidance counselors, and others who'd thought they could help her. None of them had been able to break through her mind's defense mechanisms.

Back then if she'd seen her attacker's face, it might have helped capture him. But she hadn't, and twenty years later, there wasn't much hope of her remembering, was there? Seeing the cross pendant had triggered her memory, but would it cough up anything else?

She was sort of afraid it would.

I have to do this. Any new information could help.

"I don't want to put you on the spot," Emma said as she closed the door and the sounds of the outer office became muffled. "But I know what it's like to be the target of a killer. I just wanted to let you know I'm here if you want to talk. Not as a psychologist, but as a woman who understands what you're going through."

Brooke relaxed a smidgen and sat with her on the couch. "Thank you. I appreciate it. It's nice to have a friend, rather than a therapist, and I'm sorry for what happened to you with Chris Goodsman and his fans. I can relate to what you experienced, although mine really isn't as traumatic as yours from what I understand."

Emma laid a hand on her stomach. "Being stalked and attacked by a killer is always traumatic. I was lucky."

"And smart, no doubt."

"If Mitch hadn't been there…well, let's just say, I might not be here, living a very happy life now."

Brooke glanced at Emma's hand, still on her stomach where it protruded. "My turn to put you on the spot. When's the baby due?"

Her face broke into a big smile. "The beginning of October. It's amazing how quickly your life can turn around once the right man enters it."

The right man. Brooke wondered if she'd found hers.

For now, yes. It was fun to play around with love and romance while it lasted, but in the long term? She stood by her original assessment—she wasn't Roman's type.

What's my *type?* She honestly didn't know. Men and relationships had taken a back seat to her work.

Emma talked about baby stuff—names she and Mitch had picked out, boys versus girls, the nursery. Brooke listened, fascinated. While she'd had three serious relationships, she'd never considered wanting to have a family. Hers had been so screwed up, and realizing her birth mother never wanted her had been a tough thing to get over.

But over it she was. The scientist in her kept her emotions under tight rein. Maybe that was one of the reasons she enjoyed her work so much. It was easier to deal with the ancient past than the more recent one. Easier to think about ancient people and their situations, rather than dwell on her own.

Emma stopped mid-sentence and looked abashed. "I'm sorry. When I get started talking about the baby, I gush. Which is so unlike me. I'm a forensic psychologist to the bone. I'm not usually so…hormonal."

They shared a laugh. Brooke really liked her. "I know the

feeling. Science is my comfort zone—anthropology, religion, criminals. Babies and motherhood? I don't know what to do with that stuff."

Emma grinned. "Trust me, criminals are much easier to understand, and from a forensic psychologist to a doctor of anthropology, they make handling a husband look like child's play."

"What made you want to study criminals?"

"I admit to finding the criminal mind fascinating."

Weird, but Brooke respected it. "People often think being interested in buried bones and relics from past centuries is unhealthy. They'd rather I got worked up about politics and the Kardashians."

"You're preaching to the choir, sister."

They continued chatting amicably for another few minutes. "I'd rather talk about anything but my attacker," Brooke admitted, "but maybe you could give me some insight."

"You're just saying that so I don't bore you with more stories about nursery themes and whether it's okay to let your baby sleep with you or not."

"Actually, I'd love to hear more about baby stuff, but Roman will ask me how our talk went and I want to be able to honestly say we discussed the killer."

"Smart." Emma adjusted herself on the couch, hugging a pillow to her pregnant tummy. "I haven't read your file or the reports from that night. All I know is what's been shared here today. Care to fill in the details?"

Brooke had repeated them so many times, she knew the condensed version by heart. It took less than a minute to lay out the bones for Emma. As she did so, the psychologist watched her closely.

Not the first time. But where other therapists had watched her with a clinical fascination, Emma seemed to be listening more as a friend and colleague. "Do you think the man found out afterwards that you were a witness?"

"He must have, even though the cops didn't release it to the press. Some people at our church knew. My mother told them."

"After that night, though, he never came after you?"

"His face was covered, so I couldn't ID him regardless."

"Are you sure about that?"

"That he never showed his face? Oh, yeah. If he'd removed the mask and he thought I could ID him, he had plenty of chances to eliminate me. My father was out of the picture at that point, and my mother continued her struggle with alcohol. I was on my own a lot and was even more of an outcast after the killings. People treated me like I had a disease."

"And it's your opinion the killer attacked the Dunkirks because they were black."

Brooke thought about that for a moment. "I was so young, I'm not sure I even really thought about his motivation. The police ruled it a hate crime right from the start and others jumped on the bandwagon."

"If the killer had had the chance to kill you, do you think he would have because you were a witness or because of your own ethnicity?"

Had Roman told her about the adoption?

It wasn't like the color of her skin and her kinky hair weren't dead giveaways to the fact she had some non-Caucasian blood in her, but still... "Why do you ask that?"

"I'm curious if it really was a hate crime. The records show there were no other killings in your town or the surrounding area in that timeframe, and few hate crimes of this severe of a nature. Those that were reported were attributed to the Aryan Nation."

The current mass suicide/murders were definitely in the hate crime category. The psychologist might have a point.

But then that gave weight to the theory about the "bad man."

Brooke stifled a shiver. "You could be right."

"You remembered the cross hanging from your attacker's

neck that night twenty years ago. I'm concerned you might recall more."

"Isn't that what everyone wants?"

"I saw the effect that one memory had on you and I'm sure you blocked what happened next for a reason. One that could be very uncomfortable if you begin remembering more."

Brooke rubbed her thumb across an invisible stain on her jean leg. "Those memories are part of me. I need to bring them forth so I can deal with them and move on."

"Spoken like someone who's spent too much time in therapy."

They shared a smile.

"Truth?" Brooke said. "I'm terrified to remember them."

"I don't blame you."

"You honestly don't think we should sit here and try to resurrect them?"

"Is that what you want?"

Brooke sighed deeply. "If I truly believed it would help Roman solve this case, I'd do it in a heartbeat."

"But you don't think it will, even though you're sure The Reverend is your childhood attacker?"

"I'm sure the man who broke into my rental car and left me that notecard is the same man who killed the Dunkirks. It's possible he's also The Reverend, but I can't positively say they're one and the same."

"Your intuition says it is, though."

"Maybe I just really want it to be so I can lay my childhood demons to rest."

Emma patted Brooke's knee. "Being here helping with this case? It's going to do that to some extent, regardless of whether your childhood attacker and The Reverend are the same or not."

"You think so?"

"I think all of your degrees and experience, which I completely respect and admire, are actually cushions to pad yourself from what happened to you as a kid. They make you feel worthy and able to prove to your parents, and all the people who shunned you back then, that you're not an outcast."

"You think I lack self-confidence?"

"Not in the areas of your education, but perhaps in your personal life."

Damn. How could someone know her so well after only a few minutes?

Emma showed no judgment, only open honesty. "You survived a horrific incident, Brooke, and your friend didn't. Survivor's guilt is written all over your face every time you mention her. You said yourself that you lived with an alcoholic mother and you were treated unfairly by others. Your father abandoned you. No amount of time on this couch or any other is going to heal that."

Finally. Someone who understood. "Survivor's guilt is hard to explain to people."

"I've seen a lot of it. Experienced it myself."

"People tell you it's not your fault. You know on a cognitive level that's true, but emotionally…"

"It feels like it is. Like there is no justice in the world. It sucks."

Yep, Emma definitely got it. "I didn't realize I was using my education as a substitute for my absentee parents."

"Aren't we all?"

Another shared smile.

"Truth? One of the reasons I went into religious studies and criminal justice was in order to hunt down the killer. For years, I focused hot and heavy on finding him—I was kind of…obsessed. Still am."

"As a kid, you felt helpless. As an adult, you knew you had resources and a chance of bringing him to justice."

Justice. The word rang inside her chest like a gong. They all deserved it. Aleisha, her parents, the men, women, and children killed by The Reverend and his group. "The hope that I will find him has never completely gone away, but after exhausting every avenue available, I had to be realistic and move on."

"Except you can't because of what you experienced."

"If I could put him away, that would do a lot."

"You have an opportunity for that, if the man who broke into your car the other night really is the man from your childhood. Does it frighten you that he may be targeting you again?"

Of course! "I'm trying not to focus on that."

"Understood. If you need to talk about that fear at any point, I'm happy to listen. Again, been there, experienced that."

"I'm mostly trying to distract myself with everything else."

"Everything else?"

Roman. Shooting lessons. Focusing on The Reverend's next group of innocent people. Plus, she had Conrad Flynn waiting for her inside her purse. "A little escapism never hurts, right?"

Emma held up a hand in a high-five gesture. "Amen, sister."

Brooke gently slapped it and they both stood. "Thank you for this. I appreciate it more than you know."

"You're not alone when facing your demons. Please remember that. I see you, who you are today and who you were at ten. I understand what you're going through."

Brooke's brain cramped and she was suddenly ten again.

A hand reached to move the scarf from her face. It was coming closer, closer..."I see you."

She plopped back down on the couch, her butt hitting hard and her hands flying out to brace against the fabric as the killer's voice echoed in her ears.

"Brooke? Dr. Heaton?"

Brooke blinked. Emma's hands were on her upper arms, her face in front of Brooke's. "Did you have another flashback?"

"He knew I was there," she whispered. "In the trunk."

She was torn between trying to see more of the big hand moving closer to her face and never wanting to again. "His hand. He reached for me. He said, *'I see you'.*"

"He can't hurt you now. You're not that little girl anymore. I'm here with you. Did you see anything else?"

A heavy chain was wrapped around her lungs, keeping them immobile. Closing her eyes, she let the memory hover close again. Moonlight on the gold cross, the wink of the all-seeing eye, the big hand coming down over her face.

"You can't hide from me, Brooke. Your mother tried to keep you from me, but you're going to help me get what I want."

Brooke gasped, eyes flying open. Now her chest heaved, the chain dissolving. She sucked in sharp breaths, Emma's hands anchoring her to the couch.

Your mother tried to keep you from me...

Her mother? Her *real* mother?

Fingers trembling, she wiped them across her face, clearing imaginary cobwebs. Her throat felt tight, her tongue thick. "He said my mother tried to keep me from him."

Emma released her grip on Brooke, sitting beside her. "Brooke, was the man your father?"

Brooke shook her head, not sure of anything. "Maybe it's not real. My imagination is just running wild."

"Is that what you believe?"

Brooke clasped her hands in her lap. She no longer knew what to believe.

Roman let Brooke into the house. "We should talk about what happened."

She dumped her purse on the breakfast bar, the romance novel in her hand, and headed for the den. "Not yet. I need to process."

All the way home, she'd tucked herself against the passenger door and read that damn novel, refusing to discuss the revelation she'd had during her talk with Dr. Collins. He knew from Emma that she'd remembered more about her childhood attacker, but the psychologist was reluctant to discuss the details. "That's up to Brooke," she'd told Roman. "While she's not my patient, she is my friend now. What we discussed was in confidence. She'll tell you when she's ready."

While he agreed that it was Brooke's prerogative to share when she was ready, he hated seeing her upset and needed to know first and foremost that she was going to be okay. Then, after that, if what she'd remembered might help them catch her stalker.

"I'm here when you want to talk," he called after her.

Silence met his ears. Sliding his keys onto the hook next to the door, he contemplated various ways to reassure her. To be her support system.

It's what he did—took care of others. He hated seeing anyone scared, upset, or in need.

If only Percy had let me take care of him after he got back from Iraq.

His brother would still be alive.

Be the hero.

He actually had taken care of Percy for awhile. But in the end, he hadn't been able to save him. He could—and would—do whatever it took to save Brooke.

From his wine fridge, he brought out a bottle of Sauvignon Blanc from his favorite vineyard upstate and found a wine glass in the overhead cabinet. This was the best bottle of white wine he owned and Brooke deserved the best.

Before taking her the glass, he rummaged in his pantry and found a box of chocolate truffles one of his sisters had brought back from a trip to Sweden a few months ago. He wasn't much into sweets so he hadn't opened them yet, but what woman had ever turned down fancy chocolates?

In the freezer, he found two sirloins and pulled them out to defrost. Like he'd told Brooke, he wasn't much of a cook, but he could grill a couple of steaks and cut up veggies.

Chocolate, steak, wine…what about a bubble bath? His mom and sisters liked those. Except he had nothing to make bubbles.

What she needs is time in the ring. Something—or someone—to punch a few times and work out her fear and anger.

That's what he'd seen on her face. Whatever she'd remembered about her attacker, it had scared her and that fear made her angry.

No one liked feeling vulnerable. To compensate, anger often rose to the occasion. But misplaced anger could do more harm than good. He was a walking testament to that. So many fights before he'd even become a boxer…

Snagging the glass of wine from the counter, Roman brought it and the box of truffles into the den.

Brooke was curled up at one end of the couch, knees bent and feet under her bottom with that book in her hand. He said nothing, pretending he didn't notice her gaze following him as he set the wine and chocolates on the coffee table in front of her and lit the gas fireplace. It was a warm summer evening, but the fireplace was more for ambience than heat and the sunken den was cooler than the rest of the house.

Without a glance back, he left the room and went to work on dinner.

He was opening his second beer and getting ready to chop onions when Brooke appeared in the doorway half an hour later with the empty wine glass in hand and a smidgen of chocolate on her lips. The romance book was in her other hand.

"You know, I never felt wanted growing up, especially after I overheard my parents discussing my adoption." She sat on a stool and placed her glass on the breakfast bar. "It sort of freaked me out when you wanted me for your team."

"Freaked you out?" She was talking to him again. That was good, but he had the feeling he needed to step lightly. "Why would that freak you out? You consult for Cooper's team. Mine isn't much different."

"Twice. I've consulted for them twice. And Cooper Harris doesn't make me feel like…"

"Like what?"

"Like you do."

He picked up the knife and started slicing the freshly skinned onion. "Is that good or bad?"

Her voice was soft. "I'm not sure."

Not exactly confidence-inspiring. "I like having you here, Brooke. I hope you like it too."

"Your team is great, and I admire the work you do. I hope I'm actually an asset with this case."

He stopped slicing, but didn't look at her. "I wasn't talking about work. I like having you here. In my place."

"Oh. I like that too. Those chocolates are delicious, and by the way, I noticed you have a copy of my book on your end table. Nice prop."

"It's not a prop. I read it cover to cover. Brilliant idea to make Lucy seem like a teenage girl and interview her via Twitter questions and answers. Who knew a three billion year old fossil would have so much in common with modern day women?"

"That was the idea, to bring her to life for the current generation, make her real."

"I was hoping for an autograph."

"Sure."

A peek over his shoulder showed she was staring at the romance book, which now lay next to the empty wine glass.

Wiping his hands on a dishtowel, he walked to the fridge, pulled out the Sav Blanc, and refilled her glass. "How's the book?"

Her eyes rose to the glass, then to him. "The cerebral sex is amazing."

"Cerebral sex?" He chuckled and left the bottle sitting on the bar. "And here I thought you were reading it to pick up tips on shooting a gun."

"That too." She gave him a half-hearted smile. "But honestly, it's all about the sex with an incredible hero who makes the heroine feel wanted and safe."

Exactly what he'd been attempting to do with her. And at that moment, with her sitting there looking wiped out and oh-so-vulnerable, he wanted to grab her and kiss away the worry lines around her mouth.

His cock twitched, the memories of their make-out sessions giving rise to more fantasies. Her soft skin, her gentle laughter, the wantonness he hadn't expected when she'd climbed into his lap in the Jeep and again attacked him in the elevator.

"What I really need," Brooke said, dropping her focus to the wine again as one slender finger toyed with the corner of the book, "are tips on seduction. That's why I grabbed this story. I don't know how to flirt."

Those beautiful eyes that reminded him of the ocean came up to meet his, and for a moment, he understood what she meant by *smoldering*. "From where I'm standing at the moment, you're doing a pretty damn good job of it."

"I'm serious."

"So am I."

"My last date never progressed past a kiss goodnight at my front door. I'm not a femme fatale. My serious romantic relationships all evolved over time with work colleagues. There was never this kind of...heat. Or awkwardness. I don't know how to seduce a man."

"You've had me hard as a brick since the moment you walked into the room."

One pert eyebrow lifted. "Is that so?"

"Hell yes."

"So you mean, the awkward attempts I made today to seduce you worked?"

"You mean attacking me in the parking lot and the elevator? Nothing awkward about them for me. I loved it."

"Women throw themselves at you all the time."

"They do?"

"Don't they?"

He chuckled and grabbed his beer. "In my line of work, I

don't have time to date, and I can't talk about my job. Makes for real short dinner conversation. It's nice to have someone I can talk to about a case and who doesn't want to have sex with me just because I wear a gun and have handcuffs in my back pocket."

"You're not into bondage?"

"With the right woman, sure. Like most things, it comes down to trust."

He saw her visibly swallow. "How do you know who the right woman is?"

I'm looking at her. "She has to want me for more than my badge, money, or looks."

"So no badge bunnies, gold-diggers, or arm-candy trophy hunters. Tall order."

"Probably why I'm still alone."

"Surely you've had your share of serious relationships."

He shrugged. "I was engaged once. I was sure she was the one."

Brooke's brows lowered slightly. "What happened?"

"She ditched me a few weeks before the wedding."

"Why?"

The beer cooled his throat as he took a swig, giving the old pain in his heart a chance to subside before he answered. "It's a long story involving Percy and my attempt to stop a drug deal he was involved in. In the end, he died and Melinda left me."

Brooke rose from the stool and came over to him. "I'm so sorry."

"Me too. At least about Percy."

"Melinda's a bitch. A stupid one, I might add."

"You don't know the whole story."

She threaded her arms around his waist. "I don't need to."

Her lips were right there, ready for kissing. Her eyes locked on his, inviting him to open up, share his past.

He set down his beer and touched her hair. God, he wanted her, but bringing up Percy had been a bad idea, reminding him how mixing work with people you cared about could end in tragedy. "You hungry?"

Confusion touched her face. She'd been ready for that kiss. "I just ate a bunch of truffles."

Right. "The steaks need a few more minutes to defrost. How about we hit the punching bag? I'll show you some self-defense moves. Help you work up an appetite before I throw them on the grill."

"I thought you didn't cook."

He chucked her chin. "As long as I don't overcook them, it's hard to mess up a steak."

She smiled, dropped her arms and took a step back. "I'm not very coordinated."

He'd pushed her away. Which was good.

So why did his stomach hurt?

Taking her hand, he pulled her to him and kissed her knuckles. "We'll work on that."

CHAPTER TWELVE

Twenty minutes later, Brooke was sweating. Hard.

But God, did she feel alive!

Roman had wrapped her hands before putting them inside boxing gloves, then he'd taught her how to position her feet and punch the hell out of the Everest bag in his gym.

It had made her forget about the bad man. About her parents. About her conflicting feelings for Roman and the weird vibes he'd given off upstairs. Whatever had happened with Percy and Melinda had shut down the playful banter and flirting he'd been doing with her. She'd seen the pain behind his eyes. Felt the tension in his body.

His body was loose again now, a somewhat predatory look in his eye as he stalked around her in the ring. He wore protective guards on his hands, holding them up for her to punch. "Left, right, left," he demanded, and Brooke gave him what he wanted, the sound of leather on leather echoing in the room.

It was a much bigger version of what was in his office. Weights, mirrors, the giant punching bag, a small boxing ring. Framed photos of him at competitions accepting his winner's belt and trophies lined the south wall. Some showed him in the ring with various opponents. He looked young, rebellious, defiant.

"Light on your feet, Heaton." He switched direction and started walking her in an opposite circle. "Let's see that left uppercut."

The sleeveless tank he'd loaned her was too big, hanging down past her butt, but was soft and smelled like his laundry detergent.

"I can barely hold my arms up." The tone of her voice was entirely too chipper for the complaint. She couldn't help it. Her legs shook and her arms were exhausted, but she'd never felt more exhilarated. "I won't even be able to lift my phone tomorrow."

"Cry baby."

She swung, just like he'd taught her, using her core and her hips to power the punch.

"Lightweight," he taunted, but he was grinning.

And smoldering.

Boxing turned him on.

Works for me!

She grinned back. "Don't kid yourself. I can do this all night."

"All night, huh?"

She lowered her fists and took a step back, breathing hard. "Not really. I suck at bluffing as well as the art of seduction, in case you haven't noticed."

The grin stayed in place, his own hands lowering as he stopped his predatory pace. He shucked off his guard mitts. "You did good for your first time."

"You're just saying that."

"Between shooting practice and this? You'll definitely be sore tomorrow. I'll help you with your gloves."

She stepped forward and playfully punched his rock-hard abs. His tank top's open sides showed her all of them, making her mouth water. "Why did you quit boxing? You're so good at it."

He helped her out of the ring and over to the bench where he made her sit. He kneeled in front of her, bringing them almost face-to-face. "Shoulder injury."

"That sucks."

He untied her right glove and gently guided it off her hand. "I was good at boxing, but it was never going to be a long-term career. The injury, and the rehab for it, forced me to look at different avenues for my future. It all worked out for the best."

The release of the weight from her hand was glorious, even though her fingers were still taped to protect her knuckles. She raised her other hand and let him work on the ties. "Do you miss it?"

"Every day."

He was alone, his brother was dead, his fiancee had left him. He'd given up a career in a sport he loved, no matter how casual he was about quitting it.

The second glove came off and she rolled her wrists this way and that. "I'd like more lessons."

He handed her a towel. "Any time."

Dabbing at the sweat along her hairline, she let him take her hand to cut off the tape. His grasp was firm, holding her steady so he didn't nick her skin.

"I'm sorry about earlier." The concentration on his face, his closeness, made her pulse skitter and jump. "About not telling you what I remembered."

"No pressure. I know you'll tell me if you think it's critical to our case."

Was it? "I don't think it is, but I'd like to tell you anyway."

The tape fell away and Roman massaged her hand. His fingers were warm and strong as he kneaded each knuckle and tip. "I owe you an apology as well."

"For what?"

His gaze, now tentative, rose to hers. "I can't exactly expect you to share your past if I won't share mine."

She stroked a finger over his jaw where the day's stubble already bloomed. "It's okay. I understand."

He took her still-taped hand and began gently removing the binding. "I never talk about it because it's..."

"Too painful," she finished for him. All she wanted to do was wrap her arms around him and kiss away that pain. "You're so busy rescuing everyone else, you've never let anyone help you."

"Brooke, I…"

Before he could say anything else, she leaned forward and kissed him.

It was just a soft kiss. One she hoped would convey how much she appreciated his friendship, everything he'd done for her in the past couple days. That she hoped for more…

As per normal, her attempt at seduction was less subtle than she'd planned. The moment her lips touched Roman's he came up on his knees and cupped the back of her head, moving her backward. His lips demanded a deeper response, his tongue seeking access to her mouth.

She gave it to him, grabbing onto his shoulders, her thighs spreading to allow his body to come closer. He gripped her hips, sliding them toward him while at the same time, he ravaged her mouth.

Just like earlier that day, the chemistry between them ran hot and fast. Brooke's already warm body ratcheted up another ten degrees. She was tired of cerebral sex—she wanted the real thing, and she wanted it now.

"Brooke,"—Roman drew back, his lips trailing across her jaw, down her neck. "We're about to cross a line here."

She laughed, the sound low and husky as it echoed in the training center. "Oh, Roman, we've had this conversation, and correct me if I'm wrong, but we crossed that line already. Do you really want to think about it now?"

God knew she didn't. It wasn't everyday that a Plain Jane like her got to have sex with her fantasy man. Since that night at the bar, with bullets flying and a hero saving her life, she'd done a one-eighty. Life was too wild, too messy, to hesitate and let an opportunity like this pass her by.

"If you're okay with it, I am," he murmured in her ear as his hands grabbed the hem of the tank top and drew it over her head.

His went next and they took turns fervently undressing each other while they snuck in kisses. Somewhere along the line, he produced a condom and she put it on him, enjoying the surprise on his face at her boldness.

Before she knew it, she was in the ring once more, on her back and spread eagle. Roman hovered above her, his eyes roaming over her breasts, her belly, lower. She did the same to him, letting her gaze feast on his incredible body, lingering on his erect cock that made her lick her lips.

Her breath caught as he bent his head and licked each of her nipples, sucking on them, before he dragged wet kisses down her belly. At the apex of her sex, his beautiful eyes looked up at her and his fingers kneaded her thighs.

He was so sexy, so powerful.

"Wait," she said, her voice ragged. "The first time I come for you, I want you inside me."

She saw his pupils grow bigger, darker. His nostrils flared and a moment later, he slid up her body once more, taking his time, nipping, licking, tonguing her. Her back arched, shoving her breasts into his hands, his mouth.

Wanton? Shit, she was downright shameless.

Heart kicking inside her chest, she spread her legs farther, loving the feel of his erection, of him. "I need you," she said, reaching for him. "Now."

But he grabbed her wrist and pulled her away, lifting the hand up and over her head. Pinning it against the floor of the ring where they'd just been sparring.

He caught her other wrist and did the same, causing her body to arch again, her nipples grazing his chest. "Goddamn, you're so beautiful. I can't wait to bury my cock inside you."

He sounded downright primal. Deadly. Just like he'd looked at the gun range.

Brooke had never felt hotter in her life.

"Then do it," she challenged him, wrapping her legs around his buttocks and tugging. "Give me what I want."

He kissed her, hard, and she returned it, sucking his tongue into her mouth. His cock nudged her and she arched her hips up, totally at his mercy and loving every second of it.

She'd never been so exposed to a man. Not just pinned down naked in this manner, but totally exposed emotionally as well. None of her other boyfriends had ever known so much about her. None of them had ever taken care of her the way Roman had.

"Oh, God," she moaned when he entered her, completely filling and stretching her to the max, inch by sweet inch.

His hips ground against hers, driving him in and out, the sound of their bodies slapping together echoing in the room, just like her punches had earlier. Keeping her hands pinned over her head, he lifted his upper body and watched her breasts bounce with every thrust. "Come for me," he said.

Her walls tightened as he drove into her with a frenzy she tried to match. Desperation scorched her skin. She was so close…

As if he sensed it, he bore down on her, keeping most of his weight on his elbows as he continued to hold her captive, using his immense strength to drive himself deeper and deeper. Faster. Harder.

Brooke cried out. Her pleasure, desperation, the intensity…it was all too much as the orgasm shot her into oblivion.

She writhed against his ministrations, wanting it to never end, needing more of him.

All of him.

Suddenly her hands were free. His strong fingers were on her hips, holding her in place as he grew even bigger inside her.

Clutching his shoulders, she rode the wave. "Your turn," she murmured in his ear as she thrust her hips up to meet him.

His teeth nipped at the spot on her shoulder where it met her neck. "Fuck me, I can't…hold back any longer."

"Then don't." She twisted her hands in his hair, kicked his ass with her heels. "Let go."

His already hard thrusts became harder. She met him with the same intensity, feeling a new orgasm building inside her.

Heat, lust, and desire hit her in waves, bringing her to the edge as he moaned his pleasure near her ear. She cried out as her orgasm struck, her walls milking him into his.

"God...damn." His body went rigid. He thrust again as deep as he could go.

The pulsing of his release felt so good. So right. As he dropped onto her, she hugged him close, loving his weight, the sweat they'd created. The way they fit together like they were meant for each other.

After a wonderful few minutes of floating, he caressed her face, kissed her lips. "You're a naughty woman."

Yes, she was. "Surprising, I know."

"I love it," he said, and picked her up and carried her to the bathroom.

In the shower, she enjoyed the warm spray, her legs shaking from the intense lovemaking. Roman joined her as she wet her hair, his hands kneading her breasts. She arched, giving him full access. He'd donned another condom, already hard and ready again. His penis bumped against her stomach. A finger rubbed the sensitive spot between her legs and she moaned.

Another finger joined the first, parting her engorged folds and pushing deeper. She was ready to go again as well. At the same time, he thumbed her clit, making her grasp his shoulders.

But she wanted the pleasure to be about him this time. She wanted her mouth on his cock.

Never had she asked for what she wanted. Never had she honestly craved to perform oral sex on a man. *Which says a lot about the men I've dated.*

But his erection... It captivated her like the rest of his incredible body. She wanted to touch every inch of him, kiss and lick as well.

She caught Roman's hand and drew it back, hating the loss of his touch. A touch that could bring her to climax in a few simple strokes. But it was time someone took care of him for a change.

And I'm the one to do it.

Kissing away his protests, she wrapped a hand around his enlarged penis and gave a tug before she rolled the condom off.

He sucked in his breath, then captured her by the back of the neck and kissed her hard.

She stroked him, loving the power she seemed to have over him, the water and steam making it feel like a dream. Sliding down his neck, chest, and lower to his abdomen, she finally found what she wanted.

On her knees, she kissed the head, licked the ridged length of him, sliding the tip of her tongue into the slit.

"Jesus," he swore, his hips bucking. His hands sank into her wet hair as she took him deep, sucking him into the back of her throat.

They moved together in a slow, intense rhythm, Brooke setting her hands on his powerful thighs for balance. As the pace increased, his hands keeping their hold on her head, she felt the shift in his body. The powerful drawing in of his muscles as if he were about to deliver a punch. He took one of her hands and placed it on his balls.

She had much to learn.

Gently massaging his sac, she loved the way he cursed again and pumped into her mouth.

The feel of his muscles contracting told her all she needed to know. One final deep suck and she clenched him to the roof of her mouth with her tongue.

"Fuck!" he yelled, the sound accompanied by his release.

She continued to drink him in, using her tongue, her cheeks, swallowing every last drop of his release.

His hold relaxed and he sagged against the tiles, drawing her off her knees and giving her a heavy-lidded look. "Believe me when I say…"—his chest heaved as he took a deep breath— "you do not need tips in the seduction department."

The compliment made her grin. She took up the bar of soap and started raising suds. The soap jumped from her hands and she let it fall, running her hands over her breasts and enjoying the way his eyes darkened. He got up, reached out of the shower, and came back with a fresh condom.

Roman sat on the wooden-slatted seat—cypress by the look of it—and wiggled his fingers at her. "Come here."

"I'm dirty." She grinned but stayed out of his reach.

"Yes, you are."

"I'm serious. That boxing stuff made me sweat. So you just sit there and enjoy the show."

She found the soap and ran the bar over her ankle, calf, and up higher. At the juncture between her thighs, she used it to spread her folds, then turned so he could see her butt and used it to stroke each of her cheeks.

The soap went flying again when Roman came off the seat and grabbed her, forcing her hands to the tiled wall as he bent her forward. Her heavy breasts swayed and he filled his hands with them, pinching her nipples and making her gasp.

He was hard again and had covered himself. She felt the hot length of him slide along her backside as he leaned over and ran his tongue over each vertebrae of her spine.

She spread her feet wider and welcomed the heavy fullness of him as he entered her from behind. One hand tangled in her hair, the other clutched her hip as he began driving himself into her.

Her arms shook as she braced herself against his assault, every nerve in her body sending up a cheer. Deep down, she knew that no matter how much she tried to take care of him, he would always give her twice as much.

Roman whistled as he took the steaks off the grill and slid them onto the platter. Inside Brooke napped on the couch in the den, exhausted after their workout. He liked that he could wipe the worry off her face and put her into a blissful sleep after their long, complicated day.

Positioning a steak and a pile of the grilled vegetables on each of the plates he had set out, he continued to whistle under his breath. Unlike Brooke, he was energized from the three rounds he'd gone with her from the training room to the shower, and damned if he wasn't ready to go again.

She was killing him. Every word she spoke, every look she gave him. It was all seduction and she didn't even realize it.

He didn't want to examine it too hard, but it wasn't just the physical exercise pumping him up. The sex was hot and he loved every minute of it, glad that Brooke was so unencumbered under her buttoned-up, professional image. Yet it went far beyond that. Beyond his need to protect and keep her safe. She accepted life on its terms like he did. She wasn't a drama queen, nor did she pry into his psyche, and she had a sense of humor even after all the shit she'd been through. She was tough and smart, kind and funny, all at the same time.

She made him feel better about himself.

A tough job.

He wanted to free her from her pain in return.

Unfortunately, for all his money, skills, and connections, he couldn't move enough mountains to do that for her.

But if he caught the bastard stalking her, it would be a damn good start.

He'd seen the worst of so many people over the years, it often left him jaded. Combined with his own self-loathing, he could have sunk into a rut he'd never have climbed out of. Luckily, he had a driving need to be the hero, as his brother had accused him of over and over again, and that need wouldn't let him rest.

The first time he'd seen Brooke, she'd been in front of a group of law enforcement agents talking about a growing terrorist threat in the Pacific Northwest and the group's deep-seated religious beliefs. He'd felt his world shift. While she had in no way condoned the group's actions, he'd walked out of the conference understanding them, and what mattered to them, in a way he hadn't before.

Two weeks later, his taskforce nailed the leader and shut down the cell. He'd experienced a renewed sense of purpose.

And that's when he'd known he had to have Brooke for himself.

Since he'd formed his DT Taskforce, he'd been through at least a dozen agents and half as many expert consultants that knew their job well but didn't click with the DTT's core members. Brooke had earned their respect from the first day and continued to do so.

"Hey."

She stood in the doorway, makeup free, her damp hair hanging in waves. She wore nothing but one of his button-down shirts. A single button over her breasts held the two sides of the shirt together and she was pantyless. Even though she'd picked up clothes from the store, she seemed to prefer his.

Fine with me.

He loved seeing her in his clothes. Seeing her in his house. His shower, his bed.

My ring.

He had more plans for her inside the boxing ring, and none of them involved gloves.

Or clothes.

The handcuffs were still an option.

"Hey, yourself. Ready for dinner?"

She walked over to the sliders and peered out at his large deck. "What a lovely view. Can we eat outside?"

The sun was sinking over the water, dozens of boats at the docks far below, bobbing in a peaceful rhythm with the waves.

It wasn't advisable, seeing as how her stalker could be out there, even though it would be challenging because of the sheer drop off for him to get close. But it wasn't impossible, and while the stalker didn't seem the type to take a shot at her from a distance—and he couldn't get close enough to hurt her any other way—Roman couldn't take chances. "I don't think that's a good idea."

Her hand landed on the glass door. "You think he's out there?"

Didn't that just kill the mood? "We have to assume he could be."

"Good." She unlatched the door lock. "Let's give him something to see."

She marched out on the porch.

Roman closed his eyes for a quick moment and blew out a breath. *Crazy, gutsy woman.*

He carried the plates out and set them on the glass table. She stood at the railing, the wind gently ruffling her bangs and blowing the shirt open. Roman approached her and buttoned a couple more buttons on the shirt. "I really have to advise against this."

"I know you do, but I'm tired of living in fear. He took so much from me when I was ten, I'll be damned if I let him do it again."

Roman scanned the area. It would be difficult for anyone to see her out here, with the way the house had been built against the rocky hill. His closest neighbors actually had better views of the marina, but they were all on different levels of the hill. If Brooke's stalker was in one of the boats far below with a good set of binoculars, he'd be able to see them when she stood at the railing like this, but what were the odds the bastard had a boat down there?

Roman had seen some bizarre things in his time, least of which were serial killers who would go to any lengths to keep their prey in sight. "Come sit down," he told Brooke, guiding her back to the table.

She smiled up at him, the setting sun spreading a warm glow over her face. "Ordering me around, boss?"

The term made him smile. "Damn right. Your care and well-being are on my ass right now. Get over here and eat the steak I cooked you."

She mock-saluted him and he pulled out her chair. He handed her silverware and she inhaled deeply over the steak. "This smells amazing."

"I'll get us some drinks."

He turned to go back in and Brooke slapped him on the ass.

"Don't be long."

He grabbed her wrist, heat igniting the air between them. Bringing the tips of her fingers to his lips, he let his tongue do a slow lick over the end of each one.

Her breath hitched and he released her before she launched herself at him again. He was more than happy to take her back inside and ravish her but there was no sense wasting a good cut of meat. They had all night.

"Before I give out any more sexual favors," she said a few minutes later, around a bite of food, "I want to know about your brother."

His fork stopped in mid-air. "I don't talk about him."

"I know that. I don't talk about my shit with people either, but I opened up to you." She raised her wine glass to him. "Remember? Turnabout's fair play, and as I recall, Dr. Walsh, you told me you were an open book the other day at lunch. You said you'd tell me anything I want to know."

Busted.

He went back to eating.

She didn't seem to care. "I'm serious about putting out. You want more sex tonight? Start talking."

What had brought this on? "That's a dangerous trick."

"Is it?"

The smirk on her face didn't hide the sincere solicitude in her eyes. She seemed to understand how his demons haunted him. That his driving need to take care of her, and all the others, stemmed from them.

"Percy was an Army Ranger. Three tours in the Middle East. A true hero."

Those facts were easy to recite.

"Heroes always have flaws," she said.

There was no judgment in it, just simple observation.

A not so simple truth, nevertheless.

Lowering his fork, he wiped his mouth on a napkin. "He came home with a back injury and an addiction to pain killers. Things went downhill from there."

"Usually does. What happened?"

Dog on a bone. "I got him the help he needed, rehab for both the injury and drugs. Got him clean, helped him get a job. Next thing I know, he's in deep shit with a major drug dealer here in San Diego. I bailed him out, covered it up so our parents wouldn't find out, and nearly lost my career over it."

She swirled the wine in her glass, nodded, but didn't offer platitudes.

He appreciated that. He tossed the napkin on the table and took a deep breath. Talking to her was as easy as fucking her. It was a first for him. "It took time initially, but I brought him here, cleaned him up, insisted he fess up to the entire family. He wasn't going to get better hiding his addiction. At first, he was adamant that no one find out. After a year in Narcotics Anonymous and a lot of heart-to-hearts with me, he finally agreed he had to come clean. I thought he'd turned a corner."

He chugged the last half of his beer and still she offered no comment. Her gaze was fixed on the distant view of the water and she waited, letting him take his time.

"He was going to explain everything to the family at a birthday party my mom was having for him a few weeks before my wedding. She insists on celebrating our birthdays every year and this was a biggie. His thirtieth. He'd missed a lot of them while on his tours and she was really looking forward to it. We all were. That morning, he was found in an alley, dead from multiple stab wounds. Another man, a low level drug dealer, was also dead, his neck broken. A drug deal gone bad. The cops believed Percy met with the guy, killed him, and then was killed himself by another gang member."

She shook her head. "Damn."

"My parents were shocked, beside themselves and devastated that I had withheld the truth from them. My sisters, my fiancee…they all felt betrayed and for good reason."

"They would rather you had betrayed Percy's trust and confidence?"

"Percy was an addict, and I'm one too, just not with drugs. I'm addicted to rescuing people. At least that's what I was told. I was accused of having an ego so big I thought I could save him on my own. Maybe they're right. I don't know anymore. At the time, I was just trying to help my big brother stay afloat. I thought I was doing the right thing."

"Looking back, would you change your actions in any way?"

He didn't hesitate. "No."

Saying it was a relief. Percy had wanted to suffer alone, and Roman had made sure he had the help available to overcome his injury and addiction. There was more to the story, but that he couldn't share.

"I've got news for you." Brooke ran a finger around the rim of her wine glass. "Doing the right thing usually pisses people off, especially those who love you. Few of us who are true to our inner code of ethics get through life without offending people we care about."

"I can't argue that."

"Of course not. It's true." She started eating again, peppering him with questions about his boxing career, which was easier to talk about. Soon, they were laughing over work stories, including some of her adventures at various anthropology digs.

He brought up her book and how it had made fossils cool to a whole new generation of people. "I tried," she said, "but the book and media tour wasn't the highlight of my career so far. There was a small dig in New Mexico where we uncovered a mass grave from the Anasazi area. I believe they had a serial killer among them and may never have realized it. That's the kind of stuff that fascinates me."

The love for her work showed on her face. As she finished off the last bite of steak, she wiped the corners of her mouth and sat back. "I haven't eaten this well in years."

"Doesn't the Smithsonian feed you on your adventures?"

"We're typically in the middle of nowhere with little access to anything, and it's up to us to supply our meals. Plus, I rarely work for the Smith. Usually, it's a private group, the government, or a University, and none of them have bottomless funds so stipends are next to nothing. I'd love to be able to fund my own digs, but that's never going to happen. The expenses are astronomical."

The sun gave up its struggle against the night, the last bars of peach and purple slipping below the horizon. Above them, stars began to make an appearance. The deck lights flickered on one by one.

Brooke sighed and sipped her wine. "I love it here. It's so peaceful. I'm rethinking coming after you for your money. I mean, the sex is amazing, but this view and the house? They are pretty damn sweet too."

He kicked back in his chair, watching her guileless face betray her words. "So you're going to take me to the cleaners then?"

She sent a cocky smile his way. Her bare toes touched his leg and inched up his calf. "I'll keep putting out, if that's what you're worried about."

Reaching over, he took her wine glass and set it on the table, then drew her to him across the arm of her chair. "I just might take you up on that, Doc."

The kiss started out sweet and slow, then like always, went sonic. What was it about her? He had no control, everything going from 0 to 60 in seconds.

The next thing Roman knew, Brooke straddled his lap and his hands found their way to her heavy breasts under the shirt.

He'd been hard the moment she'd mentioned sex and her toes had touched his calf. As she slid a hand past the waistband of his shorts, his cocked bobbed up to meet it.

She kissed him thoroughly, her hand working him over. A minute later, she was sliding off his lap to replace her hand with her mouth.

Damn, she loved giving oral sex. He loved that she loved it.

But it was her turn to experience that pleasure.

Lifting her from her knees, he cradled her in his arms, a soft cry of surprise parting her lips. He carried her into the house, her laughter trailing after them.

The fireplace gave off a warm glow in the den, lighting his way. He laid her on the rug in front of it, his shirt riding up over her hips and revealing exactly what he wanted.

She reached for him and he pinned her wrists to the floor, hovering over her for a moment as he watched the flickering light skim her face, neck, and bare legs. Like him, it too wanted to kiss her everywhere.

Her eyes watched him as he took his time scanning her body. They were filled with happiness, lust, something else he couldn't name and didn't want to. As long as she wanted him, he was deliriously happy himself.

He unbuttoned the shirt, revealing her breasts fully to the light and his touch. He filled his hands with them and she arched as he tweaked the already tight nipples. Lowering his head, he sucked a breast into his mouth, tonguing the erect nipple.

So hard. So perfect.

Her fingers plunged into his hair, holding him there.

But not for long. He couldn't get enough of her breasts, but he had another target in mind.

He pinned down her hips, letting his lips trail lower over her ribs, running his tongue along each ridge before dropping to kiss her flat stomach, her hip bones.

He kissed her mound, slipping his tongue in between the

folds. She gasped at the intrusion, but she was wet, ready.

Her knees fell open, baring her sensitive flesh more fully and he took advantage, gliding his tongue lower, deeper, making her arch even higher and moan.

"Oh my…god…*Roman*."

The sound of his name on her lips, raw, sexy, *needy*, echoed in his head, and a strange sensation hit his solar plexus so hard, he had to focus on breathing for a moment.

Because *goddamn*, he wanted to hear that come out of her mouth every day, every night.

Her body was primed, calling for him. His dick banged against his shorts, begging to get out and answer.

"*Please…*"

The whispered word was so faint, his pulse beating so loud in his ears, he wondered if he'd actually heard it.

He knew what she craved, but he wanted to hear her say it. He raised his head, his eyes locking with hers over her arching, naked body. "What do you want, Brooke?"

Her head moved from side to side, long hair splayed out in generous waves. A mewing sound escaped her lips. She licked them, rocking her hips as if that were her answer.

"Say it." He licked her inner thigh. "Say you want my tongue inside your sweet, tender pussy right now. You want me to fuck you with it and make you scream from the pleasure."

"Yes…"

"Say it." Her hands reached for him, but he snagged her wrists and held them. "Tell me what you want."

"I want…*you*."

The good doctor didn't talk dirty, but the words she did say—*I want you*—ripped through him, pressing against his solar plexus again, making it hard to breathe in the most exquisite way ever.

Going down on her, he found her nub with his tongue, circled it a few times, then dropped to her entrance. She moaned and squirmed under his assault, her ankles digging in to his back.

Her scent filled his nostrils, her trembling thighs vibrating against his arms that pinned them open. He had her where he wanted her.

Mine.

He drove into her opening, lapped, withdrew and flicked up to her bud again. Repeated the sequence, creating a rhythm with her rocking hips.

As he felt her drawing close to release, he concentrated on circling, sucking, building the cadence she needed until...

"Roman!"

No whisper this time, her cry rang in the shadowed rafters, her body bucking under his imposed restraints and grinding against his mouth.

She was so fucking beautiful. So...

Mine.

In the aftermath, he tongued her gently, squeezing out the last of her pleasure. Then he released her and drew her boneless body to him, tucking her inside the protection of his arms as the fireplace continued to crackle and throw its light across both their bodies.

CHAPTER THIRTEEN

The next morning, Brooke was so sore she could barely lift the spatula to flip the pancakes in the skillet.

Thankfully, Roman had let her sleep in while he attacked the treadmill and punching bag in his workout room.

It wasn't just her arms that were sore. Her thighs, her hips, the sweet spot between her legs…everything had endured quite the workout the previous day, and even though she'd thought she was in pretty good shape, her body disagreed.

But while her body ached, her heart was lighter than it had been in a long time. The connection she felt with Roman was deeper than any she'd ever had, and not just the physical aspects of it. She still had to pinch herself, since—yes, she'd counted—she'd experienced a dozen orgasms overnight, and had woken up in Roman's bed with his arms around her. He'd snuggled her close, told her to sleep as long as she wanted, and had brought a cup of that wickedly good coffee to her before he'd disappeared into his gym.

The female side of her wanted to follow after him, watch his amazing body flex, move, and make her drool. That same physical side, though, made her moan when she'd thrown back the covers and risen slowly from the bed. Even yawning hurt.

Roman was in better shape than his boxing days, and how was that possible? The man had the stamina and tenacity of a lion. He knew what he wanted and went after it. Again and again and again.

Yippee, her female parts cheered.

Because right now? *She* was what he wanted.

At least for the time being.

The thought sobered her. While she loved her career, a part of her wished she could stay right here, with Roman, hunting down a mass serial killer and ripping up the sheets with her new boss.

So unprofessional.

But that thought kept her grinning during a quick shower. She'd thrown on the clothes she'd purchased the day before, along with a coat of mascara. Keeping thoughts about serious relationships and the fact she could never have one with such a perfect guy as Roman, she'd put her hair up in a bun and started breakfast.

I'm not the type to fall in love anyway.

Like a positive affirmation, she kept mentally repeating it. Maybe if she convinced herself she didn't want a relationship with Roman, it wouldn't hurt so much when he got tired of her and moved on.

A stack of pancakes was waiting on the counter when Roman came striding in, fresh from his shower. "Damn, woman, I could smell those all the way upstairs."

Brooke plopped down a bottle of real maple syrup and his favorite jelly on the counter. "You didn't have blueberries, but I found some chocolate chips, so I threw those into the batter."

Roman kissed her hard, bending her backward before sitting down to dig in.

Droplets of water still hung in his hair and he'd left his shirt off, his broad shoulders and ripped muscles moving fluidly beneath his tattooed skin as he buttered his pancakes and drowned them in syrup. Brooke licked her lips.

As if he felt her blatant stare, he glanced her way. "Aren't you going to eat?"

Oh, she planned to eat all right.

Sliding around to his back, she wrapped her arms around his

chest and kissed the back of his neck. "If I weren't so sore, I'd make you work for those pancakes."

He chuckled. "The dozen orgasms I gave you last night weren't a down payment?"

She kissed her way down his vertebrae. "My specialty pancakes don't come cheap."

Another chuckle and he grabbed her hands, spinning around on the stool so he could grab her hips.

She laughed in surprise and let him draw her onto his lap, his hands massaging her butt cheeks. "I know plenty of ways to handle sore muscles."

"Is that so?"

He kissed her deeply, drawing her close so her breasts pressed against his chest. "I'm the best massage therapist around. I'll have you feeling good in no time."

She slipped her arms around his neck and laid her head on his shoulder for a moment. "That sounds wonderful."

His stomach growled.

Loudly.

Brooke slid off his lap. "After breakfast. Your pancakes are getting cold and you need to keep up your strength. I expect a repeat performance tonight."

He grabbed her hand and kissed her palm. "Anything you want."

The latest batch of pancakes in the skillet were starting to get too brown. She rushed over, rescued them, and piled a few on her plate.

"So what's on the agenda today?" she asked, sitting next to him a moment later.

He handed her his butter knife and scooted the syrup her way. "I spoke to the team and Polly's reviewing the parking lot footage, Shane hasn't heard from Emit Petit yet, Nadia's running a background check on Pastor Rogers, and Win's scoping for jewelry stores who carry that particular type of cross pendant. He also brought me up to speed on the gang bangers he and Thomas spoke to yesterday. So far, nothing's popped up, but we'll keep on it."

She ate a bite of pancake. Even a little too brown, it was delicious and she'd worked up quite the appetite overnight.

"While we're waiting to see if Petit's program can tag the parking lot guy," Roman continued, "I've got Shane running through all the nearby state and county police databases for any reports on violence against undocumented immigrants, especially any with ties to religion. Just because we don't have any specific matches to the mass suicide-murders that have been happening here, it doesn't mean that The Reverend and his crew haven't been practicing in other areas."

"You're running with the idea that The Reverend is the same man who killed the Dunkirks, and maybe the reason he seems to have disappeared and quit his hate crime killings for twenty years, is because he was on the move?"

Discussing a serial killer didn't seem to dampen his appetite at all. He finished his pancakes in two more bites. "A person like that can't stay in one place, there's too much heat."

The food in her stomach turned sour. "And the undocumented aren't a high priority for law enforcement."

"Patterns aren't always easy to pick up on, either. Small town departments oftentimes can't keep up with the normal stuff happening in their backyards, much less anything unusual. Budgets are slim, cops are burned out, support staff are constantly turning over and supervisors are under pressure from the bureaucrats to solve high profile cases. Even when they flag something unusual and send it up the line, it can get lost in the shuffle. At the state level, there are so many unsolved cases coming in, details never get entered into the larger FBI databases or only do years after the crimes were committed."

Brooke played with her food. "So what are you and I tackling?"

Roman's phone buzzed with an incoming text. He checked it. "It's Harris."

He read the text and smiled. "Well, looks like the first thing we're going to do is order balloons to welcome Baby Harris into the world."

The look in his eyes of happiness and the smile plastered over his face made Brooke smile back. "Blue or pink?"

"Pink. The bastard had a baby girl."

She thought of Emma and her impending birth. How happy she was talking about the baby. Usually, Brooke avoided anything to do with marriage ceremonies or births, but something in her now felt a warm bubble of fun and joy.

It's Roman.

He looked delighted, overjoyed for Cooper and his fiancee, Celina, as he typed back a congrats text.

He loves the idea of family. Of babies and happily ever after.

Suddenly, Brooke loved it too.

What was it like to have a real family? To feel loved, appreciated, and welcomed?

The whole morning had been so different than her usual start to the day. Change was coming—had already started. She saw things differently than she had only 24 hours ago.

Nations and civilizations rose and fell constantly. People were born and they died. Life was an ever-moving, ever-changing flow in the wheel of time. That's why she loved anthropology. To her, it was as relevant to study the past as it was the present.

All her life, she'd been focused on studying survival—her own and that of past cultures. Maybe now, at least for the time being, it was time to focus on not just surviving but *living*. Being present in this moment, right here with Roman, welcoming the birth of a new life.

Contemplating that, she picked up her fork and started eating again. Roman wasn't the only one who needed his strength for later.

Two days later, Roman was working the toughest case of his life.

Not involving The Reverend or any other DTT case. He was trying to convince Brooke to go to his parents' anniversary party with him.

"Just for an hour," he pleaded. "Two tops."

She sat in his home office at his desk, combing through thousands of files on killers in California who had marked their victims. "I need to stay in case Shane gets a hit on the Masked Man."

They'd started using MM to designate the man who'd broken into Brooke's car, taken her things, and left the notecard to differentiate him from The Reverend. Petit's body recognition system had gotten three different hits, but none seemed viable.

They still had nothing, and while recognition software could be wrong, Emit Petit's was better than any of the alphabet soup companies run by the US government. Although Homeland and the rest of the US government agencies wanted Emit's Shadow Force International group buried, Roman knew private companies like that could be helpful hunting down a variety of criminals. Harris agreed. Through less than official means, they'd asked for another favor—to run Brooke's adoptive parents through Petit's TrackMap, which found relationships between people even they sometimes didn't know about.

So far, they still had jack squat.

Which had only made Brooke more determined than ever to find any lead, no matter how small.

"Brooke,"—he slid a stack of files away from the edge of the desk and hefted one leg to sit on it. Outside of forcing her to eat and sleep, she'd become obsessed with the case and had been glued to his desk here at home, and to her own temporary one at DTT headquarters. "We've been at this nonstop for days. It's okay to take a break."

Her head bowed over the latest file, fingers tapping the page as she skimmed the facts about a killer in Northern California who'd killed both of his stepdaughters and their mother, covering their bodies with tattoos of crosses and draping rosaries over their folded hands before offing himself. "I take breaks. You make sure of that."

"I mean for more than lunch or to walk outside and get fresh air."

Her head came up and she pinned him with her tired eyes. "You make me workout in the gym and have sex every couple of hours."

There *was* that. "And your boxing has improved." Just that morning, he'd laid her out naked inside the boxing ring again, and the memory made his dick hard. He'd taken her hard and fast like usual, and a few minutes later, she'd rolled him over and gone down on him. The woman was insatiable. "How about after the party, we hit the gun range and do some target practice?"

That sparked her interest and her tapping finger stopped. "Bribery? Does that usually work for you?"

He couldn't remember the last time he'd had to bribe any woman to do what he wanted. Brooke was definitely different. He'd never worked a case with a lover. Never taught a lover to shoot or box. "Brooke...I need you."

"Oh yeah?" She tipped back in his chair and her fingers ran over his knee, up this thigh. "How badly?"

His already hard dick smacked against his zipper like a caged animal determined to get out. "Do me this favor and I'll return it with anything you want."

A smirk lifted one corner of her lips. "Why are you so determined to take me to meet your family?"

It wasn't about them so much as he didn't—wouldn't—leave her here alone. At least that's what he'd told himself.

At the same time, there was no way he would let his mom and dad down. "I need a favor. I'm thirty-four, still single, and my Mom and sisters are on me all the time about getting married and settling down. You know how my job is—it's not like I can share the day-to-day grind with ninety-nine percent of the women who'd be interested in me. You, on the other hand, are perfect. We can talk work, you're an accomplished PhD, and you're the most interesting person I've ever had inside my boxing ring."

"First bribery, now flattery." She stroked him through his jeans, coming out of the chair and leaning into him. "If I hold out a little longer, will you sweeten the pot even more?"

Those ripe lips of hers smiled at him, hanging like fruit on the vine, teasing, taunting him to take a bite. "No need to hold out any further. I'll marry you right now and make you sole heir to my fortune if you'll just pretend to be my girlfriend for two hours."

She laughed, tilting her head back and hanging on his neck. They both liked to play these games, and he was only partially kidding.

Partially? I'd give her everything in this moment if she'd have me.

Because she really was the perfect woman for him. The sliver of that thought had emerged when he'd first become aware of her work and seen her at a conference, but he hadn't known her. Now he did, every part of her, inside and out, and the flesh-and-blood Brooke Heaton standing in front of him was one hundred percent his ideal partner in every way.

She tipped her head back down, still grinning, and stroked her fingers along his jaw line. "It's Sunday. The courthouse isn't open today, so no quickie marriage, I'm afraid."

He grabbed her hips and tugged her as close as he could get her. "Rain check?"

Her grin grew bigger. "Be careful, or I'll hold you to it."

"I know you will."

She sighed heavily. "I have nothing suitable to wear to your shindig and I'm really not good at socializing with strangers. You might regret taking me."

He gently kissed her lips, letting his tongue have a taste. "Never."

Another sigh. "All right. I'll go. But you've been warned."

He hugged her tight, making her laugh again. "Thank you."

While she cleaned up upstairs, he checked in with his team. After nearly round-the-clock work on The Reverend case, and no substantial leads, he'd insisted they all take time off today so they could hit things Monday morning with fresh eyes.

In the middle of going through the team roster, making sure no one was at the office, a call came through from his sister, Candace. "I'm leaving in ten minutes," he said in place of 'hello,' since he knew that was what she wanted to know.

Her normally bubbly voice was tense. "Did you pick up the gift?"

"Three weeks ago. Calm down, Candy. Everything's going to be fine. Mom will love it."

"What about the wine?"

"I have white, red, and the champagne for the toast, which I'm about to load into the car, but if I have to go over the details of the party with you for the hundredth time, I'm going to be late."

"I know, I know. I'm sorry. I just want everything to be perfect."

And from her standpoint, he was the weak link in the chain. "It will be. I promise."

"I wish...but..."

A heavy pause hung in the air. He knew what she wanted to say, and he pressed his eyelids shut for a moment. In so many ways, he wanted the same thing. "You wish Percy was here."

"He hated parties."

"That he did."

Another pause, pregnant with grief and disappointment. "I'll see you when you get here."

"I'm bringing a friend," he offered. Not so much to get her mind off Percy, but he wanted the family to know so they didn't ambush Brooke when she walked in the door.

Candy's voice lightened. "Define friend. Is your friend of the female persuasion?"

"Yes. Her name's Dr. Brooke Heaton."

"A doctor?" she gasped. "Are you shitting me?"

"Her doctorate is in forensic anthropology. She also has a couple other degrees."

"Well, I'll be damned. She's like Lara Croft? Goes on amazing adventures and raids lost tombs?"

"Something like that."

"Where in the world did you find her? It was on eBachelor, wasn't it?"

A year ago, Candy had put his picture and bio on three different internet dating sites, unbeknownst to him. The fallout had been ridiculously entertaining for her, but embarrassing as hell for him. He still hadn't lived down the "highly perceptive" and "sweet" descriptions she'd used when his team had found out. "She's consulting for my team on a case."

"Oh." Candy's voice fell. "So she's not a girlfriend."

At that moment, Brooke appeared in the kitchen dressed in simple jeans and one of his white button downs over a tank top. She'd belted his shirt around her waist, emphasizing her amazing hips, and on her feet she wore a pair of stacked sandals that she'd grabbed at the local discount store where they'd picked up a Congrats on Your New Baby Girl card for Cooper and Celina.

She'd taken the braid from her hair and the wavy strands hung loose over her shoulders. Her lips sported a deep wine color that made her eyes pop.

How's this? she mouthed silently, and did a twirl.

He gave her a thumbs-up, his pulse thumping a happy beat.

"Oh, she's my girlfriend," he told his sister. "And if I'm not careful, she's going to take me for everything I'm worth."

Candy squealed so loudly, Roman had to take the phone away from his poor eardrum. He decided it was time to cut the chitchat. "See you in an hour, sis."

He disconnected and walked over to Brooke who quirked an eyebrow at him. "Who was that?"

"My youngest sister, Candace. You'll like her. She's neurotic and hardworking, just like you. But I have to warn you, you're going to get the third degree from all the women in my life."

"*Now* you tell me."

"Hey, Candy forced the truth out of me about you making me into your boy toy."

Brooke laughed. "Well, at least there won't be any secrets about us with your family."

Man, she hated secrets. "There's probably something else I should tell you."

The laughter faded. "What?"

"Melinda was kind of... Um, my mom really..."

"Your mom thought Melinda was perfect and loved her like a daughter."

How did she know? "Exactly."

"And you're afraid she won't accept me because she still has feelings for Melinda."

"You're very perceptive for someone who grew up in such a dysfunctional family and claims to hate social gatherings."

"It's one of my many talents."

Smartass. He drew her close, wrapping his arms around her. "Thank you for doing this."

The heels gave her height but she still had to rise up slightly to kiss him. "I expect a two-carat engagement ring and a whole closet full of designer shoes by the end of the week."

"Two carats, is that all?"

The grin returned. "It's a start."

He smacked her ass, kissed her to seal the deal, and went to load up the car.

CHAPTER FOURTEEN

Brooke rubbed her thumb into the palm of her opposing hand. Even though she'd kidded with Roman about meeting his family and blackmailing him into marrying her, she felt like a jittery mess. She hadn't lied to him—social situations weren't her forte, regardless of the fact that she'd probably never see these people again. He'd tagged her as his girlfriend and that alone was enough to make her sweat.

Roman wound through the hills of Del Mar with the ease of a racecar driver. "Don't be nervous."

Easy for him to say. She stopped smashing her thumb into her palm and rubbed her hands down her pant legs. "Are there any topics that are off limits?"

"Our case."

"Duh. I knew that. Anything else?"

He shifted the Jeep, made a sharp turn. "Details of our love life."

"We have a love life?"

He caught her mischievous grin and rolled his eyes. "My sisters will grill you for details. Don't let them intimidate you."

Great. "You mean like how we met?"

"How we met, how long we've been seeing each other, what your intentions are. The usual."

"I think you made my intentions clear on the phone earlier."

"I should probably apologize for that because, knowing

184

Candy, you're going to get the full Walsh interrogation, not just from her and Felicity, but Mom too."

She really wished she'd stayed back at his place. "I'll sic them on you."

"Oh, believe me, I'll get the third degree about you. They'll want to know everything, including your shoe size."

"Seven."

"I know."

He knew her shoe size? "Seriously?"

"You had me on the hook for a new pair of Shaun Maddens, remember?"

"Steve. *Steve* Maddens."

He reached over and gripped her hand, gave it a squeeze. "Him too. Whatever designer you want, you've got it."

He pulled into the circular drive of a giant brick colonial with mature trees, lovely landscaping, and a hell of a view. "Did you buy this for your parents?"

"Nah. It's the family home. Belonged to my mother's parents."

Of course it had. "You come from money."

He parked and frowned at her. "I've never taken a dime from them."

"I have no doubt. It's just…"

"Just what?"

The flowers in the window boxes looked cheery and softened the brickwork. The steps leading to the front door were wide and deep, massive flowing ferns in planters on each side. The front door was actually two French doors painted a rich hunter green with brass knockers that matched the window shutters and expensive landscaping.

"It looks like one of those million-dollar mansions on HGTV."

"Here, in this section of Del Mar, it's hardly a mansion."

"I take it your maternal grandparents are deceased?"

"Actually, they live in a retirement community in Arizona."

A woman emerged from the house, waving at them from the front porch. She had dark hair and blue eyes like Roman, but was shorter than Brooke and wore a stylish bob. Her tailored peacock blue dress matched her eyes.

I'm so underdressed. "Candy?" Brooke asked.

Roman waved back at his sister. "That's her. The youngest by a couple years but she acts like she's the oldest."

"So she tries to take care of you."

"She noses her way into my business on a regular basis."

"She loves you and she's as perfect as you are. I think I'm jealous. I want a sister like that."

He laughed, grabbing the handle of his car door as he pecked her on the cheek. "It'll pass. Trust me."

But it didn't. Candy hugged Roman, than drew Brooke into a bear hug as well, treating her more like an old friend than a new acquaintance. "Everyone's out back," she said, taking Brooke's hand and drawing her through the house.

Brooke looked back at Roman over her shoulder. He gave her a shameless grin and followed.

His other sister, Felicity, had three of the five kids running around the grounds. Her hair was lighter, her body taller and lankier than Candace's. "Nice to see my big brother is finally back on the dating scene again."

Roman kissed her cheek and accepted violent hugs from his nieces and nephews as they rushed him, heading for the back patio doors. "Hey, I'm picky. What can I say?"

Felicity patted Brooke's hand. "Thank you for putting up with him."

Brooke smiled, seeing the teasing light in her eyes and instantly liking her. "He has his good points."

They emerged onto a back patio where people laughed and conversed with drinks in hand as more kids enjoyed a bouncy house. The backyard was as tastefully landscaped as the front and included stone walkways, fruit trees, topiaries and a lush rose garden. In the center was a water fountain.

"Roman!" An older woman who had to be his mom broke free from a group nearby and hugged him. "You look tired. Are you working too much like usual?"

"Oh, please, Mom," Felicity said, eyeing her kids as they dashed through the crowd. "He looks better than he's looked in months. No doubt Dr. Heaton has something to do with that."

Felicity winked at her and wandered off to help Candace with the wine as Roman's mother turned to Brooke and looked her up and down.

A regal nose, intelligent blue eyes, and model-perfect cheekbones.

Of course. She probably had been one back in the day.

Her designer dress highlighted her lithe body modestly. The shoes on her feet probably cost as much as Brooke's Honda back home.

"My son neglected to tell me he was bringing a guest."

"Mother," Roman said, "this is Brooke. And by the way, I told Candace. Brooke, this is my mother, Theodora Walsh. Brooke is helping my taskforce with a case. She's also living with me."

Brooke nearly died right there on the spot. Theodora's eyes went hard, but she extended her hand anyway, half a dozen gemstone and diamond bracelets on Theodora's wrist clanging together.

Brooke accepted the handshake. "It's lovely to meet you."

"And you," Theodora replied, her gaze swinging back to Roman. "She's helping you with a case?"

"Yes, Mom. She's a consultant."

"I see." Those blue eyes, so much like Roman's showed tempered distaste as she took in Brooke's attire again. "And you brought her to my party?"

Roman's arm slipped around Brooke, his hand going to her lower back. "Like I said, we're living together as well as working together. Brooke has three advanced degrees, is sexy as hell, and knows how to cook. I'm nuts about her, and I'm going to get a ring on her finger as soon as possible."

Theodora's brows shot up, and for half a second, Brooke's heart stopped. Both because Roman was being totally insolent and the fact he'd just declared he wanted to marry her. He was joking again, right?

Roman's mother laughed out loud. "Why am I not surprised?" A tamed smile landed on Brooke. "Roman does his best to shock me any chance he gets. Whether or not you're sleeping with my son, I hope he's treating you right."

Brooke smiled back. "He's always a gentleman, at work and...at home."

"As he should be," Theodora said. Then to Roman, "Have you seen your father yet?"

Roman gave Brooke a tight squeeze. His gaze shot over the crowd, a smirk on his face. "Where is he? I want to show off my woman to him."

Brooke's mouth dropped open as Theodora, shaking her head, led the way around a group of men and one woman who nodded and said hello to Roman. A lot of reserved glances and greetings met them as they wound their way to one of the tables near the fountain decorated for the party.

Roman's father sat in a chair with a grandchild on each knee. All three were laughing and the sight instantly made Brooke relax a little.

"Roman, my son." The man shooed the kids off his lap and used both arms of the chair to push himself to standing.

Roman grabbed one of his arms and helped him. They shook hands, then embraced. "How ya doing, Pop?" Roman said.

"Gad! Your mother has me on some vegetarian diet and I have to drink this green crap every day. Tastes horrible! I hate it."

Theodora *tsked* and started reprimanding him while Roman slapped his father's back lightly and laughed. "You look good, Pop, so it must be working."

The wrinkled face turned to Brooke. "My, my, who do we have here?"

Roman made the introductions and Brooke found her hand engulfed by a much larger one. "Brooke, this is my father, Kylan."

"Kylan Walsh," Brooke said. "A solid Irish name if I ever heard one."

Kylan chuckled, still holding her hand. "My grandparents came from Kilkenny."

"The Walsh surname is most common there and County Mayo, although it's the fourth in Ireland as well."

His beaming eyes went from her to Roman and back. "You know a lot about the Walsh name."

She winked at him. "I have a thing for culture and history, and when I met your son, I did a little digging to see where his family roots might have come from."

"Ancestry, huh?" Kylan nodded. "Well, I'll tell you a secret, the name Walsh actually came from Britain."

"Walsh is a derivative of 'Welshman,'" she added, "which was taken to Ireland during and after the Norman invasion by the Welsh, Cornish, and Cumbrian soldiers."

Kylan squeezed her hand as Theodora rolled her eyes behind Roman's shoulder. "I think she's a keeper, Roman."

"I think she is too, Pop."

"Come sit by an old man and tell him about your work, Dr. Heaton," Kylan said, motioning her to the chair next to him.

She glanced at Roman and he gave her a nod as his mother grabbed him by the arm. "Roman, I could use your help with the food."

Brooke sensed Roman didn't want to leave her. At the same time, she knew Theodora didn't need help with the food—she just wanted an excuse to get her son away from Brooke.

That's not the effect I was going for, but whatever.

Roman's family was not a group she would easily fit into. She'd known that before she'd agreed to come along.

For the next hour, the party rolled along, a few more people arriving, food and drink flowing, and a pile of gifts growing on a side table. Roman came and went as his mother and sisters kept him busy, greeting guests, keeping the caterers on their toes and the kids out of trouble. Brooke could see they really did love and depend on him, and he was happy keeping everyone else happy.

Including her. He made sure she had more than plenty of food, never let her glass go empty, and introduced her to everyone as his girlfriend.

She found it easy to play the part.

Am I really playing?

Their relationship seemed straightforward, yet she had the nagging feeling that Roman was serious when he called her his girlfriend.

They were certainly enjoying themselves, but it was more obvious than ever that she didn't fit into his world.

I'll have to try harder.

Because, more than anything, she really wanted to be part of his life.

And that included his family.

And she wasn't one to give up easily.

She snuck into the house to find a bathroom and discovered a hallway lit with matching chandeliers and adorned with family pictures stretching back many generations. The older, larger ones appeared hand painted and were displayed in gilded frames.

Money, money, money. Everywhere she looked, it was on display, even in the family portraits.

She found herself staring at one particularly severe looking woman, dressed in a flowing gown with layers of gold necklaces draped around her neck.

"Scary, isn't she?"

Felicity emerged from a room off the hall. "That's Mother's great-grandmother. She was a countess or something."

"She's quite imposing. Is your mother's side Greek?"

"How'd you guess?"

"The jewelry. The design on her pendant has a Hellenistic flare to it with the entwined snakes around the emerald. The designer probably based it on a popular piece from that time period."

"How do you know that?"

Brooke shrugged. "I spend most of my time researching history and culture and have no life of my own."

"From what Roman says, it sounds like you have an awesome life."

"Roman is kind." She moved down the row of pictures, smiling at a couple he showed up in. Formal family pictures, his high school graduation. None of them showed his boxing fame. She came to a large photo of a man who looked much like Roman, with dark hair and vivid blue eyes, in a military uniform with a US flag in the background. "This must be Percy."

Felicity joined her. "Roman told you about him?"

"A little. He looks like Roman."

"Roman idolized him. At least growing up. When Percy enlisted, Roman went a little crazy."

It really wasn't any of her business, but she couldn't keep herself from asking. "How so?"

"Percy was the oldest. He took care of all of us when we were younger. Roman was only thirteen when Percy enlisted, and Roman had a hard time in school, always getting into fights and stuff. Percy taught him to fight, which horrified Mom, but I think Roman felt like Percy had his back, you know? Then Percy left right before Roman hit high school. It was hard on him. On all of us, really. Roman was a hellion for most of his high school career. Mom and Dad actually considered sending him to one of those military schools for awhile."

"I had no idea."

"I was just a kid when Percy left. I barely remembered him. He did so many tours, he missed all of our graduations. High school, college, Candy's wedding, mine, the birth of our kids, all of it. Then he came back and things got even worse."

War did that to people, families. "I know Roman tried very hard to help him."

"Help. Yeah. I guess you could call it that."

The derision in her voice made Brooke face her, struggling to keep the instant defensiveness out of her voice. "Roman did what he thought was best."

"By getting Percy wrapped up in one of his cases?" Felicity made a disgusted sound. "I know you're consulting for Roman's team, and I wish you all the best with that, but he should have never gotten Percy involved in that Underground Order case."

"I'm sorry. I don't know anything about that."

"Of course you don't. I'm sure Roman conveniently forgot a few details when he told you about what happened to Percy. But you should probably ask him about it. Roman always gets the bad guys and makes sure justice is served. But that time? Percy paid the price."

She walked off and Brooke stood staring after her. *What the hell?*

Had Roman not told her the whole truth about what had happened to his older brother?

Pressure pushed at her temples. She refused to jump to conclusions before she had a chance to talk to Roman, but she *would* ask him about it. Either he'd lied to his family about Percy's untimely demise, or to her.

No one's perfect.

And didn't that just suck?

Because she'd been so sure, for a little while anyway, that Roman really was.

"Hey there." He appeared at the end of the hall, a look of relief on his face. He smiled at her like she was the best thing he'd ever seen. "I've been looking all over for you."

Now wasn't the place and time to get into it with him. "I just needed to hit the bathroom."

His smile faded slightly. "Is everything okay?"

She hated the word fine, but it was the automatic way of brushing off her roiling stomach and pounding head. "I'm fine. Just tired. Can we go now?"

"Of course. Let me just say goodbye to my parents."

"I'm being selfish. You stay, I'll call a cab."

He held both of her arms, frowning down at her. "Don't be ridiculous. I'm ready to go. Are you sure you're okay?"

Was she? *Don't overreact.*

From the depths of her mind, she heard her parents arguing. The people who had raised her whisper-yelling at each other in the kitchen about secrets, death, and a whole world they'd never told her about. Her chest squeezed, her vision fuzzed in and out.

A ringing came from her purse. Brooke wiggled out of Roman's light grip and dug for it, grateful for the interruption. ID showed it was Dave. *What does he want?*

But answering it got her off the hook from responding with that meaningless word *fine* again. "I really should take this."

"Sure." Roman hooked a thumb over his shoulder. "I'll go say my goodbyes and meet you at the car."

She waited for him to leave, then sent Dave's call to voicemail.

Disappointment tightened her ribcage, but she forced it away. Everyone kept secrets—it was no revelation. All she had to do was figure out just how much Roman's mattered to her.

Brooke was too quiet, too serious. Roman took the on-ramp to the interstate. Was it from the call she'd gotten or had something happened at the party? He needed to tell her something. Something that might upset her. Now didn't seem like the right moment. Maybe when they got back to his place...

She propped her elbow against the window, head leaning into her hand with her eyes closed.

"How's the head?" he asked, giving the Jeep its freedom as they merged into the light traffic. He'd made her take some pain medication before leaving his parents' house.

Her eyes peeled open and she stared at her lap. "You know I love romance novels, right?"

Where was this coming from? "Yeah...?"

"The one thing I hate is when something comes between the hero and heroine that messes up their relationship and they don't talk about it. One or both of them is upset but they hide their feelings and if they'd just talk it out, they could resolve the issue, but *nooo*. There's all these hurt feelings, shit happens, and they don't just talk!"

He had no idea what was going on here. "I take it there's something you're upset about that you want to tell me."

She huffed out a deep breath that seemed to come from her toes. "You know I don't like secrets."

And oh shit. *She knows.* About which thing though?

Most likely someone in his family had filled her in on the details about Percy that he'd left out.

Only, even they didn't know the real truth, and he prayed they never would.

I should just come clean. Tell her everything.

Except he couldn't.

The case was sealed. Buried so deep, it would never see the light of day.

Unless he resurrected it.

Doing so would jeopardize several agents whose careers could be ruined if the truth ever got out.

Because they'd all put their faith in Percy and he'd betrayed them.

Now, their faith rested in Roman.

If he told Brooke the truth, the real story underneath all the lies and cover-ups, he would betray them all over again.

I'd be just as bad as my brother.

Yet, how could he not come clean to Brooke? She meant everything to him and she hated secrets. He should tell her. Get it all off his chest.

He needed to stall. Get her back to his place and figure out how much to reveal to make her feel she could trust him again.

Because she could trust him. The past and Percy had no bearing on his future with her, right? "Why don't you start from the beginning and tell me what's got you so upset?" He needed to deflect for now. "Was it my mom? One of my sisters? I told you they'd give you the third degree."

She shook her head and pinched the bridge of her nose. "Your family is wonderful. As a person who grew up the way I did, yours is pretty perfect."

"It's always appeared that way, but as the black sheep of the family, I can tell you, growing up in that household was far from perfect."

"Felicity said you got into a lot of fights as a kid."

"Dad always said it was the Irish blood in me. My temper used to run pretty hot all the time."

"What were you fighting about?"

This was good. They were talking about him, not Percy. "What *didn't* I fight about? I was this scrawny kid with a learning disability, an older brother everyone loved, two younger sisters that stole the show everywhere they went, and I had a big chip on my shoulder about bullies. Which were prevalent in the overpriced private school my mother put all of us in."

"You have a learning disability?"

"Dysgraphia. I have trouble putting things on paper, writing things down. Went undiagnosed during elementary and hit hard in middle school. Teachers thought I had a behavioral problem, I was misdiagnosed with ADD, the usual. Even when I knew an answer or understood a problem, if I had to write it out, I struggled. My parents thought it was laziness and puberty."

"How did they figure it out?"

"My mother is a force of nature, so while Dad put me in boxing lessons to work out my frustrations, Mom took me to a dozen different experts. One of them finally figured it out and things got a little better after that. My therapist taught me strategies that gave me some control back."

"They must have worked well since you went on to get your doctorate."

"Spell checkers and speech recognition software saved my ass."

"I'm sorry." She reached over and touched his arm. "That must have been rough."

"At least I got help. Some kids never do. They drop out of school, join gangs, end up on the streets."

"Do you still struggle with it?"

"Every day. But that's why I solve criminal cases and didn't become a writer or someone who depends on written communication."

They drove for a while in silence, Brooke keeping her eyes on the scenery. He'd managed to put the brakes on the Percy story, but wondered what he was actually going to tell her.

"Brooke, I'm not a fictional character in one of your romance books whom the author makes out to be the perfect hero at the end."

"I know." Her head bobbed but she still didn't look at him. "I don't have unreasonable expectations."

"You sure about that?"

"Are you keeping secrets from me?"

Damn. He left the highway and headed for his neighborhood. "Secrets about what exactly? I haven't told you every nitty, gritty detail about all the mistakes I've made in my life, if that's what you're asking."

"I'm asking about Percy and what happened with the Underground Order case."

Yep. That's what he was afraid of. At least she hadn't yet

found out about her birth mother and that whole hive of killer bees. "The only reason I haven't told you the full story is because it could put a lot of people's careers on the line."

From the corner of his eye, he saw her brows shoot up. The indignation in her voice echoed in the car. "But you told your sister?"

The urge to come clean was so strong, he had to clamp his jaws together for a moment. He turned onto his street. "What I told my family was not the whole truth, and the only reason I sugarcoated it was to save what little I could of my brother's memory for them."

"That sounds honorable, but I have to ask, did you do something illegal? Did your team? Who are you really covering for, Roman?"

Myself as much as anyone. "I can't discuss it with you, Brooke. I would if I could, but I can't. There are innocent people involved."

Silence reigned as he pulled up to his house. A strange car was parked in his drive. "Who the hell is that?" he said, eyeing the figure in the front seat who saw them and threw open his car door.

Roman already had his gun in reach and was ready to put the car in reverse.

"Oh God," Brooke said, putting a hand to her forehead.

"Do you know this guy?"

"Dr. David Borgman," she said, as the man stood next to his car with his hands on his hips. He was gray-haired and wearing an expensive suit. The look he was shooting at Brooke did not bode well. "My boss."

"What the hell…?"

So much for having a quiet moment to talk to Brooke about the other secret he was keeping. Not really keeping it from her—he just hadn't found the right moment to tell her.

Brooke bailed. Roman put the car in park and followed, making sure to flash his weapon before he pocketed it. He couldn't help it—the guy's whole demeanor set off warning bells in his head. What did it hurt to show a little intimidation?

Brooke went around the front of the Jeep. "Dave, what are you doing here?"

"You haven't been returning my calls."

The sun was setting over the water. Roman leaned on the Jeep hood and scanned the area. He didn't like Brooke being this exposed here. And if some Smithsonian guy could find Roman's house, surely the killer could. "A better question would be how did you know Dr. Heaton was here?"

"I had the number for that other taskforce guy, Harris. She's done consulting stuff for him too. He wouldn't tell me anything, so I went to his boss and threatened to go to the police since I suspected foul play. Got passed around, but eventually, one of the FBI's minions gave me your name, Dr. Walsh. A little digging provided me with your home address."

"We should take this inside," Roman said, although the last thing he wanted was this man in his home. "Brooke has a killer after her."

Bushy gray eyebrows went for the sky as he shifted his gaze to her. "A killer?"

"Yes. No. Maybe." Flustered, her cheeks blushed a deep rose color. "I'm sorry I didn't return your calls, Dave, but you really have to leave."

"The crew refuses to move forward with classifying anything until you're there to oversee the excavation."

Roman pushed off the Jeep and motioned at the house. "Inside. Now."

The interior of the house was cool. Roman flipped on the kitchen light and reset his security alarm as Brooke tossed her purse on the counter.

"I'm sorry the crew is upset about my absence," she said to Dave. "They're picky about who they work with. Who did you get to take my place?"

"On short notice like this?" His fists once more went to his generous waistline. "Who do you think I could get with your credentials and experience that the crew would agree to work with?"

"How about Lenny Oswald?"

"He's on a dig in South America."

"Martina Gonzalez?"

"She took a research position with the University of Oregon."

Brooke tapped an impatient foot. "I'm sorry. I can't leave right now, but maybe in a few…"

She glanced at Roman. What did she want him to say? That he could catch her stalker in a few days? Weeks? "It's not safe for you to take off on a dig until your attacker is arrested."

"This could be the biggest find in that region in this century," Dave said, pinning Brooke with a hard gaze. "Your crew is depending on you to make sure the work is done right and follows all the government guidelines. *I'm* depending on you."

"Did you not hear me?" Roman said. "Her life may be in danger."

Dave's gaze never veered from Brooke's face. "You signed a contract to handle this dig. I expect you to live up to our agreement. If that means I need to hire security for you, I'll do it, but the Smithsonian, and your country, as well as the men and women of your dig team, are all depending on you doing your job."

Brooke's foot stopped tapping. She straightened and now her hands went to her hips. "I signed that contract in good faith, and if I could uphold it, I certainly would. But like I've already told you multiple times, I'm assisting The Department of Homeland Security, the FBI, and a couple other agencies you've never even heard of to stop a serial killer, who may also be after me. I'm sorry if that conflicts with your agenda to unearth bones and artifacts that have been buried for hundreds of years if not longer, but I can't renege on my commitment to the Domestic Terrorism Taskforce."

Dave shook his head and stared at the floor, running a hand through his wavy hair. "I'm sorry it's come to this. I realize you believe what you're doing is your duty, but it seems to me that Dr. Walsh's taskforce is far more competent in hunting down a killer than you are. Can you not simply consult over the phone?"

"You can't guarantee her safety at the dig site," Roman said. "And Dr. Heaton's physical presence is of great value to me and my team. We need her here to examine evidence and talk to leads."

Dave glared at him now. "She's not a police officer, and from the looks of things, neither of you is all that busy with this case she's consulting on. Or do you regularly examine evidence and talk to leads dressed like that?"

Brooke held up both hands. "That's enough. Dave, I'm sorry, I can't go to Utah until this case is resolved. At that time, I'll get on a plane posthaste and get to work. I promise."

He shook his head and walked to the door. "That won't be necessary, Dr. Heaton. You're fired. The Smithsonian won't be using you again for any future jobs."

Just as the door slammed shut behind the asshole, and Brooke let out an exasperated cry, Roman's phone went off with Polly's ringtone.

He let it ring and reached for Brooke, but she backed away. "It's okay. Answer your phone."

As she stomped out of the kitchen, he snatched his cell from his pocket. "Please tell me you have good news."

Polly's voice was shaky. "Afraid not, boss. Pastor Rogers just found Jamison LeMont's body in front of the mission doors. He's dead."

Jamison, the kid from the mission who'd talked to Brooke earlier in the week? "Shit. What happened?"

"I'll give you one guess. He has a sigil carved into his forehead."

"Fuck."

"There's more. The Rev left a message on the kid's chest."

"A message?"

"You better get over here. I think it's for Dr. Heaton."

CHAPTER FIFTEEN

Jamison was dead. Brooke couldn't wrap her head around it.

Blue lights flashed against the brick of the church, the mission entrance swarming with law enforcement. Bright yellow crime scene tape and several police officers kept the gathering crowd back.

The kid had been so young, so full of life. He'd told Brooke he attended community college part-time working on a social psychology degree. He paid his tuition by making pizzas at a mom-and-pop joint a few blocks down from the place where he lived with his mother. The mission had once helped when they'd been homeless and she was a member of the church. They both worked at the mission every chance they got.

Now Jamison was in a body bag.

It's my fault.

"The killer knew he talked to me the other day," she murmured. Roman had told her to stay in his car with the doors locked, but she'd refused. Now her legs went weak as she saw two paramedics wheeling the gurney with Jamison's body on it toward a waiting ambulance. "This is my fault."

Roman had hold of her elbow. "I have to look at the body. Why don't you head over and talk to Polly."

Polly stood with tablet in hand speaking to Pastor Rogers just inside the mission doors that were propped open. It was all surreal, reminding her of that first night with Roman at the abandoned church.

"I'm going with you." She needed to see the body too. To say she was sorry to Jamison. To see the sigil Roman had told her he was marked with.

"It would be better to keep you out of sight as much as possible."

Her gaze darted around, taking in the gathering crowd. "You think he's here?"

"This breaks The Rev's normal MO. I don't know what he's doing or thinking at this point. We've obviously put enough pressure on him to flush him out, which is good *and* bad."

Good in that he might make a mistake and they could finally catch him. Bad because a promising young man had fallen victim to him.

Roman started to lead her to Polly, but Brooke jerked her arm out of his grip. "I need to see Jamison."

A tight sigh chuffed from Roman's lips. "Fine. Stick close."

"The bastard won't try anything with all these people around." She scanned the area again, hoping she might see him, whoever he was. But how would she know him even if she did? Frustration burned in her veins. "Plus, you'll kill anyone who so much as looks at me wrong."

"Damn straight." Roman latched onto her elbow again. This time, he led her toward the ambulance.

She let him, wishing she didn't like the way he took charge. Wishing she didn't like the feel of his hand on her arm, his rock-solid body nearly cradling her against the flow of the others in the opposite direction.

Polly caught up with them at the ambulance as Roman flashed his badge at the coroner. The short, balding man led them inside the ambulance where they took seats around the gurney.

"Body was positioned lying down in front of the mission doors," the coroner said. "Laid out like he was sleeping. Throat shows signs of strangulation, and there are markings carved into the forehead and chest, but there was almost no blood on him or the ground."

"Which means he wasn't killed here," Roman said. "Or the markings were carved into the skin postmortem."

"Correct. Based on core temperature, I estimate time of death to be two hours ago. From the condition of the body, I'd bet the markings were done postmortem, but I'll know more once I get the body on my table."

The body. Brooke's stomach turned over, anger flashing through her. *He was a living, breathing young man a few hours ago.*

"The killer wouldn't risk marking him in front of the mission doors," Roman continued, all business. "He killed the kid somewhere else, marked him, and brought the body here to make a point."

Polly eyed the length of the body bag. "Jamison was no small guy. For someone to get the jump on him and choke him to death, they must have been even bigger or well-trained in self-defense."

"Or it was someone Jamison knew and trusted," Brooke added. "It would be easy for them to get the jump on him."

Roman's sharp gaze landed on her. "Pastor Luke. He found out Jamison talked to us and he came back to shut him up."

"Quite possible. But even though Jamison knew him, he also knew Luke could be the serial killer we were looking for. The kid was smart. I don't think he'd let Luke get the jump on him."

"Unless he really did surprise him," Polly said. "If our attacker is former military or law enforcement, he might have come at him from behind and overpowered him."

"Where are Nadia and Win?" Roman asked her.

"Win's in the church on the upper story filming the crowd, and Nadia is circulating through the onlookers to see if any of them match the suspects we have from the TrackREC results."

"Good." Roman cocked his chin at the body bag and spoke to Brooke. "You sure you want to see this?"

Steeling her nerves and her churning stomach, she nodded. *Focus on the anger. The frustration.*

The coroner leaned forward to unzip the bag.

A waft of cloying metallic scent rose in the tight quarters and Brooke had to put a fist up to her nose.

Oh God.

Jamison's eyes were closed but his tongue hung from the corner of his mouth. The sigil carved into his forehead was no surprise, and yet it felt like a smack in the face to her all over again. As if the killer wasn't so much marking the young man as taunting her.

Roman pointed to the outline of blue-black bruises ringing the neck. "Do you think you'll get any fingerprints?"

The coroner held up his gloved hands. "The killer most likely used gloves, but I'll certainly check."

"Choking him is so..." Brooke shivered against the thought invading her brain. To hold someone down and choke the life from them was...gruesome, violent... "Personal."

"Exactly." Roman took a pen from his pocket and used the tip to tease the lapel of Jamison's shirt aside to show further bruising. "Which is why your theory about it being someone the kid knew rings true. He never expected the attack, and whoever did this was in a rage."

The coroner folded the sides of Jamison's shirt back, revealing the young man's chest. Brooke gasped and reeled back.

The letters were crudely drawn, but the killer's message was clear.

Doc

U

R

next.

Brooke bolted out the back of the ambulance before Roman could stop her. He'd seen the horror on her face, the belief that she was responsible for Jamison's death, and he understood what she was going through.

He felt it too, that crawling, gut-twisting sensation in his lower belly. The guilt.

The anger.

Jumping down after her, he stayed on her heels, not touching her, but not letting her out of reach.

Because he knew the killer was there. Watching. Waiting.

Waiting to get his hands on Brooke.

U R next.

If he knew anything about serial killers, the man who'd killed Jamison was not The Reverend. The sigil might fit The Rev's MO, but leaving a message on the kid's chest did not.

This guy was a copycat. Or an apostle who'd broken from the group to go out on his own. *It's Luke.*

The guy had broke rank and file initially when he'd visited the church and mission. None of the others had exposed themselves like that. Now he'd tried to cover up his tracks and scare Brooke off by killing the kid and leaving her a message.

Or maybe it's for me. He was a PhD as well.

He could only hope, but his gut told him differently.

And boy, Roman was going to enjoy grinding the man under his boot heel when he finally caught him.

Brooke headed for the inside of the mission, skirting law enforcement and crime scene techs. The horror on her face morphed into something else.

Yep, knew it.

She was angry as a hornet's nest.

Not just angry…enraged.

Roman stayed right behind her, feeling the need to shield her while keeping a lookout for anything—or anyone—out of the ordinary. She'd already had a hell of a day—finding out about his less-than-truthful confession, getting fired from the Smithsonian, now this. Yet, here she was, storming the yellow tape and flashing her brand new Homeland badge as if it were old hat.

"Who did it?" She pulled up in front of Pastor Rogers, who was speaking to Detective Clyffe. "Who killed Jamison?"

Roman exchanged a nod with Clyffe as the minister turned red-rimmed eyes on Brooke. "I was going to ask you the same thing. If you hadn't asked for his help, he might still be alive."

Brooke visibly flinched back and Roman sidled up alongside her, lightly resting a supportive hand on her back. "Did he work here today?"

Rogers turned her defensive gaze on him. "He had finals today, then a shift at Giraldi's."

Polly closed in, taking up a position on the other side of Brooke. "Giraldi's? That's the pizza joint in that little strip mall a few blocks from here, right?"

Rogers nodded. "He was glad to be done with school and was ready for summer break. He and his mother were planning a weekend upstate."

"Where is his mom?" Roman asked.

"She's on her way. She works as a night aid for Hospice. She had to find someone to cover for her with her current patient who's dying."

"Was the man who called himself Luke here in the past day or so?" Brooke had found her second wind, her eyes flashing with the need for vengeance.

Rogers shook her head. "I would have called you if he had been. Jamison would have called you for that matter."

Roman wasn't so sure. He wondered if the kid had actually tried to warn the man named Luke and ended up dead for his troubles. "Anyone around who seemed suspicious?"

"No. Like I already told the detective here, I have no idea who did this."

Polly typed on her tablet. "Ever seen this guy?" She flipped the tablet around and showed the minister a still from a video surveillance camera.

Rogers squinted as all of them leaned around to eye it. "Is that Jamison?" she asked.

Polly hit a few keys and used her fingers to enlarge the frame. "That strip mall was renovated a year ago and they put cameras everywhere from the back loading docks to the parking lots. I thought I might catch Jamison as he was leaving after his shift and I was right."

Polly's hacking skills were nearly as good as Shane's. The enlarged shot clearly showed the young man speaking to a guy in a black Chevy Tahoe behind the store. The man's features were slightly blurry behind the windshield, but there was one thing the camera had caught.

"Oh my God," Brooke said. "He's wearing the necklace."

Rogers touched her collarbone where Roman was sure lay her own copy of the cross pendant under her shirt. "I don't recognize him."

"I do," Brooke said. Her face had paled even more than when she'd seen the carving on Jamison's chest.

"Who is it?" Roman demanded.

She took the tablet, using her fingers to enlarge the picture to the max. "I'm sure it's the same guy."

"Who?" Roman, Polly, and Clyffe asked in unison.

"He was here the other day when we walked in and questioned Loretta and Jamison. He jumped up and left like his pants were on fire."

Roman's excitement evaporated. "You don't know his name, though. He was just one of the lunch timers?"

"Loretta might know him," Rogers said.

"Doesn't look like a homeless guy to me," Polly added, eyeing the nearly brand new Tahoe.

"I don't think he is." Brooke's gaze locked on Roman's. "Remember the day that you came to my lecture at SDSC?"

"Yeah...?"

"I think that's the guy that asked me the questions about The Reverend. I didn't recognize him when we were here the other day because he looked different. He wore a cap and dirty, worn-out clothes, but I noticed the ring he was wearing. A big, gold chunky one that seemed completely wrong with the rest of his appearance. But I was so focused on finding out more about Luke and the necklace, I didn't give it any thought." She tapped the picture where the man's hand was on the steering wheel, a blocky gold signet ring on his finger. It's the same guy, Roman. And the grad student at my lecture wore a big, gold ring too. He kept running his knuckles along his jaw."

Roman scanned his memory. He'd been behind the student, so he hadn't noticed. "Good work, Brooke."

Polly held up the tablet, the video rolling again. "Jamison gets in the car with him and they drive off."

"He's probably the killer." Roman looked at Polly as he grabbed Brooke by the hand. "We need copies of that picture sent to our phones. Find that vehicle and who owns it."

He dragged Brooke behind him, Polly calling after them. "You got it."

"Where are we going?" Brooke sputtered as she nearly tripped keeping up with him.

Putting her on display was the last thing he wanted to do, but he needed both of them to get a look at the crowd. "That guy knew you were on campus the other day. He's probably the one who broke into your car."

"But he can't be my childhood attacker. He's not old enough."

He pushed her toward the stairs in the back. "He's got to be the guy who smashed into your car and stole your stuff."

Their feet thudded on the carpeted stairs to the second floor where Win was filming. "And he's tied to The Reverend's killings."

"Exactly. We nail him, we'll figure out how he's connected to your childhood attacker."

Winslow was in a side room off the parish house with a window open and his phone in hand, videoing the crowd below. "Hey," he said when they came in. "Any leads?"

Roman looked over Win's shoulder at the crowd. "We've got a hit."

Win glanced back at him. "Seriously?"

"Seriously," Brooke said. She moved past Roman and Win and leaned out slightly to get a better view.

Roman joined her. "Do you see him or that Tahoe?"

Darkness had fully engulfed the city, the streetlights and flashing police strobes the only thing illuminating the crowd. Shadows hung everywhere and her eyes feverishly scanned the rows of people and the street behind the roadblock. "There're too many people and shadows. They're all looking toward the church or talking to each other. I can't make out faces of anyone past the first row or two."

"I've got video from earlier, when it was still lighter," Win said. "There weren't as many gawkers, but maybe the killer was hanging around."

Roman's phone pinged. He held up the photo Polly had sent him. "Here's the guy we're looking for and he's driving a black Tahoe. You see anyone like that while you were up here?"

"Lot of black vehicles, but none that stood out. I'll start scanning the video I already have."

"Roman." Brooke's hand grabbed his on the windowsill, her grip nearly crushing his bones. "Look. Behind the ambulance."

A man stood in the shadows as the ambulance pulled away, no lights or siren blaring. He wore a jacket over a shirt and slacks, his face hidden underneath a baseball cap.

As if he felt Brooke's stare, he raised his gaze from the onlookers and Roman jerked her away from the open window, shoving her behind him and nearly knocking Win over.

Their eyes locked.

He saw the change in the man's bearing, saw him raise his hand and offer a two-finger salute.

Then he was gone, fading into the shadows.

Roman ran, jetting for the stairs. "Stay here!" he yelled at Brooke as he barreled out of the room.

Halfway down the stairs, he hopped the railing, keeping his knees bent and going into a roll when he hit. He gained his feet, saw Detective Clyffe nearby and waved at him. "Follow me!"

They sped out of the mission doors and down the steps, heading for the spot where the ambulance had been.

But his prey had gotten away.

Roman banged a hand against the light pole and swore under his breath as he scanned the area. He had no idea which way the guy had gone.

As he explained the situation to Clyffe in between gulps of air, Brooke came hustling up.

"He went north," she said pointing. "I watched him get in his truck half a block from here. Polly already called someone at the DOT and they're scanning traffic cams for him."

"Did she get a plate from the video?" Roman asked.

"No, but Win did." She cracked a smile and showed him a blurry still photo of the back of the vehicle from where it had been parked. "We can only make out three of the numbers, but Polly says it will be enough."

"I'll get someone to plug them in asap," Clyffe said, walking away to make a call.

Roman couldn't help it, he reached out and wrapped Brooke in a hug. "We've got him, Brooke."

"Technically not yet." To his relief she hugged him back. "But we will soon. He'll never hurt anyone again."

"And whoever he's working with or for is about to go down with him."

CHAPTER SIXTEEN

Brooke's heart beat a solid, fast staccato. *We've got him!*

Whoever *he* was. After all these years, she might finally get some answers to who her childhood attacker might be.

Roman released her from the hug and held her at arm's length. "I'll take Win with me. You stay here with Polly, review the footage of the crowds, and see if you can spot that bastard on it. You might be able to get a better description of what he's wearing, if he spoke to anyone, etc."

"I'm going with you."

"So am I," Polly said, walking up behind them.

Roman shot Polly a look and shook his head before he spoke to Brooke. "I know you're upset and you feel guilty over what happened, but he's a killer, Brooke. It's too dangerous."

"I admit I feel guilty, but mostly I'm angry." She gripped his arms in return to emphasize the point. "I want to look this asshole in the face once he's in custody so I can ask him who the hell he thinks he is."

"Once he's in custody, you'll have my blessing. Until then, you're staying safe."

She huffed. "I'm going with you."

"No."

He started to walk away. She felt like stomping her foot. Instead she reached out and stopped him. "You said I was part of your team and now you're just going to dump me? I don't think so."

There was something in his eyes, something sad. "You are part of this team, but this guy is quite likely the one stalking you."

"I have a gun and you taught me how to shoot it. He should be scared of me!"

His face morphed from sadness to frustration. "It would be careless of me to let you go after him."

"*You're* going after him, I'm just riding along."

"No."

"Fine." She pulled out her cell. "I'll call a cab. I'll call the SCVC Taskforce. I'll hijack Pastor Rogers' car if I have to and drive myself, but one way or the other, I'm in this thing to the end."

"There's no way I can talk you into staying here, is there?"

"Hell no." He was teetering. She needed to give him a reason to cave. "I'll concede to staying in the car when we get wherever we're going, because truth be told, I might be tempted to draw the Glock from my purse and shoot this asshole before you get any answers out of him, but I will *not* be left behind after I've been so instrumental in figuring out his identity and helping you find him."

Detective Clyffe returned. "Name's Douglas Weber." He rattled off Weber's home address. "Got an APB on him and officers are on their way to his place now."

A ding came from Polly's tablet. "Gotcha," she said with a smile. She looked up. "Cameras caught the Tahoe running northeast. He's on S Bay Freeway, CA 54."

"But his apartment is southwest," Clyffe said, scanning the notes on his phone.

"He's not heading home." Roman pointed at Win, who came jogging up. "The guy's name is Douglas Weber and Clyffe has his home address. Call Nadia and tell her to get over to this guy's apartment, see if she can find anything that can tell us where he might be headed in case we lose him. Meanwhile, you and Polly follow us and we'll see if we can catch up to him."

"Already sent you the address," Clyffe said to Win as he pocketed his phone. "I'll tag along too, if you don't mind."

"The more the merrier," Roman said.

Brooke scoffed and Roman sent her a chastising look.

Win had his phone out, calling Nadia as all of them headed for their vehicles.

"Where do you think he's going?" Polly asked.

"He's meeting up with The Reverend." Brooke was sure of it. "Hoping he'll hide him."

Polly nodded. "Do you think he will?"

"Weber is one of The Rev's disciples," Roman said with a nod. "He'll hide him."

Roman stuck a light on the roof of the Jeep as Brooke climbed in. He handed her an earbud and gave her the quickest lesson in history on how to use the comm. A second later, she heard Polly and Win checking in on theirs.

Her fast beating heart didn't slow. She'd never been in a car chase, never hunted down a killer in person. Add to that the fact she felt hope, longing, and desire for Roman, even after he'd admitted lying to her.

Was she in love with him?

It was the only explanation and it confused the hell out of her.

She hated feeling confused, especially when she did it to herself.

Shaking away the thoughts about it, she wondered why Roman was letting her come on the chase. Did he really believe she was as competent as the rest of his team? Or did he know her well enough to know she'd be true to her word— even if he purposely left her behind, she'd find a way to tag along.

The temporary Homeland badge and the Glock in her purse didn't make her an agent. They were tools of the trade, but they were also trappings, giving her a false sense of importance and expertise. She wasn't a gun-toting law enforcement officer; she was a bookworm more at home unearthing the past than dealing with the present.

Yet, here she was, riding shotgun in Roman's car, chasing a suspect in a murder. Multiple murders in fact.

He's going to pay, Jamison, she silently promised the young man. She gripped the arm rest as Roman sped into the night. *We're going to stop him.*

And then, we're going to stop The Reverend.

Lights flashing and siren blaring, they left the downtown area behind, Win, Polly, and Detective Clyffe weaving around cars and blowing through red lights with them. They hit the freeway in short order, Brooke mentally cursing at the extremely low visibility. For all she could tell, the Tahoe could be a few cars in front of them and they couldn't see it.

Updates came in from Polly and Clyffe, traffic growing heavier as 125 merged into the freeway. "Stay on 54," Polly said over the comms. "He's on Jamacha Boulevard, heading into La Pressa."

The chase continued, through the suburb, people honking as the Jeep cut in and out of traffic. Detective Clyffe had called in backup and now several state police joined in the chase.

But Weber didn't stop in La Pressa. Before long, Polly reported the Tahoe had been spotted taking a southeast turn onto 94.

"He's taking us on a wild goose chase," Brooke said, raising her voice to be heard over the siren.

Roman killed it, his jaw tight. "He's taking us to the desert."

Understanding dawned. "The ghost town where he murdered the squatters. *Maldito.*"

"There's nothing there," Roman said, seemingly as much to himself as to her. "Why would he go back to that place?"

Brooke felt a chill. "Maybe there *is* something there. Something we missed."

"Or it's a trap," Polly volunteered over their comms.

And didn't that make them all feel better?

But there were at least seven of them, counting Clyffe and the state patrol. Still, if The Reverend had all of his disciples there, and they were expecting trouble, a second mass killing might be in the works.

"We need more backup," Roman said over the comms.

A moment later, Clyffe was patched in. "Three more squads are on the way."

"So are Thomas and Ronni," Polly added. "I put out an SOS to the SCVC Taskforce. Thomas said he'll call Mitch as well."

Teamwork. While much of Brooke's life had been spent working alone, she valued teamwork as much as the DTT did. Every dig, every research paper, required help from others.

As they left the city lights behind, the waning moon was still full enough to give them a decent amount of light. The sky seemed larger, hanging like a heavy blanket overhead, dotted with stars.

Oncoming headlights from a few vehicles interrupted their distance viewing, but even when they were flying down the two-lane road with no other traffic, Brooke couldn't see a black SUV. She didn't even see any brake lights ahead of them. It was nothing but desert, mountains in the distance, and the two-lane highway.

Had Weber somehow escaped them? Roman didn't seem to think so, his foot buried in the gas pedal, the barren landscape of southern California a dark hole of the unknown waiting for them.

As Roman sped through the darkness, a call from Nadia came through. He punched his Bluetooth. "What d'ya got for me, Fernandez?"

"Weber's place is clean. Too clean. All I can find out about him is he's finishing a Master in Business. No job, and he travels a lot. His passport is filled with stamps from Europe. I've found nothing to tie him to the murders, nothing illegal at all. Not even a stash of weed. Shane is combing through his laptop, but he doesn't have so much as a porn site in his history. I hate it when serial killers don't leave evidence lying around."

Maybe he wasn't a killer. "We need something solid. Right now, all we have is a video of Jamison getting in his Tahoe and him evading us. At best, it's circumstantial and weak at that. Unless we find a murder weapon, Jamison's blood in that vehicle, or Weber confesses, we've got nothing to tie him to the kid's murder or The Reverend."

"I'm on it, boss, but The Rev and his followers didn't take trophies that we know of, and we aren't sure what they used to carve those sigils on their victims' foreheads. I'm looking for a needle in a haystack."

Ahead, Roman saw the faint taillights of a car. Was that Weber? They had no way of knowing this far out. There were no traffic cams, and endless stretches of highway enveloped in darkness. Only the lights from their cars and the moon overhead helped to break it up. "I need that needle asap."

A heavy pause. "I'll find it for you."

That's what he liked to hear. Each of the members on his team were there for a purpose. They had a nose for evidence, analytical brains that could outthink criminals, and a drive that matched his own to bring justice to the world. He pushed them because that's what made their skills rise to the surface and shine over and over again.

"I don't like this," Brooke said.

He reached over and grabbed her hand. "None of us do, but this is where shit gets real. It's one thing to sit in an office all day and try to connect the dots when you don't have all of them. It's another when they finally lead you to the criminal you're after and you have to chase them down."

"I get that. Anthropologists and archeologists do the same thing when we search for a lost civilization or colony. There's only so much you can do at a desk. Eventually, you have to put boots on the ground and start digging. But…"

"The people you're digging up don't fight back, do they?"

She chuckled but it was from nerves, not humor. "Exactly. I don't understand why Weber attended my lecture the other day or broke into my car and stole my stuff. He's not old enough to be my childhood attacker, so how does he know about the sigil?" She put her other hand to her head and rubbed. "I'm so confused."

They passed the outpost he'd taken her to just a few days ago. So much had changed in such a short period of time. He gave her hand a light squeeze before he made the turn toward the *Maldito* site. Up ahead, he saw the flash of brakes before they disappeared into the dark again. "We're going to get some answers for you."

As his entourage left the highway, he slowed and spoke to his team and Clyffe via the comms through his Bluetooth. "The site is a few miles ahead if he's going back to the scene of the second mass killings. We don't know what we're driving into here, so everyone be vigilant."

Roman killed his flashers and asked Clyffe and the state troopers to do the same. Sirens went silent as well. It wasn't like they could sneak up on the guy, but at this point, low profile was better, especially if Weber had any friends waiting for them.

"You agree with Polly, don't you?" Brooke's voice was barely above a whisper. "This is a trap."

"Weber's been a little sloppy, but not stupid up to now. Why risk exposing himself at the crime scene?" Roman couldn't name it, but the way the guy had met his eyes and snapped off that two-finger salute had been a taunt. *Come get me.* "He either thought he was too clever to get caught or he intentionally showed himself as a dare. I'm betting on the latter."

"But I still don't get the connection to me and the sigil. How could he know about it?"

"My best guess is your attacker is now The Reverend and he sent Weber to stalk you."

Maldito was only a few hundred yards ahead now. The bowl of mountains rose around it, tree copses and cacti rising like skeletons into the sky throwing shadows everywhere. Roman eased the Jeep onto the dirt road, bumping over errant rocks and potholes, his headlights picking up the squatters' camp and the boulders sitting like silent observers in the ring.

Like ghosts.

"Those poor people," Brooke said. "Thinking they'd found salvation and a new life here and all they got was death."

She shouldn't be here. He should have left her back in town. Not only was it too dangerous for her, it was too hard on her soul.

The old familiar feeling of helplessness rose in his chest. The night of Percy's death rolled around inside his brain like a pinball, shooting off one side to crash into another. There was a line he should have drawn that night. He hadn't and it had gotten Percy killed.

Now he was repeating the same damn thing over again. Would he never learn?

Tell her. He owed her the truth about Percy. About all of it.

But before he could open his mouth, his lights landed on a man sitting on one of the boulders.

Weber.

Weber swung his hands up in a show of surrender and for a split-second, Roman breathed a sigh of relief. The man knew he was caught, didn't want to make things worse for himself.

And then he saw the glint of light off metal, his brain yelled *trap*, and bullets rained down like hellfire around them.

CHAPTER SEVENTEEN

For a quick heartbeat, Brooke wasn't sure what happened.

Douglas Weber was there, sitting on a rock with his hands raised, and all of a sudden, there was a rapid-fire *ping-ping-ping*. Roman jerked the wheel of the car, and they were spinning.

Her seatbelt locked up, glass broke, Roman swore. The landscape became a blur as the car did a 180.

"Get down!" Roman yelled and the pelting noise continued, reminding her of that night at the bar, the sound of rain on the metal roof like pebbles being dropped by a giant.

But this wasn't rain.

Gunfire.

A strong hand caught her by the back of the head and shoved her down so she couldn't see. Her window exploded, raining glass down on her and she heard a scream.

It was her own voice. Her vocal chords continued to cut loose but she slammed her eyes shut as the world spun. Only the sensation of Roman's hand holding her head anchored her.

The car stopped its merry-go-round spin and Brooke heard more gunfire, saw the headlights of the other cars lighting up the interior of the Jeep. Roman hit the gas and they jetted forward, the pressure of his reassuring hand leaving her as he used it to shift.

Brooke felt something warm on her neck. She touched the spot and her fingers came away bloody.

She felt no pain. Shaking tiny shards of glass off her arms, she scanned her body and saw no other blood.

She peeked out the hole that had been her window. The cars that had been behind them were now passing on either side. The state troopers had once again hit their sirens and lights, screaming by in a wash of red, blue, and blaring noise.

Brooke dared a look back over her shoulder. There, on the boulders stood at least ten men, one apiece. Each held a semiautomatic rifle and peppered the cars with bullets.

As the police cruisers skidded to a stop, forming a roadblock, Detective Clyffe added his car to it. Win and Polly went off-roading, driving in behind one of the lean-to structures. Return gunfire from the state troopers sent the men on the boulders scrambling for cover.

Roman steered the Jeep behind an outcropping of trees. He killed the ignition and tossed her the keys with one hand as he simultaneously unhooked his seatbelt with the other. "Stay here and stay hidden. Backup's on the way but I need you to contact Thomas and let him know what he and the others are driving into. Can you do that?"

She nodded. Before he'd turned off the car, killing the dashboard lights, she'd seen a dark spot on his right shoulder.

The blood on her neck hadn't been hers. It was Roman's. "You're bleeding."

"It's nothing." He yanked on his car door handle and started to jump out.

Brooke grabbed his forearm. "You're shot!"

"Not the first time." He gave her a quick grin, leaned over, and kissed the end of her nose. "I'm fine, Brooke. The bullet skimmed me, that's all. Get your gun out and shoot anyone who comes this way if you don't recognize them. If it looks like we're losing, get the hell out of here. Get back to the freeway and call Shane. He'll know what to do."

"I'm listening, you know," Shane's voice said over her comm.

"I've already alerted Thomas and Mitch, by the way. And for the record, this is a bad idea, Walsh."

He kissed Brooke again, this time on the lips, and bailed out, completely ignoring his computer tech. The sound of gunfire tapered off. Brooke watched as Roman retrieved something from the rear.

He closed the door quietly and scooted around the vehicle wearing a vest and carrying a large, black weapon. He didn't look back at her as he disappeared into the shadows.

Brooke climbed into the driver's seat and flipped the locks on the doors, even though the other window was busted out. Her purse was in the passenger footwell and she snatched it up, shaking off more glass pellets before pulling the Glock out. She checked the chamber to make sure a round was loaded and ready to fire.

She couldn't hear anything coming through her earbud—everyone had their comms muted. She laid the Glock in her lap, her free hand on the steering wheel, drumming over and over.

Silence now met her ears.

"In pursuit," Win's voice broke the silence. He was breathing heavy, like he was running. "Male, medium build, wearing a cap, jacket, jeans, boots. Carrying a pistol."

The sound of a scuffle ensued. A gun went off, the bang so loud in her ear, Brooke flinched. She strained her eyes, searching the area, seeing nothing but the scrubby trees blowing in the breeze.

"Suspect down and incapacitated," Win said a moment later, and Brooke released the breath she'd been holding.

A fresh shot rang out, echoing in the distance. "Gotcha," Polly said, and then, "Target acquired, but we're going to need an ambulance."

Brooke fumbled for her phone to dial 911, but of course, Shane was already on it. His voice came over the comm. "Two ambulances en route. ETA ten minutes. Thomas, Ronni, and Mitch are five minutes out."

Where was Roman? Why hadn't he checked in? Had Clyffe and the troopers caught any of the other men? Was Weber still alive?

Sitting there in the dark was a nightmare. Roman was out there with his team and the others, and here she sat, a hundred yards away from the action, useless.

But she would not be one of those too-stupid-to-live heroines in some of the books she'd read. Even though she'd had a decent amount of self-defense training and gun range practice in the past few days, this entire situation was way out of her wheelhouse.

Everything about Roman from the moment he'd walked—or shot—his way into her life that night at the bar had turned her world upside down. She'd become as close to an actual agent as she ever would, had an affair with her boss—which she'd never do in the "real" world—and he just happened to be the sexiest man she'd ever met.

Talk about being out of my wheelhouse.

Her reluctance to get involved with him in the first place had been spot on. He had major secrets, and even though she'd played the part of the romance heroine to a T, pretending to be bold and carefree about sex, in the end, she just might be too stupid to live in her own life after all. She'd fallen for the hero, all right. Lock, stock, and boxing ring.

But she could never trust him with her heart. Just like Conrad Flynn in *Operation Sheba*, Roman thought he was invincible. That his reasons for doing what he did, no matter who got hurt, were for the greater good. Maybe they were, but lies and secrets had already caused her so much pain. Ruined her family. Possibly got people killed.

All she'd ever wanted was the truth.

Could Roman ever give her that?

A few feet away, a shadow moved. Her heart beat frantically. Was it a man? An animal? She fingered the gun, her hand sweaty. Could she do it? Kill someone?

I'll aim for his knee.

She always wondered in cop shows when they were pursuing a subject on foot, running around with their guns drawn and the perp in shooting range, why didn't they actually shoot the subject? If they didn't want to kill him because they needed him to talk, why didn't they simply incapacitate him? Shoot him in the arm, leg, or foot? It drove her nuts.

But fiction wasn't real life. Cop shows had to be full of action and excitement, chases on foot, the bad guys getting the upper hand until the last climactic scene.

She had to admit that so far, real life had been pretty close to that. She'd been in two firefights now, a car chase, and was at this moment holding her breath in the dark, wondering if Roman was ever coming back to her.

The shadow didn't reappear, but she kept the Glock ready. Her eyes scanned the front, sides, rear. An owl hooted.

And then she heard another scuffle off to the right.

"Roman!" Polly's voice cut through the night. "Behind you!"

Brooke sat forward even more, scanning the area, gun raised. *Where is he?*

Shots echoed off to her right. She heard a man cry out.

"Roman!" she yelled, not caring if she was breaking some comm rule. "Are you okay?"

Her hand was on the door handle, her gun up and ready to fire, when his voice stopped her from jumping out of the vehicle and running blindly into the night.

"Suspect down and in custody." His breathing was ragged. "How many does that make total?"

He sounded funny, his voice tight. Was he hurt?

Adrenaline pumped through her veins. She flung the door open and hopped out as Polly responded. "Six. The troopers and Clyffe caught three and so did we."

Six.

Out of ten.

"And Weber?" Brooke asked, holding onto the doorframe.

Every cell in her body cried out for her to move, to find Roman, but she had no idea where he was. "Did anyone get him?"

"No," Polly said. "He and the others disappeared into the desert."

From the trees, the shadow appeared again. Definitely a man and he seemed to be dragging something.

Eep!

"Hold it right there," Brooke yelled.

At least she tried to. Her voice was a little too high-pitched and came out more like a squeak. She cleared her throat and tried again. "Come any closer and I'll shoot!"

The man emerged from the shadows into a stripe of moonlight. He was limping, dragging something large and heavy into the road.

A body.

Brooke's fingers shook so badly, it took her three tries to cock the hammer. "I said stop or I'll shoot!"

"Don't do that," Roman said. "I've got one slug in me already."

He raised his weapon above his head with one hand and dropped the man he was dragging with the other. She saw a flash of white teeth in the moonlight as he grinned at her in mock surrender.

"Roman!"

She released the hammer, tossed the gun into the car, and ran to him.

He caught her with one arm, scooping her up in a hug as she threw her arms around his neck.

"Oh my God, I'm so sorry," she said. "I thought you were Weber or one of the other men who got away."

"I know." His voice was filled with humor. "You had me shaking in my boots, though. You've got the cop speak down perfectly."

"Liar," she laughed, releasing him. Her arm was coated with his blood. "And now I'm too stupid to live because I forgot about your gunshot wound!"

"Too stupid to live?"

Flashing blue lights bounced off the far hills and sirens sounded in the distance. The cavalry had arrived. "I'll explain later. How bad are you injured?"

Polly and Detective Clyffe came running up the road from the car blockade. Clyffe went to work on cuffing the guy Roman had bagged who moaned now and grabbed his knee. "He's worse off than me," Roman said. "I shot him in both knees."

Yes! Brooke smiled. "You are so damn perfect."

He handed his weapon to Polly who removed the cartridge and flipped on the safety as he headed toward the Jeep. "So you keep telling me."

He leaned on her a little as she walked him over to his vehicle. "Where are you shot?"

"My thigh." He leaned on the side of the car and Brooke looked down to see a dark stain running down the length of his leg. "Polly, I need a tourniquet."

"Yes, boss." She stuck Roman's weapon inside the Jeep and brought out a first aid kit. "How bad is it?"

"No exit wound," he ground out as Polly took a strip of cloth and tied it around his upper thigh. "Bastard might have nicked my artery."

And shit, Brooke's surreal world spun 180 again. "You need surgery. Now."

A Bronco came flying in and Thomas and Mitch jumped out of the front seat. Ronni emerged from the back.

"Damn it, we're too late," Thomas said as they walked up to Roman. "You couldn't wait to play hero until we got here, Walsh?"

They did the guy handshake-backslap thing and Roman chuckled but Brooke could tell his heart wasn't in it. "Couldn't wait on your lazy ass forever."

Mitch cocked his chin at Roman's leg and arm. "Looks like you took a couple for the team."

The ambulances drove into the valley, picking their way

through the cars and trucks. One stopped next to the man beside the road where Clyffe stood guard over him. The detective pointed to Roman. "Take him. We'll load this guy in the other."

"I'm going with you," Brooke said.

"I'll get your car back," Polly said.

As the EMTs loaded Roman onto a gurney, Brooke grabbed her stuff from the car and gave Polly the keys. "Is he going to be okay?" she asked under her breath.

Polly looked washed out under the moonlight, but didn't they all? "He'll be okay. Nothing ever keeps him down."

Brooke prayed she was right.

———————————

Roman wasn't sure what hurt worse—the gunshot wounds or Brooke's crushing grip on his hand.

"Don't think you're getting out of our earlier discussion just because you need surgery," she said around the EMT who was hooking him up to an IV. "You're going to tell me the truth about Percy."

He was, too, but it was fun to see her acting all bossy. "Is that so?"

She pinched his leg and he yelped. "Yeah, that's so, tough guy. I told you from the start, I don't do secrets. As soon as you're better, we're having a talk."

The EMT was an older Hispanic gal named Clarice. She raised an eyebrow at Roman as she inserted the IV needle into his arm. "Sounds like she means business. I wouldn't mess with her."

He chuckled. "She's a hardass, but a cute one."

"Cute?" Brooke scoffed. "I'm a hardass, all right. A brilliant, talented one who isn't about to let you off the hook just because you ran into the line of fire and got yourself shot. You scared the crap out of me back there with your hero act."

"I was doing my job, Brooke."

She went on as if she hadn't heard him. "Since you barged into my life the other night, I've been shot at, fired from my job, forced to learn how to use a gun, and stalked by a serial killer. You owe me."

She cared. That's what this was all about. He *had* scared her, but only because she cared about him.

Not that he was surprised—he'd seen it on her face repeatedly since that first night when he'd promised to hunt down the man who'd broken into her rental car and stolen her stuff. Not many people had ever stood up for her in her lifetime. She didn't depend on anyone or let herself care for people because they always disappointed her.

As the drugs pumped into his veins and Clarice slowed the bleeding from his leg, he felt a warmth in his chest that had nothing to do with the pain killers. "Weber is still on the loose. You need to be careful."

"Are you trying to change the subject on me?"

Clarice smirked. "She has your number. You better play it straight with her."

"I'm sorry I scared you," he said to Brooke. "And I'm not trying to change the subject so much as make sure you keep your guard up while I'm at the hospital. Also, I want you to know I will find that SOB and prosecute him to the fullest extent of the law."

Detective Clyffe had assured him that a full search party would assist Roman's team in scouring the countryside, hunting for Weber and his friends. It would be tough until daylight, but they would do their best.

Meanwhile, the men who'd been arrested would have their injuries treated and Clyffe would question each and every man. With any luck, one of them would break and turn on the others. All they needed was that one solid lead and this case would be wrapped up in short order.

The Reverend and his gang were going down.

Brooke gave his hand another hard squeeze. "Do you think The Reverend was there tonight?"

"No telling. They were all wearing gold crosses, but there were only ten by my count."

Her face lost its tough expression and turned anxious. "It all happened so fast, I didn't get a good look at anyone but Douglas Weber."

"Do you have your comm still?" He'd lost his in the scuffle with the man he'd taken down.

She nodded, touching her ear. "Do you need it?"

"Raise Nadia and tell her to meet us at the hospital. I want you under guard 24/7."

A small smile split her lips. "Shane says he already sent Nadia to the medical center."

Sudden exhaustion washed over him. Or maybe it was the pain killers. His vision was fuzzy and he felt light and floaty. "Tell him...thanks."

Brooke relayed the message to Shane, her face becoming three as he tried to keep his eyes open.

"You need to rest now," Clarice said, patting his arm. "We'll have you at the hospital in no time."

"It's okay, Roman." Brooke's face looked like it was smiling at him. He couldn't feel her hand anymore. "Don't worry about me. Close your eyes and relax."

He didn't want to. He wanted to keep staring at her, make sure she didn't disappear on him. For the first time in a long while, he wanted a woman in his life. Not just for a weekend or a short-term fling. He wanted someone who understood what drove him, who didn't flinch at his lifestyle. "I promise to tell you...everything," he said as his lids fluttered shut.

"I'll hold you to it."

He heard her say something else, but she sounded far away. He floated on the darkness for a long minute before coming back hard as Brooke's voice broke through.

He heard Shane's name, felt the low buzz of anxiety under

his skin as Brooke's voice spiked again. Something about the sigils. What was that? What was she saying? An ancient alphabet?

The drugs took him under once more, away from her and whatever had upset her. Darkness enveloped him, the pain slipping away…

Sirens jarred him… *bambambam*…the dream pounded against his skull. Screams. A loud, reverberating boom like thunder. His body went sailing through the air, floating, gone…

Lights and sounds assaulted him, lifting his too-light body from the shadowy dream. He tumbled over, hit something hard. Pain exploded in his temple right before something heavy hit him in the back. He tried to raise his arms, found them too heavy. Pushing against the thing at his back, he half rolled over, forcing his heavy lids to crack open.

One obeyed, the other didn't. Lights flickered, he heard a moan. His one good eye saw the inside of the ambulance, but nothing looked right.

It wasn't a dream. The ambulance lay on its side, the gurney and IV pole tangled around him. Clarice was knocked out, lying pinned under the gurney.

A whisper. "Romaaan."

Brooke! He searched for her and saw her at the end of the ambulance by the back door. She reached for him, her slim hand floating in the air. He struggled to grab it, his vision from the single eye blurring. He blinked, got both to slit open this time.

There! Contact. The ends of their fingers brushed and they clawed at each other. Brooke tried to crawl toward him to get a better grasp.

He shoved at the mess of paraphernalia that covered his body, trying to shift toward her, but his limbs didn't want to cooperate. Something heavy weighed down his right thigh.

God, he was so tired.

"My ankle is trapped," she said. As he blinked again, he noticed blood coming from her lip. "I think it's broken."

He had to pause to get his breath and realign his body around the weight holding him down. He fought through the sedative and pain killers, feeling like he was drunk.

What the hell had happened? Had someone T-boned them, flipping the ambulance on its side?

The echo of gunfire from his dream surfaced and he shook his head, trying to clear the cobwebs. Through the confusion in his brain, a spike of primal fear hit his solar plexus. "Brooke..." His lips didn't want to form words. "Where's...the gun?"

She stopped trying to kick at what had pinned her ankle and looked around. "I...I don't know. I can't see my purse."

"Find...it. Now. Get a...weapon. Any...thing."

Her gaze met his and he saw the fear written there. Just as she started to shove at the blanket near her head to find the purse, the rear door opened.

Fuck.

Whatever had fallen on Brooke's ankle went careening to the ground. She gasped and a man in the doorway, silhouetted by the moon, smiled at Roman.

"No!" Roman yelled, but it was too late.

The man grabbed Brooke by the ankles and jerked.

"Roman!" she screamed, her hand still reaching for him as she was hauled out of the ambulance.

The man threw her over his shoulder, her screaming and kicking, as Roman surged upright, knocking the gurney away and jerking the IV from his arm.

He crawled over Clarice and shoved debris from his path, but his balance sucked and he fell sideways. "Brooke!"

Shoving himself forward, he slid out of the ambulance to the ground. The vehicle was in a ditch and he used his arms to pull himself up the embankment.

He had no leverage, no balance. His right leg was worthless. He listed sideways, still calling for Brooke as the man who'd taken her set her down next to a jacked up truck with a brush guard on the front. Brooke, God bless her, rammed an elbow into the man's side, making him grunt.

Good girl.

She started to stomp on the top of the man's foot, but he slapped her and knocked her into the side of the pickup. She sagged, then rallied and took a swing at him. She was no match for him with her injured ankle, and the man grabbed her by the back of the neck and slammed her head into the truck's door handle.

Goddamn it. Roman pulled himself up to the road.

Her body went limp and the man picked her up and tossed her into the truck as if she were a doll.

Roman forced himself to his feet and started dragging his injured leg behind him when another man appeared in his peripheral vision. The last thing he saw was the butt of a rifle coming at his head.

CHAPTER EIGHTEEN

Brooke hurt from one end of her body to the other. The only thing that hurt worse than the sharp pains radiating up her leg was the hammering going on in her head.

She tried to lift a hand to her pounding temple but both were bound behind her, around a wooden chair back that cut into her shoulder blades.

The bare room sported walls made of concrete blocks. The light overhead shone from a single, bare bulb, and was so bright, she had to squint. Because of its blinding brightness, she could barely make out anything more than a few feet in front of her.

Shadows darkened the block walls and she almost missed spotting the outline of a wooden door.

Where am I? What happened?

Her throat was dry, making it hard to swallow the fear rising like bile into her mouth. Fragments of the accident, of Roman, flashed through her memory.

Where was he? Was he hurt?

Of course he's hurt, idiot. He'd already been shot twice and needed surgery before the ambulance had been rammed by that truck.

Memories beat against her temples. The man who'd pulled her from the ambulance hadn't been Douglas Weber. He was older, taller. She seemed to remember a gray beard, piercing eyes.

The Reverend?

Her head throbbed even worse, making her sick to her stomach.

Do not throw up.

She had to get free, find Roman.

But how? She wasn't Julia in *Operation Sheba*. The self-defense and the shooting skills Roman had taught her would do her no good when she was tied to a chair with a concussion and broken ankle. Especially when a serial killer lurked somewhere out of her field of vision. Any minute, he would open that door and...

Apprehension toyed with her lungs, making it hard to breath.

Don't panic, she heard Roman's voice say in her head. *Think.*

"Shane?" she whispered, hoping her comm might still be in her ear and active. He'd been talking to her right before everything had gone sideways. What had he told her? Something about The Reverend's sigil not being a symbol, but a letter from an ancient alphabet. Glagolitic? Cyrillic? She couldn't remember. "Shane, can you hear me?"

"No," a familiar voice said from behind her, "but I can."

Brooke jumped so hard, she nearly yanked her shoulders out of their sockets. She whipped her head around, to the detriment of her pounding temples, and tried to get her eyes to find the speaker through the glare. "Roman? Oh my God, is that you?"

"Yep, you can't get rid of me that easily."

She felt the brush of his fingers against hers. He seemed to be tied up like her, their backs to each other.

"I've been trying to wake you up since I came to," he said. He sounded as dazed as she felt. "I was afraid your concussion was serious."

"It may be, since I'm pretty sure I must be hallucinating you."

"I assure you I'm real. My head is killing me. It wasn't easy maneuvering my chair so close to you."

"My head feels like someone took a hammer to it. Did they knock you out as well?"

"Yeah, but I'll live. How's the ankle?"

"Hurts like hell and it's swollen. What about your thigh and shoulder? Your gunshot wounds?"

"Shoulder is nothing but a scratch, and Clarice put blood clotting compound in my leg, so I won't bleed out."

"Where are we?"

"I wasn't awake for the drive, so I have no sense of which direction they took us or how long we were in the truck. From what I can see and smell, this seems like an old prison of some sort. Or maybe an empty warehouse."

Great. That sounded fun. She sniffed the air and picked up dust and mildew. Something else too. Urine? Sweat?

The tang of old blood?

A chill rose from the concrete floor up her legs and she shivered. People had probably been tortured here. Maybe even left to die. "Why did they kidnap us? Why not just kill us?"

"They want information is my guess. Information that only you or I can give them."

"Or this is some sick game."

"Could be that."

"You could at least argue and try to make me feel better."

He chuckled tiredly. "Sorry, I don't have the energy at the moment."

"The man who hauled me out of the ambulance...do you think he's The Reverend?"

"He wasn't with the others on the boulders, but he must have been nearby. He picked up Douglas and ambushed the ambulance."

"They shot the driver. Shot out the tires. We skidded, went into the ditch, and ended up on our side."

His fingers brushed hers again and tugged at the plastic ties around her wrists. "I'll get us out of here, Brooke. All we have to do is stay alive."

His voice brokered no doubt—he truly believed he was about to save the day. He was worse off than she suspected, but ever the hero, he'd finally stepped up to reassure her.

The clink of keys at the door made Brooke tense. Her eyes had at least adjusted to the bright light.

The door swung open and Douglas strolled in. "The princess is awake," he called over his shoulder to someone she couldn't see.

He bent to her eye level, close enough she could see the flecks of brown in his eyes. "We meet again face-to-face."

At least he didn't seem to notice that Roman had moved his chair. Maybe Douglas hadn't been the one to put them in here.

Just how many were here?

Brooke steeled her nerves, swallowed past the lump in her throat. "I know who you are, Douglas. What I don't know is why you brought me here."

"My name isn't Douglas, bitch. It's Mikhail. Mikhail Zion. And you're about to learn your place in the family."

Family? "My name isn't *bitch*, it's Brooke, so if you want me to call you Mikhail instead of Douglas, you'll do me the same courtesy of using my given name."

Behind her, Roman hissed at her brassiness. She expected derision, maybe even a slap from her captor. Instead, Douglas—*Mikhail*—smiled at her and chucked her on the chin. "Well, well. My sister has stones."

Sister? If Brooke hadn't been tied to the chair, she would have fallen over.

A tightness that had nothing to do with fear for her and Roman's life sat like a pit in her diaphragm. "I assume you're using the term *stones* as a euphemism for testicles, which if you think about it, are the most sensitive parts on a male of any species and the easiest target to hit in order to disable one. It's not a compliment to say someone has stones. And I'm not your sister. I don't have any siblings, and if I did, I certainly wouldn't be related to the likes of you."

Mikhail chuckled. "Listen to you, being all flippant and smartass as if you don't know who your real mother is. Of course, if I were you, I wouldn't claim that cur either. Let's hope you have more Zion blood in you than American."

...your real mother.

Sister.

Family.

Her brain cramped just thinking about it. "Zion...blood?"

The brush of Roman's fingertips brought her back to reality. First, she needed to find out what she could about where they were and if there was any way to get out. That much she knew.

Then she could go digging for information about her family—if Mikhail actually knew what he was talking about.

He called me his sister. He claims to know my birth mother.

The realization that the man in front of her might hold the key to her past made her heart trip over itself. Was it possible she could find out the truth about her biological parents? That she might walk out of here knowing who she really was?

That was crazy, but...

Was Mikhail really her brother?

It was like a second blow to her head. She couldn't wrap her mind around it. "You sniffed my camisole!"

For a second, he looked perplexed, then Mikhail laughed. "You saw that, huh? I thought that'd freak you out."

"Freak me out? It disgusts me. Especially if you think I'm your sister. You need serious help!"

A figure appeared behind Mikhail in the doorway. He cleared his throat and Mikhail moved aside. "Meet your uncle, *Brooke.*"

There was the derision she'd expected earlier. He spat her name like it was a curse.

Maybe it was to him.

"Uncle?" Brooke forced a sneer. "Sorry, but I'm not buying that either of you is related to me."

"I am Uri Zion." The man stepped into the room, eyeing her

with something akin to a hunter eyeing a trapped animal. "Head of the Zion family."

"Wait," Roman said. "The Russian criminal organization?"

Uri's chest puffed and Brooke's stomach dropped.

"Where is your mother?" Uri asked.

"My mother?" Her voice came out shaky. Was he talking about her adoptive mom or her birth mother? Did it matter? She didn't know where the one was and she wasn't giving up the whereabouts of the other. "What do you want with her?"

"To kill her." His accent came through on the word *kill*. *Keel.* "Why else?"

Whoever they were and whatever they wanted, Brooke knew she couldn't tell them anything. They were cold-blooded murderers and apparently part of some Russian mafia.

The villain monologue! It happened at the climax of every good book. When all was lost and the bad guy had you in his clutches, you kept him talking, played along, hoping to buy time until the hero showed up or you found a way to free yourself.

Unfortunately, her hero was tied up with her. *What would Julia do?* "Look, I don't know who you are, but I think you have me confused with someone else. I don't have any siblings and my mother is in a nursing home with early onset Alzheimer's. Why would you want to *keel* her?"

His lips twitched in a bemused smirk. "Do you work for CIA?"

Brooke sputtered. Playing stupid wasn't as hard as she'd expected it to be. "I'm an anthropologist. I know nothing about the CIA or spies."

Except that you never ever cop to being one.

She gave him her best innocent look.

The man cocked his chin at Roman behind her. "Homeland has trained you, then?"

He knew Roman was Homeland. Mikhail and Uri had done their homework.

Her stomach flip-flopped. She didn't like where this

interrogation was going and she had no idea how to get out of here. *Buy time. Keep him talking.* Roman would come up with a plan, and if he didn't, she would.

Riiight. The demon on her shoulder was back and laughing hysterically.

Instead of answering Uri's questions, it was time to ask a few of her own. "Are you The Reverend?"

He lifted one bushy eyebrow, the bemused expression still on his face. He shrugged slightly. "The Mexicans are bottom feeders. They're cutting into the Zion trade from here to Brazil. I had an itch."

An *itch*? "You call murdering dozens of innocent people scratching an itch?"

"I murdered no one. They are so stupid. It was easy to get them to drink their own death."

Even though her legs were bound to the chair, her ankle swollen to twice its normal size, the anger sent her to her feet, raising the chair legs up and nearly toppling her over. Mikhail grabbed her by the hair and jerked her back down, body jarring on impact.

"Brooke,"—she was closer to Roman now and he grabbed her bound hands with his and said softly—"take it easy."

"So sweet," Mikhail remarked, cuffing Roman on the shoulder. "That's why we kept you, Homeland. My sister is foolish over you. She'll do anything I want if I threaten your life."

"The sigils you carved on the victims' foreheads?" she hissed. "Why did you do that?"

"The Zion trademark." Mikhail refocused on her just like she wanted and grinned maliciously. "We mark all of our enemies when we kill them. Sends a message."

Shane had been correct—the sigil was a variation of a pre-Cyrillic letter, bastardized to represent the crime family.

It wasn't often she missed the mark. So much for her expertise helping the DTT. They'd done more for her than she had for them.

"Your mother was CIA," Uri continued as if bored with talking about mass murder. "She escaped the family once. I will not let her again. It does not matter if you work for Homeland or CIA, she will come for you."

Brooke's jaw fell open and she pictured her adoptive mom in her mind as she spoke. "My mother was a bank teller, and a waitress, and for a while she worked the counter at a Starbucks. She had a drinking problem. A severe one. Believe me, she was not CIA."

The man sighed and did an impatient eye roll. "Not the woman who did such a poor job of raising you, Brooke. Your blood *mother*. Aurora Adams."

Aurora? *My mother's name is Aurora?*

Aurora Adams. It was the smallest piece of knowledge, yet it sent a thrill through her heart.

And if this man and Mikhail were telling the truth, they believed her mother was an American spy.

Holy crap.

Brooke swallowed hard. They knew she'd been adopted, so there was no reason to pretend differently, but there was no way she'd let them see how much they'd rattled her. "I don't know Aurora, and even if she *is* the woman who gave birth to me, she obviously has no interest in me or she would have stayed in my life. I don't know why you think I'm compelling bait to draw her out. *She left me.*" Even playing this crazy game, the truth made her breath hitch and her eyes burn. "You haven't answered me yet. Why do you want to kill her?"

Mikhail slammed his hand against the concrete wall, making Brooke jump. "Stop acting like you don't know! She killed our father in order to keep you away from us! You know she will stop at nothing to protect you."

Killed our father...

Ditto on the holy crap.

Either Mikhail was completely nuts or her birth parents had been.

"Let's all take a deep breath," Roman said. His voice was low, soothing. The ultimate negotiator. "We can sort this out. Dr. Heaton doesn't know anything about her birth mother or what happened to your father, Mikhail. Why don't you fill us in? Then maybe I can help you find this Aurora. Being a Homeland agent, I have many resources."

She loved him in that moment. Here she was on the verge of losing her shit, and calm, cool, collected Roman was negotiating on her behalf. Offering to help Mikhail and Uri find Aurora.

Would it buy them time? Would the DTT find them?

Uri strutted in front of Brooke, seeming to contemplate Roman's offer. Finally, he stopped pacing and stood, feet apart, hands on hips. "Aurora Adams infiltrated our organization, seduced my brother, and became pregnant with his child. I didn't know all of this at the time because I was in South America, running operations there. Aurora set a trap for Victor, and he ended up in an American prison for nearly seven years before I got him out. I brought him home, but he wanted revenge and once he got his strength back, he started trying to track her down. Although he did not share the information with the family, he knew Aurora had been pregnant with his child before she turned on him. He wanted revenge, and he wanted his child."

Here, Uri looked directly at Brooke. He must have seen the shock on her face because, being the bastard he was, it made him smile. He hulked over her, trying to make her feel small. "He insisted on returning to America to hunt her down. He couldn't find her—CIA had given her a new identity and there was no trail—but he found you, Brooke. It took three years and every contact he had in America. He nearly bankrupt our family, but eventually, he narrowed it down to a dozen possibilities. He told me the moment he saw you, he knew." Uri leaned down so his face was level with hers. "It's the eyes. Your mother had the same color."

A tremor raced up Brooke's spine. This had to be true, didn't it? It matched up with what little she already knew. "He was the bad man," she whispered to herself.

"Victor wasn't bad, just soft in the head when it came to your mother. He actually thought she loved him."

"Did he kill the Dunkirks that night or did you?"

Uri cocked his head. "You were nothing to me. *Are* nothing to me. A gnat to be squashed. I only wanted Victor to return to his real family and help me run our empire. But he wanted to bring you into the fold. He was determined to kidnap you. Aurora interrupted him before he could snatch you that night. Why did he kill that family?" A shrug. "Who knows? Maybe he believed they were helping Aurora hide you. Maybe he was sloppy and one of them woke up. Who cares at this point?"

"I care."

Uri rolled his eyes. "He went after her, your mother. You know what happened?"

Mikhail's words rang in her ears and Brooke had to look away. "She killed him?"

A muscle in Uri's face jumped. "His body turned up across the border six months later. Aurora and some of her Mexican dogs killed him and dumped the body in a remote area."

"It's been twenty years," Roman said. He gripped her hands again, but his fingers ran around the plastic bindings at her wrists, feeling, searching. "Why come after Brooke now? She doesn't know anything. It wasn't her fault that Aurora duped your brother and killed him."

Mikhail pushed off the wall. "It's because of me. I was conceived when my father returned home after Uncle Uri got him out of prison. I never knew why he left my mother and four sisters again for America and ended up dead."

"I continued to search for Aurora all these years," Uri said. "But she's hidden herself well. Mikhail will be taking over our North American operations soon. It was time he knew the truth."

Mikhail puffed up his chest. "You played right into my hand, sister. The moment I saw you at the university, I knew it was time to make you and your mother pay. She will die by my hand." His eyes flashed with hate as he put a fist to his chest. "And you will bring her to me."

She'd always known her family was dysfunctional, but this topped the cake. "Screw you," she said, glaring at her captives. "I'm not doing a damn thing to help you."

"You don't need Brooke," Roman said. He tugged on Brooke's bindings ever so subtly. She felt one loosen around her left wrist. What was he doing? "You have me. Like I told you, I have many resources, and the truth is, I already know all about Aurora. I have a contact number for her. Give me a laptop and let me make a few calls. I'll have her here in an hour or two tops."

What?

Brooke nearly turned her chair around to look at him, felt him squeeze her fingers.

He was making this up, right? This was just a trick to buy more time.

Except the conviction in his voice was so real.

He's a damn good actor.

"No way," she said, playing along. "We're not giving my mother up to anyone, especially not these turds."

"Do you think we are stupid?" Mikhail yelled, his gaze still on Brooke even as he spoke to Roman behind her. "We're not turning you loose, Homeland. The only reason you are here is to make sure my sister cooperates. Aurora keeps tabs on her. It's only a matter of time before she shows up."

"Stupid? Nah," Roman said. "I don't think you're stupid. But dead? Yeah, you're about to be that."

Before Brooke knew what was happening, Roman tipped her chair sideways and all hell broke loose.

Adrenaline was an amazing drug. Better than the pain killers Clarice had pumped into him in the ambulance. Those had worn off some time ago anyway.

And pain had always been his drug of choice. It fueled Roman's body, always had. It was one of the things that had made him such a tough fighter.

Add to that the fact Brooke was hurt, and her own family was about to use her to lure her mother to her death, and he had all the stimuli he needed to kick some Russian ass.

While Brooke had impressed the hell out of him as she kept Uri and Mikhail talking, he'd managed to slip the zip ties from his hands, slide the tiny knife from the hidden compartment in his watch, and cut through hers. He'd had to dislocate one of his thumbs to get out of his plastic cuffs, but hey, that was the least of his physical pains at the moment.

And stupid? Yeah, he actually did think Uri and Mikhail were to leave him sitting close to Brooke.

His feet were still bound, but as Brooke screamed and toppled sideways, he jumped up and came down hard on the chair, busting the wooden legs into multiple pieces and freeing his ankles.

The impact jarred the hell out of his injured leg, but he didn't have time to worry about it as Mikhail sprang and Roman hit him with a quick uppercut to the face that sent Mikhail sprawling and brought Roman great satisfaction.

Especially when he saw the amount of blood that came gushing from the kid's broken nose.

Uri wasn't leader of the Zion mafia for nothing. Before Roman could jump over Brooke, who had realized her hands were free and caught herself before she smacked her head on the floor and was now trying to free her bound ankles, Uri pulled a gun and pointed it at Brooke's head.

"Go ahead," he taunted Roman. "I'll kill her dead."

God, he hated that phrase. "If you kill her, she's dead, there's no way around it, so saying you'll *kill her dead* is redundant."

The crime lord didn't expect a grammar lesson and the split second of mental head-scratching he did gave Roman the opening he needed.

In one swift movement, he grabbed the gun, forced it upright as Uri pulled the trigger and shoved the man into the wall. The bullet hit the ceiling and rained plaster down on them.

The old guy tried to knee him in the balls and was stronger than he looked, but Roman evaded the incoming danger to his family jewels while keeping his head from becoming the receiver of a bullet.

And then *whap*, something laid into his lower back, right about kidney level and brought him to his knees.

Mikhail had decided to use a chair leg as a bat.

Roman rolled, banging into Brooke, who cried out as the chair leg came down at both of them. Roman threw up an arm to block it, taking the full force of the blow so it didn't hurt her.

Unfortunately, it was his injured arm and upon impact, it went weak.

Natural-born fighter that she was, Brooke took both her legs, still zip tied to her chair and managed to boot Mikhail in the shins with the chair.

The kid cursed and went down on one knee, dropping the chair leg. Roman rolled again toward Uri to take him out and found himself staring at the end of Uri's gun.

Brooke didn't realize that though. She scrambled to her hands and knees, grabbed the dropped chair leg, and raised it above her head to bring it down on her half-brother.

Uri swore in Russian. The gun went off, but not at Roman.

Brooke screamed. The chair leg dropped from her hands.

Roman didn't see blood, thank God, but the chair leg was now in three pieces.

Uri had shot that and not Brooke.

As the gun swung back to point at Roman, he swiveled his body and used a roundhouse kick to knock Uri's legs out from under him. The old man sprawled to the ground and the impact sent the gun skidding across the floor.

Mikhail smacked Brooke across the face, knocking her flat as he scrambled over her to lunge for the gun.

Roman lunged at the same time.

They grappled with each other, punching, kicking, and shoving each other, both trying to reach the gun first.

Roman had just delivered a gut punch to Mikhail when he heard Brooke let go of a banshee yell that made the hair on the back of his neck stand up. As both he and Mikhail looked her way, she towered over them, a different chair leg raised above her head and a look of sheer determination on her face.

She brought the chair leg down on Mikhail's calf, following it up with a second strike to his hip. *Whack, whack, whack.* She kept swinging.

The kid flailed; Uri swore and staggered to his feet. Roman brought an elbow down on Mikhail's temple and knocked the kid out just as Brooke reared back with her chair leg bat and swung for the bleachers at Uri's head.

The old man was a more controlled fighter than his nephew. He had an uncanny ability to move fast and efficiently. He grabbed the end of the bat and yanked Brooke forward.

She spun slightly, letting go in order to grab Uri.

As Brooke knocked Uri into the wall once more, Roman rolled to his feet and grabbed the gun in one quick motion. Uri shoved Brooke aside and she went down.

Roman fired.

The first bullet hit Uri in the shoulder. The second in the thigh. If Roman had his way, he would have put three center mass, then done the same to Mikhail, but Brooke needed answers about her family, and he wasn't about to rob her of that chance.

As Uri writhed on the floor, a figure appeared in the doorway. The woman wore black from head to toe, her hair pulled back in a tight bun. A sizable black handgun complimented her outfit and her eyes did a sweep of Roman, Uri, and Mikhail. They paused for a moment on Brooke, who lay motionless on her side, eyes closed.

"Looks like I'm late to the party," she said to Roman. "As always, you seem to have things under control."

The adrenaline was wearing off, his body going into shock. He needed to sit down. "I do my best."

She lowered her weapon. Her eyes were sad as they seemed to feast on Brooke like she longed to go to her. Hug her. "Is she okay?"

"Battered and bruised, but you'd be proud of her. She kicked ass."

A twitch of the corner of her lips. "I've always been proud of her."

"She won't be happy when I tell her the truth."

"So don't tell her." The woman's gaze came back to him. Those eyes…Brooke's eyes…startled him. "That was our deal."

"I'm not keeping secrets from her anymore. Yours almost got her killed today. She deserves to know the truth."

A noise came from down the hall. The woman pocketed her gun and gave him a disconsolate look. "The truth is ugly. She'll never understand."

"You should give her more credit. She's smart and capable, just like you."

Brooke stirred, blinking and moaning Roman's name. Aurora hesitated, longing written all over her face. "Tell her that I really did love her father. Victor and I were just caught in terrible…circumstances."

Brooke pushed herself upright, leaning back against the wall, her gaze taking in Uri and Mikhail, and then bouncing to Roman. She turned her head and caught sight of the woman.

But Aurora had already moved away and was heading out. The sounds of others echoed in the hallway.

"Who was that?" Brooke asked.

It seemed such a simple thing to tell her. To no longer be

bound by the pact he'd made with her mother only a day ago. Or was it two now?

He'd truly believed he was helping protect Brooke. Aurora had told him a group of men from her past were looking for her daughter, that she needed help keeping Brooke safe. He'd never dreamed how it would all play out.

He had to tell her the truth. Would she ever forgive him?

"That was Aurora," he said and watched her already pale face go another shade whiter.

"Aurora…Adams?"

He sagged against the wall and slid down next to her. "Yes, Brooke. That was your mother."

Winslow and Thomas came through the door, weapons raised.

"Don't shoot," Roman said. "We're clear."

He handed off Uri's weapon to Win. "Cuff them and get them out of here."

Win hit his comm. "Clear," he told the rest of the team. "You okay?" Win asked Roman.

Roman closed his eyes for a second and leaned his head back against the cool concrete blocks. He reached for Brooke's hand, but she pulled it away. Warm blood was running down his thigh again. "Hell, yeah."

Thomas pulled out a pocket knife and cut through Brooke's leg bindings, tossing her chair aside. Win cuffed Uri and suddenly Brooke was leaning over him, her shirt in hand.

"You better have an ambulance outside," she said to Win as she tied the shirt around Roman's leg.

"Two, in fact," he replied.

She gave a jerk on the ties, tightening the knot so hard, it sent pain shooting into Roman's groin and brought his back off the wall.

Yep, she was pissed.

Thomas cuffed a still-unconscious Mikhail. Nadia, Ronni, and Polly appeared in the doorway.

"Jesus," Polly said, "you scared the shit out of us, boss."

"Good thing Shane had that tracking device in your watch," Nadia added.

Brooke stared at him, eyes hard and flat. He needed to explain things, tell her why he'd done what he had. "Could you guys give us the room for a minute? I need to talk to Brooke."

Two EMTs came through the door with a gurney and their medical bags, everyone forced to move out of their way.

"You need to get to the hospital," Brooke said. "We'll talk later."

And then she, too, moved out of the way so the paramedics could go to work on him.

He argued but Brooke quietly slipped out the door and was gone before he could order anyone to stop her.

"Don't leave her alone," he told Nadia and Polly.

"I've got it," Ronni said, waving them off. "I'll get her to the hospital and make sure she's okay."

She wasn't, that he knew.

Worse…it was all his fault.

CHAPTER NINETEEN

Two hours after his surgery, Roman was sitting up in bed when Brooke blew in, a bucket of double chocolate fudge swirl in one hand and a box of tissues in the other.

"That's a lot of ice cream," he said, his eyes wary as he scanned her face. "I don't know what they told you, but I *am* going to live."

"The ice cream's not for you." She plunked it down on the tiny table and pulled up a chair. His family had left a few minutes ago, his team was on the way to see him. She needed to get her answers and get out. "I figured I was going to need solace food and tissues when you explained to me exactly what happened with my birth mother."

"How's the ankle?"

"It's sprained, not broken. They gave me some serious pain meds that I'm fully enjoying." She withdrew a spoon and the Glock from her purse and set them on the table next to the ice cream bucket. "Start talking."

His eyes didn't miss the gun. "First, I want to apologize for not being upfront with you."

"Yada, yada, yada." Peeling the lid off the bucket, she motioned with the spoon for him to get on with it. "Spill. I want the whole truth and nothing but the truth, or you're going to need another surgery. Understand?"

That got his attention.

He told her everything. How her birth mother had initially

contacted him after Brooke's rental had been broken into on campus. The message had been anonymous, cryptic. Brooke was in trouble, needed protection. He'd already figured that out.

From the information Brooke had told him, he'd contacted Cooper Harris's friends on the East Coast again and asked Petit and Beatrice Reese, the former NSA gal, to do some digging. It hadn't taken long for a few details to emerge, thanks to a retired CIA agent who currently did work for Shadow Force International. Not only had the man known Aurora back in the day, but had trained her.

Like Mikhail and Uri had confessed, Aurora Adams had gone undercover for the CIA to get into the Zion criminal organization. Aurora was a cover name—her real name was Justine Amour.

She'd become pregnant with Victor's child and refused to abort it.

Knowing the Zion family would come after her and the baby, she'd gone into hiding, given birth, and then found a couple who didn't ask questions to adopt Brooke. There was no paperwork with Aurora or Justine's name on it, only a fake birth certificate that claimed Brooke was indeed the child of Krissy and Everett Heaton.

Roman had put two and two together, figuring that the anonymous message had probably come from her biological mother and had put Shane on the task of searching traffic cams, parking lot surveillance, and satellite feeds for anyone who might be following Brooke. Shane had found two hits of the same woman following them to the discount store and outside the Laudlin Towers. "She's still got it," Roman said. "I checked and double-checked that we didn't have a tail, but I never saw her."

"What else?"

He continued, explaining how Justine had sent Roman a new message, this time with a contact number *in case.*

"I never actually knew where she was or what she looked

like," he told Brooke. "In the videos we caught of her, she's wearing a scarf over her hair and sunglasses to hide her eyes. She made sure to keep her head turned away from the cameras. Shane couldn't get a positive facial rec on her, and the CIA refused to provide her official photo to me, even though she hasn't worked for them—or so they claim—in thirty years."

Brooke swallowed the cool ice cream and focused on the *so they claim* part. "You think she's *still* working for them?"

"No idea." He eyed her bucket. "You didn't happen to bring two spoons, did you?"

"You think I'd share my favorite ice cream after you lied to me?"

"I was trying to keep you safe, and honestly, I wasn't convinced that first anonymous message was even legit. A lot of people knew your car was broken into and you could be in danger. Anyone could have sent that message to me."

"And after you found out about Aurora—Justine—and my birth, you didn't think that was worth sharing?"

"I planned to tell you after my parents' anniversary party, but you got off on the Percy tangent and blew my timing."

"The Percy *tangent?* Oh, Dr. Walsh, you haven't seen a tangent yet."

"I have a feeling I'm about to."

She threw the box of tissues at him. She didn't feel like crying, but she seriously considered making him cry.

He flashed a smirk but it lacked luster. His whole demeanor was off. Might have been the drugs in his system or the fact he'd been shot twice, lost a lot of blood, and had required a three-hour surgery. Physical therapy, and lots of it, loomed in his future.

Good. He deserves to suffer a little.

Or it could be he was actually worried that she was about to walk away and never give him the time of day again.

She toyed with the spoon a moment, considering that.

The devil on her shoulder urged her to climb into bed and

hand-feed him ice cream, but her heart still felt like it was in pieces. She slapped the devil with her spoon. "I'm glad to know about my birth parents—I think—but since my mother didn't stick around to chat, I guess that's a dead end once again. Let's get back to you. Now would be a good time to tell me the truth about Percy."

"I can't."

She considered throwing the spoon again, and dug into the ice cream instead. "I've already promised myself that no matter what it is, I won't throw you or anyone else under the bus, so stop worrying. I'm not looking to get anyone in trouble, or tarnish your brother's image with your family. I just need to know what really happened. I need to be able to trust you again."

Roman took a deep breath and leaned his head back against the pillows, closing his eyes. He was still for so long, she thought he might have fallen asleep. It wouldn't surprise her, since he'd only been out of post-op for a short time and probably needed rest.

But she kept eating her ice cream and watching him, just to be sure he wasn't faking it to keep from answering her.

Questions about Justine circled her brain.

Why would she run away from me a second time?

It was too much. Tears welled behind her eyes and she blinked them away. She would *not* cry for the mother she'd never had. The woman who claimed to care so much for her, but had abandoned her. Twice.

Roman cleared his throat, and then opened his eyes, startling her back into the present. He lifted his head from the pillows and met her gaze. "Are you okay?"

No, she wasn't. Brooke dashed at her eyes. "Fine. Tell me about Percy."

He sighed. "What I told you the other day is basically the truth. I helped Percy get over his drug addiction. He had a felony drug charge looming over his head though, and I got the DA to cut a deal with him. At the time, I was running a different taskforce, one working to break an international drug syndicate. If Percy helped us, he wouldn't end up in prison.

"He worked his street contacts and we put a sting into motion. Percy got in deep enough that the cartel's main buyer wanted to talk to him about moving product to and from the Middle East. A place my brother was very familiar with. But the night the sting was supposed to go down, I got cold feet and called it off.

"It was a huge break for us, but I couldn't send him into that meeting. My gut kept telling me something was off. That this buyer had found out Percy wasn't who he said he was."

Brooke stuck the spoon in the ice cream and sat back. "How did he end up dead?"

"Percy was pissed when I pulled the plug an hour before the op was to go down. Some of the taskforce members were upset too—they'd put a lot of days and nights into laying the framework, but they respected my position. Percy didn't. He went to the meeting anyway, and he sent a text to three of the taskforce guys after he was there telling them it was going down right then, that I was with him and needed their help. They all scrambled to get there and set up surveillance, not realizing he'd played them. Before they could get hold of me and confirm whether or not I'd okayed the op after all, Percy was dead, and the other three guys severely injured trying to save him."

Crude. Brooke shook her head, not surprised that Percy had a hero complex—it seemed to run in the family—but really, what the hell had he been thinking?

Roman shifted his leg and winced. "The cartel was in the wind again. All the long hours, being away from their families, and risking their lives to stop this international cartel, and what did they have to show for it? A dead CI who'd blown the operation and nearly gotten three men killed in the process."

"I'm sorry, Roman."

She was too. Like her mother, Roman's brother had no doubt meant well.

"I covered for him with the family because I had to. I couldn't let them know what his final act on this earth had been. I also took the blame for the failed op, claiming I had tried to pull it off at the last minute. The men who were injured all survived and still have solid careers and that means a lot to me."

"You couldn't just tell me that from the beginning?"

"I promised those guys I would never tell anyone. Promised myself I would take Percy's actions to the grave. My family doesn't need to know the truth. It would serve no purpose to soil Percy's memory."

"It appears taking the blame didn't hurt your career."

He shrugged and the action drew another wince as he disturbed his bandaged shoulder. "I'm here on the West Coast, as far away from Homeland headquarters as they can put me outside of Hawaii or Alaska. The higher-ups see it as punishment, but it actually works well for me. I get to stay close to my family and work a job I love with the DTT."

The taskforce was a good group. She envied him in many ways.

Cleaning off the spoon, she put the lid on the ice cream bucket, then retrieved her box of tissues and stuck both in her purse. Without the Glock in there, she had room for them. She dropped the strap over her shoulder. "Thank you for telling me the truth."

As she limped toward the door, he called after her. "That's it? You're walking out after I told you everything?"

She turned back. "I need some time to myself. I have a lot to process, and unlike you, I don't have family and friends to lean on for support."

"Brooke, I'm here for you."

He was too. She could see it in his eyes, in the way he was throwing back the covers to try to get up and come to her.

She held up a hand. "Don't. I know you feel guilty about

withholding the truth from me, but I do understand. Mostly, anyway," she fiddled with her purse. "But I'm not cut out for this. I thought I was, but I'm not. I need to go analyze some bones and artifacts and get back to what I'm good at. What I feel comfortable with. I need you to respect that and give me some space."

He sat on the edge of the bed, holding onto the bed's railing. "I don't want you to leave."

All he had to do was say he needed her. That he loved her.

But he didn't.

"The taskforce needs you, Brooke."

The taskforce. Not *him*. "No, they don't. Shane figured out the sigils, not me. I added nothing to solving this operation. If anything, I endangered you and your team, and Jamison died because he talked to me. It felt like a game, a really fun one, until it wasn't anymore."

"We wouldn't have solved the case without you."

He was being kind. She appreciated it, but what else would the perfect hero do?

Confirmation bias. This time, however, her bias was accurate. "Do you think I'll ever see Justine again?"

"I don't know."

At least he was telling the truth about that.

"What I do know," he said, "is that she loved you enough to give you up in hopes of protecting your life. She told me to tell you that she really did love Victor, and I believe her. We don't know the whole story between them."

"I wish I did, because maybe then, I wouldn't feel so…lost."

His face screwed up. "I know."

"No, you don't. Your family is nearly as perfect as you, and you should tell them the truth about Percy. Stop playing the hero, Roman, just once."

He sucked in a breath like she'd slapped him.

Then the surprise passed and he set his jaw again. "Uri and Mikhail are going to prison and Mikhail has given up enough in return for a lighter sentence that the CIA, NSA, and Homeland will be able to systematically disassemble the Zion organization. I was hoping you might want to help."

Brooke chuckled. The sound was dry and hoarse. "Thanks for the offer, but I'm an anthropologist and its time I quit playing undercover agent. Although I will miss the sex."

She hugged the damp ice cream bucket to her. "Maybe some day, our paths will cross again, preferably not during a bar shoot out, and we can start over. Until then, I wish you well, Roman. You're an incredible person."

The tears she'd held back earlier trickled down her face as she hobbled out and soldiered down the long hospital hallway. Roman hadn't originally trusted her with the truth about his brother, or her birth mother, and yet she still loved him.

Talk about soft in the head. Maybe I take after my father.

But how could she not still love Roman? He was a hero, if not quite as perfect as she'd once believed.

So yeah, she loved him. To the very marrow of her bones, and she'd always known he had to have a flaw, like romance heroes always did. Even Conrad Flynn had betrayed Julia. Somehow, she'd been able to forgive him and move on.

Unfortunately, real life wasn't that easy. *At least not for me.*

If only Roman's flaw had been something else.

In the immortal words of Conrad Flynn, the only person who can betray you is someone you love.

Boy was he right. The only thing she'd ever wanted since she'd found out she was adopted was to have someone in her life who would tell her the truth. Someone she could trust one hundred percent.

As she walked out of the hospital into the early morning light, she wondered if she'd ever trust anyone again.

Fourteen days later
Utah

Even with the padded saddle, Roman's butt was killing him.

The ten hour ride up the mountainside had sounded like fun. Now he was sunburnt, sweating like he'd just spent nine full rounds in the ring, and he smelled like the ass he was riding into camp on.

Tents ringed the site, six or seven people, straw hats on their heads, squatted in various delineated squares in the buff-colored ground. Some used paintbrushes, others seemed to have dental picks, and still others worked with wooden boxes with screens, sifting through churned up dirt and creating a series of conical piles off to the sides of each square. To the north and east, broken hills rose around them, piñon and other scrub trees dotting the slopes.

His guide, a native to the area, pointed and Roman tipped the brim of his hat up and followed the old man's bony finger. For half a second, his heart stopped beating and he dragged in a ragged breath.

Like the heroine from an Indiana Jones movie, Brooke worked in khakis and a white button-down, boots on her feet and a straw hat on her head.

Is that my shirt?

Yep. The woman had stolen one of his shirts. The thought gave him hope.

As she took off her hat and ran an arm across her forehead wiping off sweat, he saw her cheeks were flushed and a warmth invaded his belly that had nothing to do with the blazing sun. The white shirt was unbuttoned and the breeze parted it long enough for him to see she was wearing an "I love Lucy" T-shirt with a picture of the famous skull underneath.

He remembered those flushed cheeks as she'd lain under him, her beautiful eyes filled with lust as he moved on top of her, making her moan and beg for release.

Had he given her enough time? She'd said she needed to process what she'd been through and he'd totally respected that even though he'd cursed himself every minute of the day since. He hoped for the sake of his still-healing body, which was yelling at him after that blasted ride, and the person he'd blackmailed into coming with him, that Brooke was ready to forgive him and grant him a second chance.

The woman he hoped would be his future mother-in-law had said little on the ride, enduring the harsh conditions as if it were nothing compared to her normal life. Maybe it wasn't. Justine had been through the CIA's farm, infiltrated a Russian mob, and given up her child, all in the name of survival. No telling what other trials she'd seen and lived through.

Even if Brooke never wanted to see him again, it was the right thing to do, bringing Justine here and introducing them. Justine needed to know what an amazing woman her daughter had become—not just from a distance, but in person. And Brooke needed to know that there *were* people in her life who loved and supported her.

A man emerged from one of the tents and spied them. The guide waved and the man kicked up dust as he made his way over to greet them.

Roman slid off the donkey and nearly fell down. They'd taken a break every hour but his butt and legs were stiff and sore. His feet tingled from lack of blood flow.

He shook out his legs, the rubbery sensation familiar from his days in the ring but unwelcome just the same. As the man from the tent neared, Roman recognized him.

Dr. David Borgman. Brooke's boss from the Smithsonian.

"You," Dr. Borgman said, hands going to his hips. "What the hell are you doing here? Dr. Heaton is not available for one of your consults." He made air quotes around *consults.*

Roman forced a smile and brushed past him to go see Brooke. Flagging tape created a sort of runway, showing where people were allowed to walk.

He'd waited two full weeks, restraining himself from calling or texting just to see if she was okay. He had his sources that could keep tabs on her, but none this deep in the high country. He'd lost cell service ten miles into the ride.

"Hey," Borgman called after him. "Where do you think you're going? This is an official government site. You can't just—"

Roman heard the man make a startled sound and he glanced back to see Justine had grabbed the man by the collar and was now speaking directly in his face in a low, threatening voice.

Hearing the commotion, Brooke glanced their way. She still had her hat off and her eyes went wide when she saw him.

Roman smiled for real this time, and worried that she might not be happy to see him, he waved.

He never waved. But he felt like a lovesick teenager who'd never had a girlfriend.

To his surprise—and relief—Brooke did the same.

Sure, it was a bit hesitant, but he hoped that was because he'd truly surprised her in a happy way and not in an *oh hell no* manner.

"Roman? What in the world are you doing here?" she asked when he reached her.

Okay, not exactly the reaction he'd hoped for, you know the one where she threw her arms around his neck and kissed him, but...

"I came for you."

"Ten hours up the mountain on a donkey? Why?"

"To tell you something important."

Her face fell. "Is everyone okay? Polly? Win? Nadia?"

"Everyone's fine, but they miss you. *I* miss you."

She blew right over his admission as if she hadn't heard him. "Did Uri get loose? Is he coming after me?"

"Uri, Mikhail, and the other men who were part of The Reverend ring have been rounded up and are awaiting trial. What remains of the Zion family back in Russia have been arrested. Their empire continues to crumble and we're dismantling their international operations. You're safe."

She breathed a sigh of relief, her gaze running over him from head to toe. "Sorry to be so self-centered, it's just been a concern of mine. I didn't want to put my colleagues here in danger. How are you? How's the leg and shoulder?"

So polite. So...professional.

"I. Miss. You." He moved closer, touching her arms, letting his fingers trail down to her hands. "My body is healing. My heart not so much."

He saw her throat work as she swallowed. She took a small step toward him, her gaze searching his face. "What's wrong with your heart?"

"You broke it."

Fake surprise lit her face. "I did, huh?"

"I love you, Brooke Heaton. I know I screwed up and betrayed your trust, but I'm hoping you can forgive me and let me make it up to you."

Her lips quirked. They had an audience now, her colleagues watching. "How do you intend to do that?"

He leaned in, putting a hand on her warm neck as he whispered all the intimate things he planned to do to her if she would take him back. The pulse in her neck sped up under his fingers, her breath hitched at the last suggestion.

Moving back, he let go of her and motioned behind him. "And then there's this."

Justine took her cue, coming forward, her eyes, so much like Brooke's, filling with tears as she met her daughter's shocked gaze.

She held out a hand. "It's nice to finally meet you, Brooke. Roman isn't the only one who owes you an apology. I have so much to make up for, and I hope you'll at least give me the chance to tell you what really happened between me and your father. Your biological father."

"M...Mom?"

A sad smile spread across the older woman's face. "I'm so, so sorry, Brooke, for putting you in danger. I thought I was doing the right thing. I thought I was keeping you safe. I never meant for you to get hurt. I love you more than..."—her voice broke—"anything."

"So do I," Roman said. "We both want you to know it, and we couldn't wait any longer."

"The grand gesture," Brooke murmured.

Justine sent Roman an inquisitive look. He shrugged, not really understanding. This must be another term from her romance books, like cerebral sex.

Brooke smiled, dashing at the corners of her eyes as she chuckled. "I can't believe it. I cannot freakin' believe it."

"Believe what?" Roman asked. "That we love you enough to come find you in this godforsaken place and ask for forgiveness?"

Without warning, Brooke threw her arms around her mother's neck, then around Roman's. She held on tight to him. "You are the perfect hero after all."

He hugged her close, winking at Justine. "Far from it, I'm afraid, but I hope I'm worth coming home to when you're done with this job."

Brooke broke from the embrace and eyed him. "Home?"

He took the small, blue box from his pocket. It had pressed ceaselessly into his leg the whole way here, reminding him he was about to make the biggest decision of his life. Risk it all for a woman who'd turned her back on him and walked away.

He swallowed the lump cutting off the air in his throat and opened the little box in front of Brooke's face. He'd given it plenty of thought and risking his life without her was far worse than risking his pride right here in front of these people.

"Brooke Heaton,"—he dropped to one knee, trying hard to do this the proper romance-hero way—"will you marry me?"

She started laughing, and her eyes went skyward. Was she rolling her eyes or asking the heavens for lightning to strike him dead?

"I can't believe this," she muttered again. "What are you doing?"

He hesitated, his stomach flopping like a fish out of water. "Proposing?"

She raised her hands and looked around. "Here?"

"Is there a place other than this that will up my chances of you saying yes?"

Another laugh and Justine joined in. She tapped Roman on the shoulder. "I think my daughter is purposely putting you in the hot seat," she said.

Brooke waved a hand at herself. "I'm a dirty, sweaty mess. Not exactly the scene I had in mind for a proposal."

Roman stood once more. "I wouldn't want you any other way."

Her eyes met his. "Are you sure about this?"

"I've never been more sure of anything in my life." He raised the box a little higher, making sure the rock caught the sun. "You said two carats wasn't enough, so I doubled it. What do you think?"

"Oh, Roman."

He waited but she didn't say anything else. The others, now gathered closer, seemed to be holding their collective breath along with him.

"Sorry, Brooke, but my romance hero knowledge is a little rusty," he said. "Is that a yes or a no?

She sighed, looked down at her dusty boots, and sighed again. When she raised her face, she was grinning. She threw her hat into the air. "It's neither. It's a hell-yes-what-took-you-so-long!"

She jumped and he caught her, nearly dropping the ring box, but not caring. A cheer went up around them.

As she laughed long and hard in his arms, he twirled her around and laughed with her.

Then he set her feet on the ground and slid the ring on her finger before she could change her mind. "I love you, Brooke."

"I love you too." She glanced at the ring, sparkling in the sunlight and nearly blinding him, then jumped into his arms again. In his ear, she whispered, "But I still expect you to do all those nasty things to me you just mentioned. I want to be your badge bunny, treasure-hunting trophy wife."

His feisty, lusty romance heroine was back. He kissed her long and deep before smiling down into her beautiful, flushed face. "Anything you want, Doc. Anything—and everything—you want."

"Including that pair of shoes you still owe me?"

"I cleared an entire wall of my closet so you can fill it with shoes."

She laughed. "Now we're talking."

ABOUT THE AUTHOR

USA TODAY Bestselling Author Misty Evans has published over forty-three novels and writes romantic suspense, urban fantasy, and paranormal romance. She got her start in 4th grade when she won second place in a school writing contest with an essay about her dad. Since then, she's written nonfiction magazine articles, started her own coaching business, become a yoga teacher, and raised twin boys on top of enjoying her fiction career.

When not reading or writing, she enjoys music, movies, and hanging out with her husband, twin sons, and two spoiled puppies. A registered yoga teacher, she shares her love of chakra yoga and energy healing, but still hasn't mastered levitating.

Learn more and sign up for her newsletter on her website at www.readmistyevans.com.

Printed in Great Britain
by Amazon